A PINCH OF COMMITMENT

A MARRIAGE OF CONVENIENCE ROMANCE

JEAN ORAM

COMPLETE LIBRARY OF CONGRESS CATALOGING-IN-PUBLICATION DATA AVAILABLE ONLINE

Oram, Jean.

A Pinch of Commitment / Jean Oram.—1st. ed.

Large Print ISBN: 978-1-989359-58-7, 978-1-989359-59-4

Paperback ISBN: 978-1-928198-81-9, 978-1-928198-42-0

Ebook ISBN: 978-1-928198-34-5

First Oram Productions Edition: November 2021

Cover design by Jean Oram

ACKNOWLEDGMENTS

A big, generous thank you goes to Allison Fentriss who supported the annual CLIC Sargent Get in Character charity event that helps raise money in the U.K. for families with children with cancer. She was the winning bid to be named as a character in this book. Any errors in my representation of Allison are on me. Thank you for helping families in need, Allison!

I'd also like to thank Donna W. and Mrs. X., Rachel B., Margaret C., Erin D. and Emily K. for their help with fine tuning Ethan and Lily's story.

And as always to my online writing support network which expands with every year. Writers are the best!

XO,
Jean Oram

A NOTE FROM THE AUTHOR

Growing up, a friend and I often baked like Lily and Mandy did in this story. However, neither my friend nor I started a newsletter or went on to start any culinary-related businesses. But we did learn how to make a mean (that roughly translates as: unrivalled and delicious) Nanaimo bar (it's a Canadian dessert) that her father liked to consume. In my friend's kitchen I learned you can make a 'pumpkin' pie with carrots. You can separate an egg white and egg yolk without a fancy contraption and much more.

However, learning to shop for groceries was a skill I picked up from my parents—especially stocking up on good deals. I still remember being embarrassed as a teen as I pushed an entire cart full of discounted two litre containers of pop (soda) through the store and was stopped by a neighbour who asked if we were having a party. Nope. We were just stocking up because money was tight and the deal was unreal. Now, I shamelessly load my own cart with deals, excited to be saving money on groceries as I feed my own family of four. Oh, how times change!

I hope my readers enjoy this tale of friendship, family and love. (And that the pages within don't make them recall their own silly, embarrassing stories from their youth.)

Happy reading,
Jean Oram
Alberta, Canada 2017

To Emma and Kristal. For the baking.

A Pinch of Commitment

CHAPTER 1

*E*than Mattson needed out. He needed a buyer to finally follow through and take his restaurant and catering business off his hands so he could focus on what he truly enjoyed—his web design company. Not slapping ham and cheese on rye multiple times a week.

Ethan leaned back, peeking through the doorway that joined the kitchen's prep area to the dining room of his sister's café. He also needed to figure out why the hottie chatting with Mandy seemed familiar. The two were chatting as though they were long-lost friends and he wondered if the hottie was going to help out around the place when Mandy's soon-to-be adopted newborn son arrived next week. If so, Ethan could use the distraction of a fling. Not that he had the time and energy for something like that these days, but it could be fun.

Although the way the hottie held herself, bubbly and free, reminded him of Mandy's old high school friend Lily Harper, a woman who'd definitely be off-limits. Then again, Lily had been more of a tomboy growing up, rejecting anything feminine, and this woman at the counter? There was nothing tomboy about her whatsoever. She was not Tagalong Lily. She was voluptuous, fit, and the sexiest thing he'd ever seen in the small town of Blueberry Springs, including his ex-fiancée the international model, who had left him a decade ago.

Massaging a kink in his bothersome left shoulder, Ethan went back to making sandwiches for the town hall's order. He should be grateful for the reliable business that his brother, Devon, the mayor, sent his way each month. He should also be grateful for how his sister had passed on her catering company when the café had taken off, helping him get a start on the road to independence and recovery after a particularly bad car accident had left him wheelchair bound for several years.

But catering wasn't his dream, his passion. It had once been construction. Putting up walls, roofs. Creating a home out of nothing but a pile of lumber and nails. The physical satisfaction of a hard day's work. There had been nothing else like it in his life.

And then a massive avalanche had swept his car off the road and down the side of the mountain on his way home from visiting his then fiancée, Dani Demare. The accident had taken everything away from him. His independence. His savings. His apartment. Even his fiancée when she found out he might never walk again.

He still owed his dad and stepmom nearly six figures even though they said to forget the debt. And that was why, even though he received no joy from working in the food business, he had purchased the town's biggest restaurant, Benny's Big Burger. But the place, even though it was fully staffed and only needed him there for a few hours a day, was proving to be more headache than profit and he needed it gone. Sold.

Ethan fitted a slice of cheese on another sandwich. What he really needed now was luck. Lately, whenever he seemed to get close to a sale for his catering company and restaurant, something weird happened, chasing away the interested party. If that happened one more time he swore he'd cave and accept the disgustingly low offer he'd rejected several weeks ago. Anything so he'd have the time to pursue the lucrative web design contract business magnate Burke Carver had offered him.

Ethan picked up a bamboo skewer to begin the task of creating colorful fruit kabobs. He ought to take the skewer and jam it through his eye. Every week it was the same order. Sandwiches. Fruit kabobs. Over and over again. If there'd been more profit in the job he'd have hired it out long ago.

Finished, he tossed his tea towel across the prep area and turned down Mötley Crüe, then scrolled through the list of unread emails on his phone. He was slowly losing track of his web business.

Ethan heard a warm voice say "Hello" and looked up, expecting to see the hottie from the café in the dining area's doorway. Nobody was there. He turned, spotting a tall woman standing in the alley's delivery entrance, her handcart ladened with boxes of lettuce. She was cute.

"I like your uniform," Ethan told her. The light blue shirt brought out her dark skin, the beige shorts showing off the fact that she worked out.

She smiled shyly, her lashes lowering. "Thanks. I like your shirt."

He checked to see what he was wearing. Just a regular cotton number which was a bit small, causing it to pull across his chest. She was flirting with him. Nice. That didn't happen often.

"You can set the lettuce there." He pointed to a corner. If he asked her out before she noticed his limp, his chances would be better. At least, if his history down at the local pub Brew Babies was any indicator. Women wanted men who were whole and capable, and his personality and general low level of charm weren't quite enough to bring them past the fact that he was still slightly crippled despite numerous surgeries and years of physical therapy.

A bumblebee buzzed in through the door behind the woman and she panicked, her ponytail swinging as she tried to duck. "Kill it!" she squealed as she swatted the air.

"Aw, no. The poor thing's just hungry." The bee was hovering over his uncovered fruit platter. "It's heard about my amazing kabobs and wants a taste."

"Bees freak me out!" She wrapped her arms around her head, ducking low as she scurried through the open door and out into the alley again.

The bee finally settled on the fruit and Ethan gave it a moment to take a nibble, even though he knew he shouldn't due to the food regulation acts his sister was always spouting on about. Then he slowly cupped his hands around the insect so he wouldn't damage its wings.

"Come on, little guy." He gently lifted it as it buzzed in his hollowed hands, and ambled to the back door, his left leg dragging more than he'd like. Maybe the cutie would overlook that when she saw how he'd saved the day.

"They don't sting," he said from the alley as he opened his hands. The bumblebee flew away, its wings hardly seeming able to carry its large, fuzzy body.

"They freak me out." The woman's shoulders were still hunched, her eyes wide and on the lookout for more winged attackers.

"Would you like an iced tea? Lemonade?"

She watched him move. "Are you okay? Did you hurt yourself?" Her eyes had drifted from his leg up to the thin scar that lined the edge of his mouth, her expression changing to one of caution. If he smiled, the scar would look like a charming laugh line. He didn't smile. He could see her reassessing him, his manhood, his possible value to her within her able-bodied life. He didn't blame her. She looked like she did the things he couldn't—hike up steep mountain trails and camp out on the ground without waking up with frozen joints. It didn't matter that he could still perform as a man should —he'd engaged in an experiment with one of his nurses after his accident to see if he still had his mojo, even though his legs hadn't yet been work-ing. He'd been able, but lying there had stolen what felt like the last thread of his manhood and he hadn't bothered with another "experiment" since.

Ethan shook off his thoughts with a scowl.

"I'm fine and walking, aren't I?" His tone was

slightly curt. "It's almost lunchtime. Care to join me?"

"I'm sorry, I've got more deliveries." She brushed past him, collecting her cart from the kitchen.

"Another time then," he said gruffly as she handed him her clipboard.

"Yeah. Sure. Please sign."

Ethan scribbled his initials and returned to the kitchen, grumbling about women not wanting half a man. He found himself face-to-face with his sister and her friend the hottie. He quickly turned away, embarrassed that they'd likely witnessed him being rejected.

He went to push past Mandy, but she stopped him, giving him a light smack on the chest. "What's your problem?" she scolded.

"What's yours?" he retorted just as quickly. Having a sister who picked up on his every mood— and he had plenty—was a colossal pain in the you-know-what. It was as if she thought him smiling more would fix his life.

Ethan glanced over at the hottie, who looked even sexier from the front. All curves and low neckline and high hemline. She dressed like a powerful businesswoman from the city and his mind spun down Dirty Avenue before his gaze had a chance to make its way up to check out her pretty face, which was quite likely to be filled with pity.

She had beautiful eyes, no hint of pity, and a familiar pert nose speckled with freckles.

Aw, man.

Hottie was totally off-limits.

He'd been jonesing for his sister's childhood friend, Tagalong Lily. Sure, she wasn't a kid any longer, but she was like a sister to him, a year younger than Mandy and several more junior to him. Not that it mattered as adults, but you didn't think about a woman's legs wrapped around your waist so you could fall into her if she was essentially family. You protected her from men with thoughts like his.

He shook his head, disappointed in himself.

"Hey," said Hottie. Scratch that. Lily. Lily, Lily, Lily and her newfound hotness.

Her cheeks were pink, her eyes filled with happiness at seeing him. Or something else. Probably something else. People generally weren't delighted to see him. Something about his stormy moods that frequently rolled in. He should probably do something about that. If, say, he desired a social life and didn't mind his bad days becoming a burden on others—but he believed his family and friends deserved more than that. They had their own lives to lead and he didn't need them constantly worrying over him anymore.

"Hey, Lilypad."

She gave him a sassy head tilt that exposed an expanse of smooth neck. Then, as though unable to hold back any longer, Lily yanked him into a fierce, brief hug that left him stumbling, his mind imprinted with one impression—she felt amazing pressed up against him.

Last he'd heard from Moe—the bartender at Brew Babies—his younger sister, Lily, had been working in the city as some fancy-pants chef after cooking school or whatever it was called, and had broken up with the latest douche in a long line of men not good enough for her. Was she here to stay, or just to torment him with the fact that he hadn't been with a woman in what felt like long enough to re-grant him his virginity and her middle name had been changed to Hot Stuff? Lily Hot Stuff Harper.

Hello, libido, so nice of you to pop in and turn me into an imbecile with a one-track mind that likes to play in the gutter like a neglected orphan.

Lily leaned in, her perfume soft and sweet, her hands light on his elbows as her lips neared his.

He flinched, jerking away. Too late, he realized she was only going in for a polite cheek kiss to top off her hug.

She gave a smile, but the hurt in her eyes wasn't easily masked. It reminded him of when, as a family guest at his high school graduation, she'd tried to kiss him goodbye since her family was moving to South Carolina to be closer to cousins. She'd been vulnerable, and it had been his job to protect her like a sibling, not take advantage of her. He'd pulled away, receiving the same look of rejection she was giving him now.

"She wants to relieve you of your burdens," Mandy said, jabbing a thumb in Lily's direction.

"She what?" His mouth went dry. Surely not *that* burden.

All right. Gutter mind needed to take some time off. His eyes drifted to her long legs again before he caught himself.

"Lily wants to buy your catering biz as well as Benny's." Mandy was speaking slowly, letting the lifeline hit the water, swirl around him, tempting him to change his drowning tune, grab hold and haul himself in.

He could ditch this job.

He could accept the contract from Burke Carver and his fashion-conscience company, Sustain It, Honey. Ethan could change the course of his business, helping him repay his dad and stepmom for the way they'd made their home wheelchair accessible so he could leave the rehab facility and eventually get his life back in order. Return the down payment they'd placed on his current home.

He glanced at Lily. She seemed serious about buying him out.

He could be free.

"I've already done a pile of research and have asked around about it," Lily said. "I'm interested."

"That was you?" he asked, taking her in. She'd requested detailed accounts, contracts, the works. He'd assumed it was some sharp-eyed business conglomerate checking things out, not his kid sister's friend who'd become a verified foodie.

Not that it surprised him. She was smart, but he found the idea of her as a savvy businesswoman attractive in an unexpected way.

"Yes." Lily tipped her chin up in that defiant way he used to find cute when she was about ten. But there was a hardness to her expression now that spoke of a challenge—a challenge he wanted to pursue with a throaty growl.

"You want to buy my businesses?"

"Yes."

"Fine," he said, leaning against the counter. "Name your price and they're both yours, Lily Harper."

"HERE'S THE THING," Lily said, leaning against the doorjamb, thrown by Ethan's "name your price" offer. It hadn't been what she'd expected to hear from her friend's brother—a guy she'd had a crush on ever since he'd pulled her out of a mud puddle when she'd been pushed there by her own brother, back when she was six. Ethan had not only pulled her out, but scolded Moe, then walked her home so she could change her clothes, drying her tears as they went.

He'd always been a nice guy. Steady, reserved and quiet. The kind of man she could trust, who she knew would look out for her and ensure she wasn't nudged aside by others even when he grumbled about her tagging along and cramping his style.

And now he was offering her two thriving businesses at whatever price she wanted? There was nice guy and then there were offers that were too good to be true. This time, she knew what the catch was, unlike with her boyfriend Skip, who, it turned out, had had a wife on the side. Or rather, Lily had been the one on the side. They'd met at a job fair and he'd convinced her to move from South Carolina back closer to the place she considered home—Blueberry Springs—to work in his kitchen in the nearby city of Dakota. He'd claimed that if she put in a little sweat equity he'd make her full partner in his restaurant. She had. And a year later he'd turned around and sold it all, collecting a tidy profit he then used to buy a Mexican beach house for his wife.

Meanwhile Lily had been tossed aside, fired from the job. She'd been left with a broken heart filled with deception, her bank account dipping even further into overdraft, her student loan debts nowhere near paid off.

After that Tanner had come along, looking like a knight. He was a chef, too—unmarried—who loved creating new recipes. They'd had fun being creative in the kitchen and it had felt so real, so much like love and everything she wanted there, surrounded by stainless steel and knives that cut better than a Blueberry Springs winter wind. They'd indulged in delicious, rich flavors, the scents of sauces and baking constantly in the air like an olfactory track to the movie of their life.

Then Tanner had taken full credit for their recipes, publishing them in a cookbook he'd been contracted to write prior to meeting her. She'd unsuccessfully tried taking him to court, merely adding to her debt load.

But that wasn't the worst part. Even now he kept begging for forgiveness, kept trying to find a way back into her life.

Her years in the city had taught her some very

important lessons. One being that nobody was going to help her succeed; she had to do it on her own. There was no more living off someone else's kitchen. The next time she worked in a restaurant, the kitchen would be all hers. Her rules, her world. She got to choose the people that would become her family, her trusted circle.

Even if the debt and responsibility finally killed her.

That was where Ethan and his reasonably priced, established restaurant came in. He wanted out and she wanted in. And she had just enough credit left to make it happen—assuming she found a way around the catch in his offer.

"Here's the thing," she repeated, as Ethan's ice-blue eyes met hers, striking in their intensity. For a moment she couldn't breathe, couldn't think of anything other than what those impatient, frowning lips would taste like.

Pull it together, Lil. Pin him against the wall with your business sense. You're tougher now. You can handle a complete hunk staring at you.

"On the real estate listing," she continued shakily, "it says the businesses come with everything. Recipes, contacts, agreements, discounts. Everything down to the grains of salt in the shakers."

Ethan nodded, slowly crossed his arms, looking stiff. Not good. He was preparing to play hardball.

No, she could play hardball, too. She'd survived being an intern, a kitchen lackey, a sous-chef's assistant right on up to chef. She'd been underestimated, undervalued, underpaid, discounted and used. It was a hard business with demands that broke many, but she hadn't faltered, hadn't let it shake her off her course.

"When I talked to your suppliers," she continued, "they said new owner, new deals."

"Who said that?" Ethan asked, his eyes narrowed. He seemed predatory, defensive, ready to protect. He used to pull out that look when bullies tried to put her down for her ragtag appearance, her dad's inability to afford the right outfits for her. Now Ethan was using the look on her and it made her feel like an outsider, an enemy.

Lily whacked Ethan's chest with a roll of lists and papers, trying to remain tough. She'd spent two days talking to people. She knew what had to be changed in the offer of sale. "Nobody will honor the current contracts."

"That's true." Mandy piped up.

"How do you know?" Ethan looked surprised.

"Because I'm one of them!" his sister snapped, putting her hands on her slim hips. "You can't sell your business and expect me to provide my prize-winning whiskey-and-gumdrop brownies to some stranger at cost. That's a special deal between you and me. And I'm also not letting a stranger use my kitchen free of charge for their catering business."

"Why don't you prep catering orders in the kitchen at Benny's?" Lily asked.

"It's too busy with regular orders." Ethan turned back to his sister. "Lily's not a stranger. Why can't you give her the same deals?" His voice was low, rumbly and warm, in a way that shot straight to Lily's core, nudging all her girlie parts into paying very close attention to the man in front of her.

"You can't expect me to treat others like I'd treat family," Mandy replied.

"But Lily *is* family." Ethan faced off with Mandy.

Lily tried hard not to swoon, but figured she must have, judging from the glance Mandy darted her way.

Her friend's tone softened. "I know she is. Always will be. And if she buys your businesses we'll work something out. But my point isn't about Lily. You can't expect everyone to honor deals and contracts that were...were for you." Mandy wasn't looking at Ethan and Lily figured she knew why. He had received some primo deals based on his like-family status, as well as pity due to him being in a wheelchair when he'd started out. Years later, those deals were still helping his bottom line.

Which was a bit ridiculous seeing as he was obviously back on his own two feet now.

"Renegotiating the contracts and current arrangements could easily eat up most of the profit margin," she said. The success of any restaurant—even well-established, popular ones—was always iffy in a small town such as Blueberry Springs, and more so with a change in ownership.

"It can't be that bad," Ethan said uncertainly. He looked frustrated. Maybe a bit desperate.

"This is my cue to head back to work," Mandy stated. "I only have a week before our baby arrives." She gave an excited grin and a hop as she left the kitchen with a parting "Good luck."

"I'm taking a huge cut in proceeds with the amount of taxes I'll have to pay when I sell," Ethan said. He waved his hands as though shooing off pigeons. "But whatever. Make me an offer. I'd rather sell to you than a vulture."

"I'm not done."

Ethan gave her a pained look, crossing his arms again and making his shirt stretch over his biceps. There was a thin white scar along the side of his mouth that gave him a look of rugged imperfection. Slightly bad-boy and compelling.

"It says in this contract—" she dug through her shoulder bag "—that none of the recipes from Benny's can be sold with the business."

"Technically, I'm not selling the recipes. I'm giving them away to the new owner, since they're not listed under assets."

"Didn't you read this thing? You can't give them away, either." She waved the contract. "Blueberry Springs doesn't do well with change." Such widespread menu changes could chase off even the most loyal customers.

"So I'm stuck with the restaurant?"

"It's going to be difficult for the new owner to make money unless you cut your price by at least 20 percent."

"Twenty?" He looked aghast. "I owe more than that on it still."

They stared at each other for a long moment. Then Ethan rubbed his eyes, which were looking suddenly bleary. "What do I have to do to sell these businesses to you without taking a huge financial hit? Any ideas?"

She felt a surge of hope, a renewed belief that maybe she could find her way home again, that she could finally have her own kitchen—a place of belonging, a place to fit in. A place that nobody could take from her.

She blinked back the dampness in her eyes and decided it was worth the risk of possible rejection. There was one catch preventing them from getting what they wanted and she knew the way around it.

"Most of your suppliers said they'll leave the deals in place if your family takes over."

Ethan rubbed his eyes again, appearing defeated. "Mandy already has a business and there's no way Devon could do this without wrecking it all—plus he's not interested. I asked." He picked up a tea towel, then tossed it away, his other hand resting on his hip. He studied the floor for a moment, then looked up. "They're really being that fussy?"

"Your sister struck some hard bargains with the catering business, and Benny has several decades of loyalty that extended to you because…" She didn't dare say it. *Pity.* Everyone thought the man in front of her was a cripple, even though he was strong, virile, and totally capable. She could see it in the no-nonsense way he held himself, the broadness of his shoulders and the appealing quality of his presence. Sure, she'd heard him muttering about being only half a man when the delivery lady had shut him down, but even Lily could see why the woman had shied away. Ethan was too gruff, too quick to reject her, when she'd only been trying to figure him out.

Her loss and Lily's gain. Maybe.

"I just need a chance to prove myself as a worthy partner and I'm sure they'll change their minds," she said.

"I'd do anything to get rid of these businesses." Ethan gazed up at her soulfully and she knew he was telling the truth.

"There is a way," she offered tentatively.

"Yeah?" He looked hopeful.

"We could both follow our dreams..." Her palms were growing damp, her doubts over-whelming.

"I'm listening."

"It wouldn't be that difficult. We're friends." Sure, she still kinda had a crush on him, but it would be okay. He was good at keeping bound-aries, just like when they'd had their subscription recipe newsletter in high school. He'd done the email newsletter bit and she'd provided the content for their list, which included a combination of family, teachers, and strangers that had found her basic site on the web. They hadn't made much money, but he'd been happy enough working alongside her. And he'd always made it clear that he didn't want anything more than friendship be-tween them. His disinterest would keep things simple, uncomplicated.

It would also help her stay away from love in the kitchen, which seemed to be one of her biggest downfalls.

"Well?" he said impatiently.

"Family." She swallowed. "They want to work

with you or your family." She waited to see if he clued in.

He gave her a blank look and she closed her eyes, still in disbelief that she was willing to put her plan into words. With Ethan.

She held her breath, ready for him to reject her like he always did when she tried to cross the line. She released the air from her lungs as she blurted, "A wife counts as family."

UNABLE TO HELP IT, Ethan began laughing as he put two and two together.

Marriage? Him and Lily? Not likely. She was like…a sister. A sexy, forbidden sister.

The idea was utterly ludicrous.

"I'm not asking you to take me into your arms and make sweet, steamy love to me," Lily chided, her lip gloss shining under the kitchen lights, her lower lip looking plump and juicy. Ethan abruptly stopped laughing as the not-so-hard-to-imagine visual popped to mind.

"I'm just asking for a chance to prove myself." She picked at her thumbnail, no longer looking up. Ethan knew it was difficult for her to ask for help, and he caught the vulnerability in her request, causing his mind to still.

Family came first, and if she needed someone to help her, then that man should be him.

But marriage?

"I'm only asking you to consider a way around everything," she said, glancing at him again. "To help us get what we want. I'll work hard, Ethan. Really hard."

"I know you will." She was one of the most hardworking people he knew, and she had a new toughness to her that he suspected would take her far. "But you're asking *me* to marry *you*?"

"You have a problem with that?" Her chin tipped up again and her eyes flashed. What he wouldn't give to tangle his hands in her soft curls and kiss that pretty mouth as if they weren't old friends with so much at stake.

"I just didn't see it coming," he said, clearing his throat. "That's all. It feels a bit much for the situation."

"If we were married…" She lowered her voice, stepping close enough for him to pick up another hint of her perfume, feel her body heat. "…your deals would be extended to me. We could keep everything in your name while I run the businesses for a year. Then we separate and I buy you out at today's agreed price. A marriage of convenience, on paper—nothing beyond that. Platonic. Business."

He felt a slight sting of rejection as she put special emphasis on "platonic." He knew where she was coming from, but hearing the woman he'd thought would always adore him suggest they avoid anything sexual took him down that last peg of manhood.

"They seriously won't extend the deals to you?" That didn't seem right or fair.

She nodded.

"Everyone?"

"Everyone on the list the agent gave me. I called them all."

Ethan was surprised. Lily was tenacious, charming and determined, and yet she hadn't managed to sway a single one?

Somehow that didn't seem possible.

He pulled out his phone and dialed one of the long-standing suppliers of both Benny's and the catering company.

"Hey, it's Ethan Mattson." After a minute or two of chitchat, he said, "I have a question for you. When I sell my companies, will our discounts be extended to the new owner?"

There was a telling pause and Ethan glanced at Lily, who raised her eyebrows in question.

"Ethan," the man said hesitantly, "I'd like to but...well, I worked with Benny for almost two decades and he vouched for you. Plus I already knew you and your sister from the catering company. We had a relationship."

"Like family?"

"Exactly. And I knew Mandy would kick your butt if you messed up or failed to pay." They both laughed at the truth of that statement. "But with a new owner there are risks. Your discounts are based on years of history."

"Well, it sounds like I have an interested party. She's a good friend." He glanced up at Lily. "Like family. But the lack of carryover discounts could pull the venture under."

There was another long pause. "I'm sorry, Ethan. I just can't."

Ethan felt frustrated by the man's refusal. Lily had been cooking and working in restaurants for years and would do a much better job than he ever had. She knew this stuff better than he did, and she deserved a chance.

"What if I told you she was my wife?" Ethan said, hardly believing he was doing so.

"You got married? No way! Congratulations!"

"Well, we're just thinking about it."

"Don't let her think too long and hard—she might change her mind."

"Tell me about it." Ethan smiled at Lily. "But say she took over for me as the new owner, she'd still get the discounts, right?"

"Of course! She's family."

Ethan thanked him and ended the call. Family.

That's all it would take? Bring Lily into the family he already knew she was a part of? That was easy.

"So?" she asked. "I'm guessing from your expression that I'm not considered family unless we're married?"

Ethan nodded. "You might have to keep the menu and orders fairly similar for some time. Big alteration could result in discount changes."

She nodded, barely able to hold back a grin. "This is Blueberry Springs. I'm not going to turn Benny's into Asian fusion."

Ethan tapped the counter, thinking.

She would get discounts and deals, but only if he vouched for her. Married her.

It was ridiculous.

But marriage would get her a kitchen—something she obviously longed for. Plus, acting married would be easy enough, seeing as they were old friends, his family adored her and nobody expected him to act lovey-dovey.

They'd have a walk-in, walk-out marriage between friends, with her slowly taking over the companies to ease the transition, preventing waitstaff, customers and suppliers from being scared off. And after they separated, things could carry on like they had before, only they'd no longer live together. An amicable breakup. Two friends who'd tried to take their friendship one step further and had failed.

The town would love her, support her.

It was a perfect plan.

Other than the fact that his libido wanted to snag a taste of those cherry lips. Then again, all he had to do was wait for the look of pity from her when he couldn't do something a regular man could, such as hike up a mountain or carry a heavy box or not limp. That would throw ice on his mojo. And everything would remain perfectly platonic. As she'd emphasized. Repeatedly.

Okay, she had only once, but he'd taken the hit hard, like a big baby.

"You're sure about this?" he asked.

"We'll write up solid prenuptial agreements that focus on what to do with the businesses in case of divorce."

"You think a year is long enough to prove yourself?"

"I can build relationships and deals in that time frame."

"You know," he said thoughtfully, "because of the divorce, it won't be considered a sale, so no capital gains taxes. It's brilliant." He felt hope swell inside him, resurrected from the ashes.

If Ethan could pay him back, his dad might be able to quit consulting for the mine a few hours away in Chesapeake. Cory Mattson was retired, but because he'd spent a chunk of his nest egg helping Ethan, he was working again here and there. If Ethan could repay him, he could retire once and for all.

Ethan leaned against the counter, impressed with the simple brilliance of Lily's plan.

"It's an unexpected angle and I honestly can't see a lot of potholes." Other than the fact that they'd have to deceive the whole community, his family and her dad. "Although won't suppliers know it's a ruse, since you were just asking everyone about deals?"

She paused. "Maybe." She shrugged. "You seeing anyone?"

"No. Are you?"

Her expression darkened slightly and she worried her thumbnail again. "I could actually kind of use a fake husband at the moment."

Ethan's instinct to protect her reared up and whinnied. "Say what?"

"Nothing." She waved a hand. "Just an ex who doesn't understand that I'm no longer interested in helping him or…well, anything that involves him." Her chin went up again, but Ethan could see the hurt in her eyes. Someone hadn't treated her well, and his desire to make that man pay was mighty strong.

"How's he bothering you?"

"Never mind, it's not a big deal." She sighed, looking suddenly weary. "I'm just worn-out from the constant confrontation and deflection, you know?"

They faced off for a long moment, unspoken words drifting between them as they settled on a decision.

"I'm a horrible actor," he said.

"You do have a crappy poker face."

He laughed. He'd been stupid enough to play poker with Lily only once and he'd lost badly. He'd had to provide six months of recipe newsletter support for her at no charge. It hadn't been a hardship, though. She'd been fun and easy to work with.

He grew somber as he met her trusting gaze. "You deserve better," he said gently. "A husband who loves you."

Her cheeks turned pink and her eyes darkened. "And I'll find him after you and I are done. This is business, nothing more."

"What if you find him while we're together?"

"Does that mean you agree?" A flicker of excitement washed over her face and she rolled up onto her toes.

He picked up the tray of sandwiches, then set it down again. His family would be excited about the marriage, but what about hers? "How's your dad?"

It had been just Lily, Moe and her dad while she'd been growing up, and her father had been absent a lot, as he worked long shifts in the nearby mines. Dinner had rarely made it to the table unless Moe or Lily were cooking. As a result, she had spent a lot of time with Ethan's family, and he knew she'd missed the hubbub of their home when she'd moved away with her dad at sixteen. Especially since Moe had just graduated high school and had been old enough to stay in Blueberry Springs on his own.

Lily shrugged. "The same, basically."

She was hiding something. Money problems? Ill health? A big fight?

The poor kid didn't have much in the way of family and was likely trying to move closer to her brother. There were a lot of reasons to agree to her plan, but something kept holding him back from saying yes, despite his desire to step in and help. He settled on the truth. "Lil, the thing is…I'm tough to be around. I'm not a marriage kind of guy and I'm happy being alone."

CHAPTER 2

*L*ily felt the sting of rejection.

Ethan didn't want to help her.

She hadn't realized how much she'd been counting on him until he'd told her he wanted to be alone in life, and had picked up his domed tray of sandwiches and walked out of the kitchen.

What had she expected? For him to suddenly see her as a mature woman and not reject her or her advances, even if they were only business related?

Men wanted her for what she could provide in the kitchen, and for that reason she'd thought Ethan would accept. But then again, he was Ethan, and he probably thought he was protecting her.

"It's a *business* arrangement, Ethan. Purely platonic. Nothing at all like a real marriage," she said, catching up to him in the alley before he turned onto the sidewalk. It didn't her take long, as it turned out the new Ethan liked to mosey. The teenaged version she'd known had been more like Devon, never slowing down, always pushing the edge. "We don't have to do anything other than work together a bit."

"You'd have to live with me, and I like my space."

There was that new grumpy act of his again.

She slowed her pace to match his. He was holding the tray awkwardly, as if it was precious cargo.

"I promise not to sing opera in the shower."

"Do you still snore?"

"That was one time and I had a cold!"

"You woke up the whole cabin."

"Well, I don't snore, and I'm a clean and helpful roommate. I'm actually more worried that *you'll* fall in love with someone while we're together."

"We're not together." His mouth was set in a determined line. His eyes cut to hers, then dropped to her legs. She suddenly felt warm despite the cloudy August day.

"Come on. Please?" she begged, making her eyes large.

He shook his head.

"Don't resign yourself to a lonely life. Mandy says you hate those businesses."

He gave a harrumph, but she could tell his heart wasn't in it.

She smiled at some people who passed by, and allowed herself to bump against Ethan, who gave her a dirty look, pulling his tray closer to his chest.

"Maybe you could just run the businesses for me," he suggested.

She reacted without thinking. "No way! I get control. I own it. I'm not working for anyone else ever again."

Ethan seemed surprised by her vehemence, but only asked, "What if I gave you free rein?"

"No." She knew what she wanted, and she was not putting herself in a position to be walked on ever again.

Ethan sighed. "You're still stubborn." He stared up at the town hall, then began easing his way carefully up the ramp, as if he couldn't take the stairs and carry a tray at the same time. Either he had a ton of injuries left over from his car accident years ago or he was so out of his comfort zone with this food business that it was making him move like a marionette. Her guess was the latter.

She let out a breath. "I want to own the place because I want to control my cash flow. Plus my dad could use some money and I'd like to be able to help him out." Maybe even leverage the new assets to buy him a small trailer, so he no longer had to worry about rent back in South Carolina.

Ethan's attention swung to her.

She shrugged. Her family and money problems. What else was new? Her dad was still working, even though his hours kept getting reduced and some weeks he could barely feed himself.

"Is Moe sending him money?"

"He tries to cover his rent when he can."

She froze as a familiar form became visible in her periphery. The man's voice slid over her. "Lily, baby. I've been looking everywhere for you."

She turned to face Tanner. "What are you doing in Blueberry Springs?"

Ethan swung the tray of sandwiches between her and her ex. "Hey, I'm Ethan. Pleased to meet you." He awkwardly offered a hand to shake.

Tanner ignored him.

"I've been calling all week. Where've you been?" He reached over to tuck a strand of hair behind her ear, but she backed up, Ethan moving into the space she'd opened up.

"Tanner, I don't want to speak to you. What we had is over."

"I want to work on my next book with you."

"Do I look stupid?"

"The critics love my berry crumble."

"*My* berry crumble!"

Ethan was watching her intently, and Lily felt foolish and embarrassed for having allowed herself to be taken advantage of by Tanner. Plus now couldn't get him out of her life. She wanted to feel grown-up around Ethan, prove herself, and here she was, flopping around like a dying fish.

"Come on, Ethan." She reached for the door to the town hall.

"Lily." Tanner snagged her arm and she whirled on him.

"Don't. Touch me."

"Baby, come on. We had something good. We *belong* together. We were like family in the kitchen. Remember that time we had a food fight? Nobody makes me laugh like you do." She felt her anger lessen slightly. They *had* been like family and had had some good times. Before he'd shown his true colors.

"I miss you," he added softly. "I know we had some troubles—"

"You taking credit for our recipes and profiting off them?" Her anger sharpened once again, reminding her exactly why she'd shoved his no-good butt off her front porch in the first place. "Yeah. I'd say those are some troubles. I'm no longer interested in being used."

"It's time for you to leave," Ethan said quietly to

Tanner. Lily recognized the voice. Ethan was mad. To an outsider he might look affable, calm. Harmless. But she knew he'd already shifted into protective mode. He had been her constant shield against bullies until she'd left Blueberry Springs. And as he edged her away from the conflict now, she realized how lonely it had been not having him at her side.

"Let's go," she replied, not wanting to cause a scene. She could see Mary Alice and her sister, Liz, approaching, chatting and enjoying the sun. They were both huge gossipers and would love to insert themselves into the middle of something juicy.

And this was juicier than a plump, overripe peach.

"Baby, come on. Give me another chance." Tanner had sidled closer, trying to pull her against him. She wiggled away, like she'd become accustomed to doing whenever he tried too hard, but his grip was firm. He reached to tuck her hair behind her ear once again, a sure sign he was trying to convince her of something, and she panicked, feeling trapped. What happened next was a blur, with Tanner's fingers never making contact because Ethan was suddenly in Tanner's face. Tanner tried to shove him out of the way, but Ethan swung, delivering a quick uppercut that landed with a crunch. Tanner's head snapped back, sending him tumbling to the ground.

Lily squeaked, jumping backward. Tanner swore at Ethan, clutching his jaw as he rolled into a sitting position on the concrete steps.

Ethan turned his back to him, his expression somber. "Come on, Lily."

His container of sandwiches was upside down on the sidewalk, but still intact. She scooped it up and hustled after him as he ushered her inside, saying to Tanner as they went, "Stay away from Lily or you'll be messing with me. Understood?"

A zing of awareness zipped up Lily's spine at Ethan's possessive words. He might not be ready to marry her, but the man she'd once known as her protector seemed to be back, as well as her extra large crush.

SHOOT.

Ethan had just assaulted a man. That wasn't his style. Not at all.

But having him move in after Lily told him not to touch her, then seeing that panicked look in her eyes had taken Ethan back to when she'd been picked on as a kid. Nobody deserved that. And as an adult she deserved better from both men.

"I'm sorry. I shouldn't have resorted to violence." He'd gotten lucky with that punch. He could have easily ended up in a fight he knew his body couldn't finish. What a stupid, moronic thing to do, acting like a caveman. What had come over him?

He knew better than to act like that.

But Lily... He'd do anything to keep her safe, and that guy had a serious lack of boundaries.

"Does he bother you often?"

Lily was pale, and he worried that he'd scared her.

"I'm sorry. You're safe with me. I'd never hurt you," he assured her.

She released an exasperated-sounding sigh. "Ethan, I know that. He...Tanner sometimes forgets we've broken up."

Ethan didn't like the sound of that.

"Thank you, by the way," she said softly.

"For acting like some primal beast who can't use his words to resolve a conflict?"

She gave him a small smile as he led her into the meeting room where he was supposed to deliver the lunch. He got the feeling Lily was underplaying things. The guy was obviously acting against her wishes and she was putting up with it due to a fear of causing a scene. Ethan's best guess was that Tanner took advantage of her politeness and sent unwanted texts, made frequent phone calls and likely added a few unwanted drunken middle-of-the-night visits. Basic harassment that she shouldn't stand for.

If Ethan had the right to act on her behalf—more than he already had—he'd give that guy a free trip to the moon, courtesy of his—

No, no. He needed to take it down a notch. He couldn't stoop to Tanner's level and infringe on Lily's life, her world. Even though he was like a big brother to her and really wanted to send Tanner out of her life forever.

But she should speak up, even if it hurt Tanner's feelings. He had it coming.

Lily had lifted the dome off the tray of broken, mixed up sandwiches. Some fine day this was turning out to be. Now he was going to have to go all the way back to the kitchen and remake them. Plus he'd completely forgotten the kabobs.

And his hand hurt. He hadn't punched anyone since the days of he and Devon play fighting, and he'd forgotten how much it hurt to smack your knuckles against someone else's jaw.

Lily had cleaned her hands with one of the disposable towelettes he often tucked in with the sandwiches and she was studiously rebuilding the sandwiches, her bottom lip tucked in as though fighting to control her emotions.

She looked lost, alone, vulnerable. She needed

someone to help her build the independent life she so rightly deserved.

If he said no to her offer it meant leaving her to face it all alone. He couldn't imagine denying her the opportunity to enjoy her passion, which happened to be his least-loved work. He also couldn't imagine going home to his quiet house and waiting for something better to come along.

This was it. And it was Lily. Family.

She looked up slowly as he came to stand beside her. He ignored the sandwiches, watching her face instead.

"I want to help you, Lily, and I think we should get married."

Her expression opened like a ray of sunshine after a week of rain, and she threw her arms around him, hugging him close. So close he thought she might feel a little bit like home.

LILY DIDN'T WANT to let go of Ethan. She wanted to hang on forever and fight the happy sobs threatening to burst forth. But he was already easing out of her grip.

"Thank you so much, Ethan."

"And whenever you want out, whenever you

feel you have a good grasp of the reins, we'll break up and it'll all be yours, at today's value."

The tightness in her chest eased up and she smiled at him in gratitude. She not only now had an ex on the run, but possibly a job, a livelihood and even a home. And a family—the Mattsons. It would be like she'd never left, plus now she'd have her own kitchen.

No more being on her own.

"We'll keep it low-key," she offered.

Ethan was looking nervous, as if afraid she might hug him again, and she forced herself to hold back, listen to his conditions. But in reality, she'd do just about anything.

"Walk in, walk out," he agreed. "No party, no wedding. Okay?"

She nodded quickly.

Unable to resist, she threw herself at Ethan again. "Thank you, thank you," she whispered into his neck. He held her close, his aftershave smelling so much like him, so familiar, that it brought tears to her eyes. He was her safe place, and like always, she felt like she belonged, a part of something wonderful.

"Well, would you look at that?" said an amused voice. "Ethan's got himself a girlfriend."

Lily slipped out of her fiancé's arms—*fiancé! Ethan!* Oh, would wonders never cease?—and turned to see his older brother leaning in the doorway, looking surprisingly dapper in a shirt and tie.

"Devon!" She began laughing at the sight. "Is that really you?" She knew the man best with grease and grime coating his jeans and T-shirt, from work he'd been doing under his car. "Mr. Mayor?"

"Lily Harper." He grinned and opened his arms; she threw herself into his hug. "I heard you were in town."

She stood back, flicking his tie. "What's this?"

He smoothed it down. "I have to dress the part, according to my wife."

"I still can't believe you're mayor. And married."

When Ethan stepped forward and slung an arm over Lily's shoulders, Devon gave them a curious look. "Speaking of wives and life changes and all that…why are you two acting like a couple?"

Lily cut a glance at Ethan, who cleared his throat. "We're getting married," he said quickly.

He looked just like he had when he'd confessed to breaking a window to his father. The shattered pane had been her fault, but he'd taken the blame, knowing she couldn't afford to replace it.

Just another reason to love the guy for all eternity.

He'd even refused her attempts at repayment, saying he was an accessory, since he'd been trying to teach her how to hit a softball hard enough that she'd stop being picked last in gym class. It hadn't worked, but she'd enjoyed spending the time with Ethan—until she'd broken the window.

"Get real." Devon's jaw was hanging and he looked from Ethan to Lily and back again. "You two? Married? To each other?"

Lily felt her cheeks flush and she began to stammer. "I—It's just—We, um…"

"Buzz off," Ethan said, scowling at his brother as he snugged Lily closer.

Mmm, that felt nice. She could get used to it.

"No, I get it," Devon said with a knowing smile. "Ethan, you're a lucky man, but Lily…" He gave a chuckle. "You can't do better than my grumpy little brother?"

Ethan shoved Devon off as he tried to give him an affectionate hair rub.

"Welcome to the family. Ethan, where's her ring?"

"I just proposed. Give me a chance, man."

"Usually you get the ring before you propose. You should know that by now." Devon quickly changed the subject, and Lily suspected it was for reasons to do with Dani Demare, Ethan's ex-fiancée. The story was that she'd left him when she'd found out he was paralyzed. "Let me know if you guys need anything—my wife designs wedding gowns if you want something special."

"I met Olivia a few months ago," Lily said. "She seems nice."

"And will be your sister-in-law," Devon said with a grin.

Sister-in-law. Lily felt her eyes dampen again. She was gaining a big family filled with love and joking and...everything. She'd have Devon as a brother, her best friend, Mandy, as a true sister at long last. Add in Mandy's husband, Frankie, plus Ethan's mom, dad and stepmom...

It was overwhelming.

Her life felt inexplicably full all of a sudden. Even if it was just temporary, it filled a well inside her she hadn't realized was dry.

"I'm going to make everyone a nice big meal," she announced. She'd learned to cook in the Mattsons' kitchen and couldn't imagine a better way to reignite the old feelings of gratitude, acceptance and home than with a big dinner.

"I thought we weren't doing a party," Ethan said.

"It's just a way to say thanks and bring everyone together." She could pour her love for them into a tasty pot of soup or a crusty loaf of homemade bread.

"Lily's back! Let her cook," Devon crowed. "Can

you make that coconut upside-down cake you used to bake back in high school? I haven't had that in forever."

Lily felt her world grow bigger. "I sure can."

"Oh, and those cookies you used to send in those care packages back when I was earning my degree. And your bean soup." He wrapped an arm around her, sneaking her away from Ethan. "You know, my brother's a bit of a bear. Maybe you could come work as a cook for Olivia and me. If nothing else, we smile a lot more."

Lily caught Ethan glowering at his brother. "If you want her cooking you can get it at Benny's, or here through catering. She's not your personal slave." He shoved the tray of sandwiches toward Devon.

His brother frowned, obviously noticing the ones she hadn't finished putting back together. "Huh?"

"I dropped them," Ethan said, turning to leave. "Bon appetite."

Lily giggled.

"Welcome to the family, Lily," Devon said. "And good luck with grumpy-pants."

ETHAN DROVE HOME, exhausted from dealing with Lily and her marriage proposal on top of his day. He'd been on his feet for hours and his body was rebelling at the effort he'd put into hiding his limp and bad shoulder from Lily. All he wanted to do was curl up in bed and let himself slip into sleep. But he was going to have to pull an all-nighter if he wanted to get through the thirty-nine emails waiting from clients, update a website to ensure its online checkout system remained secure, as well as relocate a few sites to a more reliable, robust server.

Never mind the fact that in twelve hours the offer to accept the contract for handling Burke's website would expire.

One thing at a time, he reminded himself. Dr. Leham had warned him to chill out and prioritize, let the less vital things slide. Plus it was only four thirty. Still lots of day left. Ethan could work for a few hours, take a supper break, work some more, stretch, work, catch a few hours of sleep, then get up early and begin working again. And somewhere in there determine what exactly he and Lily were going to do in regards to the whole marriage thing.

He turned his SUV onto his street, grateful for the shade provided by the large trees overhanging the road. How was marrying Lily the only way to get everything he wanted? And why was she set-tling for him, a broken, messed up, grumpy man?

He was going to marry her, though. He already knew that. They just had to figure out the logistics before the news carried far and wide and expecta-tions of a big wedding began to grow. Because in Blueberry Springs, weddings, graduations, baby showers and funerals were big to-dos. To deny the town the opportunity to come together and cele-brate their "love" was akin to…well, he wasn't sure, but he knew it was bad.

And that meant he and Lily had to sneak off and get married soon. Really soon.

Ethan worried that he might have given her the wrong impression today, though. One that sug-gested he had the ability to keep her safe, protect her like a man—a husband—should be able to. He'd lucked out with a well-timed punch to Tanner's jaw, but was certain he wouldn't get that chance twice. He was going to have to talk to a friend, Logan Stone, who worked in private security, to see if there was anything he could do to help pro-tect Lily.

Ethan parked outside his small house, surprised to see his mother sitting on his front step.

"Mom?"

"My TV broke."

He checked his smartwatch as he climbed out of

his vehicle. Her favorite TV shows were long over. "Why didn't you let yourself in?"

"I did." He noticed the cup of coffee on the step beside her.

"Is that fresh?" He could use a pot of java right about now.

"Decaf."

Leaves rustled on the tree beside him as the wind picked up, bringing with it a weather change he could feel in his thigh. He eased onto the step next to his mom, massaging his leg where the steel rod had been placed through the bone. The persistent ache made him feel like an eighty-year-old man instead of one nearing his thirties.

He was a modern miracle though, and should count his blessings. That's what his mom had told him ten years ago when he'd woken up from the medically induced coma two weeks after the accident. Most doctors believed he shouldn't have even survived the accident, and there had been many dark moments during his five-year recovery that Ethan had wished he hadn't.

He'd been told it was sheer luck that his truck hadn't been buried under the mountain of snow that had slid off the side of the mountain and across the road, taking him with it. More luck that his truck had been found. But it hadn't been pretty. It had taken rescuers five hours to free him and get him to hospital, and he'd been in the intensive care unit for several weeks, released into a rehabilitation facility four months and a dozen surgeries later. It had been a long, slow recovery, full of more surgeries, and more hope. But Ethan's family had been there every step of the way and still seemed to be looking out for him despite his renewed independence.

"What are you up to?" he asked his mom.

"Waiting for you. Is your leg okay?"

"It's fine." There was no need for her to worry about it. It was what it was. "I'm thinking of getting married." He settled in beside her even though he knew his joints would pay for sitting on the shaded, cool concrete for any length of time.

His mother, who'd just been taking a sip of coffee, spit it out all over the step, her painted-on eyebrows arched high in disbelief.

"Nice. Thanks, Mom." He reached for the railing and struggled to stand.

"You're doing too much. Sit."

Ethan complied, only because it felt nice to think his mom had sat and waited for him after seeking him out.

"So? Married?" she asked, peeking over at him, her coffee secured on the step below.

"Yep."

"I don't know who we'll ever find, though." She

said it in a kind way, but it still brought up a well of hurt, rejection and failure. "You're on your own too much and have been ever since spending your twenties in rehab to get your mobility back."

Before he could speak, she added brightly, "Lily Harper's back in town. She brought me scones, the sweet thing. I can't believe she remembered." His mother smiled, obviously happy to be thought of. "You used to bring me things, too, you know."

As a kid he'd bring home things from his day, such as a four-leaf clover he'd found in the square on Main Street, a library book he thought might interest her, soup from Benny's restaurant. He didn't do that any longer and he wasn't sure why. Probably because he'd grown up and realized there were only so many dandelion bouquets a mom could act thrilled over.

"Did she say anything?" he asked, referring to her visit with Lily.

"No, she sat there like a statue. Of course she said stuff!" His mom laughed, suddenly in good spirits. She smelled like coffee and candies. "She wants to buy your restaurant, you know."

"What would you say if I told you I was thinking of marrying her?" He had a sudden lump in his throat, not for the deception, but from something else. Something he couldn't even begin to identify.

His mother was stunned into silence, hands frozen to her thighs.

"Why?" she asked slowly.

Okay, that hurt.

"Do you love her?" His mother was looking at him as if he'd said he'd made contact with aliens. Half intrigued by his looniness and half—okay, more like nine-tenths—in utter disbelief.

He put his bad arm around her shoulder, pulling her closer. "Oh, Mom."

"What? You two aren't even dating. Are you?"

"Well, we were talking about marriage today."

His mother leaned into him, taking away some of the empty feeling inside—what moms were so good at doing.

They remained silent for a few moments.

"Do you need a ring?" his mom asked.

Ethan blinked at the sudden shift in topic, his mind devoid of anything useful such as thoughts or words. The lump in his throat was back.

"Oh, Ethan." His mom tsked, shaking her head. "You *are* a special boy, you know that?" She cupped his chin, gazing at him with affection. "Marry her before she changes her mind. You might not do any better."

Any better than a fake marriage?

Unfortunately, she was probably right.

"YOUR FATHER TOLD me you're going to propose to Lily."

Ethan put his grandfather on speaker as he copied files from one server to another.

"It's a thought," he replied carefully, hoping to downplay the arrangement. Gramps was the only one still willing to bust Ethan's balls, and he had a special knack for hitting where it hurt the most. Even Devon tended to back off when push came to shove.

"Well, your father plans on meddling."

"What else is new?"

His grandpa chuckled.

While Ethan appreciated all his father had done for him over the years, he didn't want him heavily invested in what amounted to a lie. He didn't particularly want to lie to his grandfather, either, but he did want to help Lily.

Ethan turned up his phone's microphone volume and stood, stretching out the stiffness in his back. He'd been hunched over his computer since his mom left hours ago, furiously trying to get caught up, and had worked through the supper break he'd promised himself. His stomach rumbled and he huffed out a sigh as he started to pace. The last thing he wanted was to make another sandwich, even for himself.

Walking through the small, empty house, phone in hand, he searched for an easy snack. His brother had hired Katie Leham a few years back to do some decorating at his place, which had earned Devon a good teasing. But today Ethan understood the need to paint over the starkness, to fill the barren space with some color and life. It was like living in a hotel room, except without the mass-produced art or throw cushions.

"Tell me three things you love about Lily," his grandfather suggested.

"What?" Ethan opened his fridge, confused by Gramps's request.

"Three things and I'll stay off your back."

Three things about Lily. That should be easy.

He rifled around in his refrigerator while he thought. Everything in there seemed to have expired. How could that be? And where had all of July gone? He opened a container of yogurt—his usual go-to snack, since it was easy and relatively filling. Plus he figured the calcium was good for his patched up bones. He gave the container a sniff, then stirred it and took a bite.

Still okay.

"Three things," Gramps prodded.

"She's got great legs."

His grandfather let out a satisfied grunt. "I do love a set of good legs." Ethan smiled. "But I didn't ask what gets your Johnson up," Gramps scolded. "And don't lie—I know it's waving because I've already heard about you punching out the lights on her ex-boyfriend like a possessive fool."

"I didn't KO him, Gramps."

"The ladies go for that, by the way. Smart move. I hope you hit him in a soft spot so you didn't hurt your hand."

"The hand is fine," Ethan said, testing it and feeling slightly dazzled by his prowess. Man, had he lucked out. It felt good. It was like he'd temporarily put his life back in the ring again, enjoying a flash of his former self.

"Anyway," his grandfather said, his thrill over Ethan's pummeling seemingly passed, "I asked for three things you love about her."

Ethan sighed and rubbed his face, knowing he'd be unable to put off his grandfather.

"If you can't rattle that off in your sleep you're not ready for marriage."

"Fine." Ethan ran through his thoughts, picking up things he admired about the woman he'd known most of his life. "She's sweet and kind."

"That counts as one."

Ethan grumbled silently. Then he thought about her determination to get what she wanted.

That was pretty cool. Respectable. Plus she hadn't backed down or acted wounded when he been grouchy, either. Another thing to admire. But he wasn't going to admit that out loud.

"She's willing to pursue her dreams with determination. She has a new toughness to her."

He got an approving sound. "You need someone strong. One more, Son."

Ethan stumbled. He couldn't think of anything. He didn't want to. Already, visions of her smile, the one that lit up everything around her, was filling his mind, drawing his attention away from his secret fears that he might end up back in a wheelchair one day. He knew it would sound cheesy, but she made him want to claim life, to not give up.

"One more," his grandpa prompted.

"I don't know," Ethan exclaimed, suddenly realizing just how deep their deception was going to have to go. And how easily he could begin to think it was real, when he knew it never would be because he couldn't be the old Ethan she'd once admired.

He sagged into a kitchen chair. He needed this. He needed Lily to take over his two businesses so he could focus on the third, and lower his stress levels a notch like Katie's husband, his doctor, Nash Leham, had been advising. For the past year his aches and pains had been growing worse, and

Nash believed Ethan might be heading into some early onset debilitating arthritis. Something that could make him a burden on his family once again. He needed to earn enough money that he could hire someone to take care of him if something bad happened with his health. He couldn't ask his family to drop everything for him. Not again.

"Gramps, it doesn't matter. We're getting married."

"Don't take the tone with me. Answer the question."

"She's…smart. And she doesn't take my moods personally. She trusts me more than I deserve to be trusted. She sees me as…" His voice grew weak. "She sees me as a real man, Gramps."

He'd seen the way she'd looked at him when he'd punched Tanner today. She'd looked at him with admiration, as if she knew he would always keep her safe. He wanted to be that man. Desperately.

Before his grandfather could speak, Ethan added, "She's a perfect ray of sunshine and I'd be lucky to have her in my life."

"Then you have my blessing."

Ethan just about hit the end-call button in panic. He was going to deceive some of the most important people in his life in hopes of being able to give Lily what she wanted, the life and stability she deserved. What if he failed? What he hurt her in some way?

"I can't do this," he said.

"Which is exactly why you must," Gramps said cheerfully. "There's a sale on rings downtown. I recommend something classic." He ended the call.

Ethan stared at his silent phone before pressing it against his forehead.

He was going to buy another ring. Only this time it would be for a woman who wasn't going to reject him for his physical weaknesses before they tied the knot. This time it would be for a woman he already knew wasn't in it for the long haul.

Because he'd learned long ago that men like him didn't get to find true love.

CHAPTER 3

*L*ily was staying at Mandy and Frankie Smith's until she figured out what she was doing, which sounded like marrying Ethan. That meant she was buying a restaurant and would finally have her own kitchen. She'd be the boss. She'd make or tweak the menu and decide on everything from schedules to flatware. Everything. All her. And she'd be surrounded by employees who loved their jobs and were like family, friends. Not like her old bosses, who were gruff and practically inhuman. She'd be friendly, approachable, and it was going to be fantastic.

Lily thought about calling her father to share the news, but decided it would be wiser to wait until she'd tied the knot with her protector, Ethan, in case things went awry with their tentative deal.

She found herself smiling as she pet Mandy's fluffy gray cat, Portia. She was getting married! She knew it was temporary and completely platonic, but even so, a thrill kept zipping through her. Especially when she thought of the way Ethan had socked Tanner today. Wow. Out of nowhere, ready to protect her.

Lily sighed in contentment. She'd missed Ethan.

Her phone buzzed with an incoming text and she picked it up to read the screen, hoping someone was bored and looking for something to do.

It was Tanner. All apologies. She sighed and deleted the text while upping the volume on the TV. Mandy and Frankie were in their bedroom, apparently enjoying their last week of being childless, and Mandy's giggles could be heard every once in a while, punctuating the lulls in Lily's TV show.

Someone knocked at the front door and Portia took off, a flurry of sharp claws, while Frankie's big black dog, Heart, burst off the floor, barking.

Lily waited for Mandy or Frankie to reappear and answer the door, but when the giggling continued, she got up with a sigh. Ethan was standing there, looking nervous. The setting sun lit him up, giving him a glow that highlighted the rugged slant of his jaw, the seriousness of his expression.

Her fiancé.

Mmm.

"I don't know how to do this," he announced.

"Do what? Visit someone?" She opened the wooden door wider to invite him in, but Ethan remained in place, looking as skittish as a teenager meeting his girlfriend's father for the first time.

He was staring at something in his hands and her gaze followed his. He was holding a square ring box and her heart thudded harder.

"If I get down on one knee I might cause a scene."

She couldn't think. Couldn't breathe. She'd imagined this. The way she'd jump into his arms, kiss him, make love after.

It was here—that day was here! It was coming —*shut up, Lily. Just. Shut. Up.*

This was a business deal. No emotions or dreams or any of that complicated stuff. She was getting a restaurant, not being swept off to bed.

Platonic.

Ethan handed her the box. "Please, Lily Harper, say you will take these dang businesses off my hands."

She laughed at his earnestness and the lack of romance in his request. She took the ring box. "Sure. Let's do this thing."

His shoulders sagged in relief and she believed he'd never looked sexier.

"I have some ideas for the prenuptial agreements you mentioned," he said. His voice was deep, slightly shy, and it commanded her awareness in a way that shouldn't be legal. She wished she had the right to step up to him, touch him, make him smile with just her presence, but most of all, wished she had the power to make him hers.

That? That would be…heaven.

"Are Mandy and Frankie home?" he asked. Just then laughter burst through the house. Ethan quickly added, "How about we go to my place?"

"Yeah, good idea." Lily grabbed her suit jacket off the coat rack by the door and followed him down the front steps. She was still in her business nonsense outfit with the tight skirt from earlier, and she felt slightly silly for being so dressed up.

Ethan walked slowly and she fell in with his easy pace, reminding herself she was in Blueberry Springs now, not the city. Everything was slower here. Relaxed. At ease.

A few blocks away, Ethan ushered her up the walk to a house slightly bigger than Mandy and Frankie's, but not by much. He'd left the lights on, giving it a homey feel as the sun set behind the mountains surrounding them.

She was going to live there. A romantic vision

of them happily married, living their dream careers, flashed before her and she smiled.

Mary Alice, the world's biggest gossip, went by, walking her small dog. Ethan gently placed a hand on the small of Lily's back, guiding her up the steps. She waved at Mary Alice, who was walking faster, trying to catch them to chat before they entered the house. Ethan hit a button on a remote, unlocking the front door before they reached it.

"Slick," Lily whispered. Was there anything sexier than a gadget head? He probably could dim the lights and lower the music from his phone, too. She almost purred, thinking about it.

"Hurry," he urged quietly, nodding at Mary Alice before following Lily into the house and quickly shutting the door. He let out a gusty breath that blew his nicely trimmed hair off his forehead. "Close call." He kicked off his loafers and tossed his keys inside one.

She giggled, loving how he seemed less grumpy and more like the old Ethan she knew from high school. Deadly cute.

"So we're getting married?" she asked, testing the idea out loud.

"If you're still game."

"How soon?"

"How about yesterday? I need to work on a

project that'll take me away from Benny's and catering. I need you to take over ASAP."

Oh. His intentions for an immediate workload shift were slightly disappointing. But no, that was what she was looking for—to dive right in.

"That's music to my ears, honey bun."

He lifted an eyebrow in disgust.

"No? How about baby cakes?" she teased. He needed to loosen up, smile more. She laughed at his expression. "We have to play the part, my sweetie pie."

"Whatever you say, Lilypad."

That nickname never failed to make her feel like she was ten years old again.

Unsexy. That's what that feeling was.

"I'll start calling you Either."

He shrugged at the despised nickname his brother had given him years ago, but she noticed the corners of his lips almost lifted in a reluctant smile. Almost.

Give her time; she'd get him there.

He was focused on her hands. "Does the ring fit? I picked it up on the way over—store's open late."

The ring. Right. She patted her jacket pockets, bringing out the box. She paused, then extended it to him. "Did you want to…"

He frowned, his scowl back. "It's just a prop."

He turned on his heel, heading farther into the house which was in dire need of some homey touches. From the outside it had looked welcoming, but inside it was stark and a bit cold.

She opened the box and held in a gasp. It was the most beautiful ring she'd ever seen. And it was for her. Her eyes dampened and she blinked the tears away so Ethan didn't think she'd been affected, that she couldn't handle this. She slipped the simple, classic and bold solitaire onto her finger, testing its size. It was perfect. Absolutely perfect.

LILY SWIVELED her engagement ring around and around on her finger, nervously tapping her foot outside the Blueberry Springs law office run by John Abcott. It was nearly noon on a cloudy August day, but that had nothing to do with how her suit was sticking to her back as doubts swirled through her mind.

She was going to have to be uncharacteristically firm and jaded in the office in order to be sure she got what she wanted. She'd been too trusting in the past when it came to agreements, and this time she wasn't getting short-changed. Ethan was trustworthy, but who knew how things might change once money and marriage were involved?

She straightened the long, fitted suit jacket she wore over a slightly longer skirt. Business sexy, as she called it. The second-to-last outfit outside her jeans and sweatshirt repertoire, and her personal favorite because it said in the same breath "look at my legs, but don't mess with me."

Ethan came around the corner, his brow furrowed in a way she realized was now typical for him. He gave her a nod, holding the door for her.

"Good afternoon," she said, with a hinting tone.

"Good afternoon," he grumbled in reply.

"You know, you might want to try acting as though you wouldn't mind spending the rest of your life with me."

He grunted, and she placed a smile on her face, hooking her hand into the crook of his elbow, trying not to act insulted when he jerked away in surprise. They were definitely going to have to work on this whole being-in-love thing.

"When's the big day?" Liz Moss-Brady asked, smiling up from her desk as they entered the office. Lily remembered the gossipy Mrs. Moss-Brady from back when she lived in Blueberry Springs. Not exactly the person she wanted to see while arranging a prenup that might contain some questionable clauses. "I didn't even get to place a bet with my sister on when the engagement might occur. Did a one-night stand go wrong?" The woman laughed at her own joke and Ethan's scowl deepened, making the sexy scar near his mouth stand out.

"Is John available?" he asked.

"Will you be taking over the restaurant for Ethan?" Liz prodded. "I hear you went to baking school."

"It was a culinary arts program," she corrected automatically. "I thought you worked for the local paper."

"In my spare time." Liz smiled, folding her hands on her desk and giving the couple an expectant look.

The door behind Liz's desk opened and a man a little older than Lily's father smiled at them, ushering them in.

"Congratulations," John said, shaking their hands before gesturing for them to take a seat. Lily made her handshake a quick hug.

"I haven't seen you since I coached you in soccer as a teen," he said, adjusting his reading glasses. "How have you been? Do you still play?"

"I haven't in years. Are you still coaching?"

"Just the little kids now."

Ethan offered Lily the closest chair, then awkwardly made his way around to sit beside her. "The draft looked good," he said. "Do you have a final copy for us to sign?"

"Almost." John leaned back in his chair, spinning to lift a box off a hidden coffeemaker. "Coffee? Water?" He poured himself a cup when both Ethan and Lily shook their heads, then covered the machine again.

"Why do you hide your coffeemaker?" Lily asked.

"Liz makes horrible stuff, but would be insulted if she knew I made my own." John took a sip of his secret coffee. "I'll admit I don't do many prenuptial agreements. Did you want to add anything about possible children? Custody, et cetera?"

Lily's heart dropped and Ethan shot her a quick look. "Whatever's standard."

What did that mean? He wanted kids? He thought this was real?

She gave herself a mental shake. No, he was just being careful not to lend suspicion to their situation. Still, she worried how much adding extra clauses would cost them in fees. She didn't have a lot of cash on hand right now, even with Ethan planning to let her crash with him, rent free.

"And could I also give Lily power of attorney so she can act on my behalf if anything happens?" Ethan asked, leaning forward, his expression more serious than she'd ever recalled seeing.

"But we're young," Lily said. And healthy. As well as getting divorced in a year.

"That's not a bad idea. Especially with several businesses involved." John began scrawling on the draft in front of him. "If one partner becomes incapacitated, unable to make decisions or take care of things for any reason, you want the other to be able to step in and keep everything running."

Lily felt a wave of fear. Suddenly everything felt too big, too real. They were adults. Adults responsible for real-world things, who might be faced with real-life problems. Big ones.

"Lil? Is that okay?" Ethan asked, consulting her.

She gave a fast nod.

"I'll give you the boilerplate version I give all business owners, as I heard you two want to get moving on a wedding date. Then, if you want to modify it later, we can do that at no extra charge."

"Thanks," Ethan said.

"Is the date set? I'm sure the town will be eager to see you two walk down the aisle."

"We might elope," he admitted uncomfortably.

"Well," John said with a chuckle, "if you manage to get that past your stepmother, Ethan, you're a better man than I."

Lily smiled. Trish was a force to reckon with at times, that was for certain. When she believed in something she had a way of digging in her heels.

For example, she'd decided years ago that Lily needed to know how to grocery shop and had taken her to the store several times, filling her head with knowledge about the best cuts of meat, how to tell whether fruit was ripe and more. She'd also let her buy whatever ingredients she thought she might need for a recipe, turning her kitchen over to the teen as if she was Lily's own mother.

John turned to Lily. "You're okay with purchasing the two culinary businesses at today's market value, while Ethan keeps his web company if you two choose to part ways?"

She nodded.

John scratched his head, looking at them. "I must admit this is quite unusual."

If he caught on, so would suppliers. She'd lose the ability to run the business and turn a profit before she even had it. In other words, she'd spend another year working for someone else, with nothing to show for it but exhaustion and a mountain of debt.

"It's fair. They're his, but I'll be taking them over," Lily said calmly.

John turned to Ethan. "The market value may increase."

Ethan nodded. "I'm sure it will with her at the wheel."

"It could also go down," Lily pointed out.

The lawyer seemed uncomfortable as he looked from Lily to Ethan, then back again. "So we're good then?" he confirmed. If he suspected something, he didn't let on. "I'll add a clause about kids and a boilerplate POA and you'll be set."

Lily leaned back in her chair as John typed in the clauses and hit Print.

That was it.

No fighting.

Exactly what they'd agreed, plus two things.

But kids? The very idea shot a thrill right through her. She smiled at Ethan, knowing she was getting her hopes up.

John gave her a wink. "I'll go grab the copies." He left the room.

Ethan had a faraway gaze as he turned to her. "Are you going to serve that meatball soup?"

"Meatball soup?" What did that have to do with adding a clause about babies?

"The one you and Mandy used to make when you were teenagers."

"Oh! Right. That was pretty good, wasn't it?" Fond memories flowed through her. The soup was definite comfort food that would be delicious with a warm, crusty bread. Maybe add a side of salad and a slice of rich chocolate cake for dessert. "I might have to see if I can find the recipe."

"Mandy still has it. She makes it now and again."

"For her café?" Nuts. So much for using the recipe—she couldn't take a recipe from her friend.

Ethan shook his head. "Just when I fake a funk and she wants to pull me out of it." He gave Lily a secret smile that lit her up from toes to nose. Those smiles were rare and special—always had been.

"Should I add it to the menu?" Her earlier apprehension was melting like snow off a black roof. She curved toward Ethan, curious what his thoughts were.

"I think there's always room to add more—or introduce new things as a weekly special to test them out."

Lily reached over, tangling her fingers in Ethan's as John reentered the office. This time, instead of looking startled, Ethan gave her a slight smile that warmed her insides like homemade jam.

"You know, I have a feeling you're not going to need this," the older man said, sliding the documents, still warm from the printer, toward them. "And not to brag, but my gut is usually right about couples."

Lily pointedly kept her eyes lowered as they scrawled their names on the indicated lines, then swapped copies before doing so again.

Done.

She could hardly believe it. In one year she was officially going to own a restaurant as well as a catering business.

John gave them a smile as he stood to shake their hands, offering them congratulations.

For the first time, Lily felt as though they truly might be able to pull this off.

"No," Ethan repeated to his stepmother. Trish had her mouth set in a firm line and wasn't about to back down, but neither was he. They'd fought plenty during his teenaged years and he could bring back that sulky, stubborn-mule side of his personality in a split second. Everything was already getting out of hand with Lily and they'd been "engaged" for less than twenty-four hours. She'd held his hand in the law office an hour ago like she had the right to claim it. Claim him.

The very idea made his ribs feel ten sizes too small for his lungs.

Yes, it was an act. But people expected a wedding. Parties. Kisses.

Didn't they see it was a mismatch? Why couldn't they just ignore it? Look away and avoid the fact that Ethan was going to be left in a year.

They should have eloped before saying anything. People liked Lily and were excited for her, which meant he needed to drag her off to a court-room and marry her and end the expectations. Quickly.

"I said no party," he repeated when Trish opened her mouth to speak, a list of guests clutched between her long, shiny red nails. How had she even had time to create the list?

He was the forgotten child, in the middle—the third and last kid to tie the knot. They were sup-posed to be yawning over another wedding, not tricking him into coming over by sending a text about his dad needing help with his email program, so they could ambush him. They'd have him spend every last dime on this fake wedding if he caved even one tiny little bit.

They meant well, but they didn't know the truth.

"Ethan, you listen to me," his father interjected. "Trish didn't once complain about your foul moods, making her home wheelchair friendly. You found someone, you're having an engagement party at the very least. It's time to let the world back in."

"What's that supposed to mean?"

"Son, you owe us this."

"Have you set a date?" Trish asked.

"This evening," Ethan mumbled, turning to escape. Ten steps to the door.

"What?" Trish cried. His father laughed, not believing him.

Five steps.

"Afraid she'll run away?" he called, still chuckling.

Ethan opened the door. "When you know, you know. No need to wait," he muttered, closing it behind him.

It opened immediately, Trish poking her head out. "You had better be joking. And you'd better be here by seven for the party. And make sure it's still a surprise for Lily."

"Trish, we don't want a party." He turned on the landing to face her.

"All women want to be fussed over."

"Lily's a tomboy." Or once was. Today's outfit had been just as sexy and feminine as yesterday's. And those high heels? He wished she didn't walk so easily in them so he could catch her, have an excuse to hold her in his arms.

"All women want to be fussed over and be the center of attention," she repeated.

"I have a massive project in the works and can't deal with all this wedding crap."

Trish let out a horrified gasp and he softened his tone, struggling to be patient. "We know what we want and it's to get married. So we're going to do that and leave the rest. You guys always say it's about being together."

Trish bit a knuckle, trying to hold back a flood of tears.

He hated the tears.

"I'm just so happy you found someone," she squeaked, holding out her arms for a hug. "She's always been such a ray of sunshine and you were always so sweet to her. You took her under your wing and now she's taking you under hers. We can stop worrying about you."

Ethan shifted out of her embrace, sighing. He hated that they still felt responsible for him. Sure, he couldn't do everything, but he was able enough even on his bad days to be entirely independent. He'd even hired out his yard work so if he didn't get to it right away his brother wouldn't feel he had to do it for him.

He loved his family, but he didn't know how to get them to stop worrying and fussing.

"What she means to say," his father added, slipping his arms around his wife's slender waist as he joined them out on the step, "is that it'll be nice for you to have someone."

Trish shook a finger at Ethan. "You keep being good to her!" She dabbed at her eyes. "I remember Lily and Mandy upending my kitchen with their baking." She smiled wistfully and Ethan realized how much she'd enjoyed the teenagers, even though she'd been stunned and overwhelmed at the time. To go from no kids to a pile of them running rampant through her home, and not-so-subtly making fun of her breast enhancements behind her back. "She needed us just as much as we needed her."

Ethan sighed and looked up at the sky. Now she was just being dramatic.

"Are you sure we can't talk you up to a decent-sized wedding?" his dad asked.

"Elopement."

"We could help pay."

And never retire because of it? No, thanks. He'd waylaid their plans enough as it was.

"You guys have already done enough for me over the years. But thank you."

His father looked concerned, that same expression he got when he thought about Ethan's endless surgeries. Not quite pity, but something that usually caused him to back down, to not push Ethan in the way he pushed Mandy. Ethan tried not to use it to his advantage, but sometimes you just had to.

He made a show of limping down the steps, wondering how fast he could get a wedding band on Lily's finger.

LILY STEPPED into Veils and Vows, Blueberry Springs's bridal shop. Her future sister-in-law now worked in the store as a gown designer and over the years Lily had purchased many bridesmaids dresses from the shop.

Not that she expected to purchase a gown anytime soon, seeing as her engagement basically amounted to a business arrangement, and neither she nor her father could afford anything extravagant. But ideally, she'd like to pick up a simple sundress that could double as a wedding dress so she'd feel at least a little bit done up for their elopement, and the families could have a little something to put in their albums.

"Is Olivia in?" Lily asked the shop's owner, Ginger McGinty, an old high school friend.

"I heard you're engaged!" Ginger squealed, giving Lily a monstrous squeeze. Recently, Ginger had taken over her grandmother's shop, then become a mother figure to a special needs young woman, Annabelle, when she married a massive man, Logan Stone. As a teen, the man must have eaten his parents out of house and home building a physique that rivaled a bunker. Only, you know, a good-looking bunker. If something like that existed.

"Girl, you move fast!" Ginger said. "Weren't you single only last week? It's not that blind date I suggested when you were in town months ago for that bridesmaid fitting, was it?"

Lily shook her head. Ginger had tried to set her up with some mountain man—cute, but totally not her type.

"Who's the lucky guy? No, don't tell me. He's a prison pen pal who needs bail or a woman on the outside." She laughed as she tugged gowns off nearby racks, holding them up against Lily's frame. Ginger's lips would purse as she considered each dress before discarding it and choosing another.

"Ethan. It's Ethan Mattson." Lily pushed one of the offered dresses away.

"Ethan? I thought everyone was kidding." The quiet surprise in her friend's tone didn't go unnoticed, nor did the sudden slackness of her jaw and arms. The A-line dress she was holding brushed the floor before Ginger snapped to, lifting it high enough that its hem wouldn't gather any dust. She laughed again, her eyes dancing. "How did you manage to get him to move so fast? Then again, he's always been sweet on you in a protective, brotherly sort of way." She winked. "And I heard what he did to your ex-boyfriend in front of town hall."

Before Lily could think of a reply, Ginger

waved a dress at her. "So? What do you think? High waistline? That would really enhance the girls. No? Too flashy?" She held up a fitted gown, saying, "Too much like a mermaid," before she discarded it, as well. "I liked the last bridesmaid dress you bought. It had a nice shape." She shook her head, laughing yet again. "Ethan probably didn't even see you coming. Poor man."

There was pity and sorrow in the way her friend said "poor man" that caused Lily to frown. Her husband-to-be was the last person in need of pity. He was strong, smart and successful.

"There's nothing wrong with Ethan," she said carefully. Sure, he had a limp from his accident and a facial scar… Lily's spine straightened suddenly as she thought back to Ethan's request for a power of attorney when they were getting their prenuptial agreement. It had felt odd at the time and now she feared that there was a genuine reason for him wanting one, as well as wanting to move two of his businesses into someone else's hands.

"He's recovered fairly well for someone who was confined to a wheelchair," her friend hedged.

"Yes, I know. But what's wrong?"

"He's just…different since the accident. More reserved. That's all." Ginger was watching Lily with concern. "I'm sure if anything is wrong he'll tell the woman he loves."

Lily tried to keep her expression neutral even though her stomach had begun to plummet.

"How do you feel about a specially designed gown?" Ginger asked.

"What?"

"For your wedding," she teased.

"I was thinking of a sundress," Lily said weakly. Something was wrong with Ethan. "Something simple, since we're eloping."

Ginger rounded on her, looking as unimpressed as a scorned lover. She had one hand on her hip and a look so lethal Lily took a step back.

"What do you mean, eloping?" her friend asked slowly.

"Ethan just got a really big account for his web design business—it's for Burke Carver..." She needed out of the store. Needed space to think.

"Jill Armstrong wants to talk to him about her soaps and lotions line," Ginger said. "And?"

"What?"

"Never mind." She waved a hand through the air. "I heard you'll be taking over the catering and restaurant right away, so there's really no time to plan anything."

Lily nodded quickly, finding her excuse for not buying a gown. "That's right."

"If you're worried about planning a wedding," said a woman as she approached them, "this town can pull off a wedding with minimal effort from the bride and groom."

It was Olivia, her future sister-in-law. She winked at Ginger and the two shared a secret smile that Lily was certain must have had something to do with Olivia and Devon's own wedding.

Olivia hugged Lily. "It's so good to see you again. Welcome to the family."

"Thank you."

Olivia was elegant, blonde, and so beautiful she used to model for her family's company, Carrington Cosmetics. And she was surprisingly down to earth—a fantastic match for Devon.

"I love your perfume," Lily said. It was classy, sweet but sophisticated.

"It's Dani Demare..." Her voice faded away as she obviously realized her faux pas. Dani was Ethan's ex-girlfriend. The one who'd left him after his accident. That felt like so long ago—how could the woman still have the power to be a name best whispered? And if she was that bad, why was Olivia wearing her scent?

Because it smelled awesome, that was why.

But why would she send gifts to Ethan's brother? Was she still involved with the family? Was she going to be competition? Lily wondered.

And did it matter? It was a marriage of convenience. One to a man with secrets, apparently.

"Sorry, it was a gift," Olivia was saying. "We used to model together sometimes and she sent it when we got married. I didn't want to snub her and so I've been wearing it because..." Olivia caught Lily's expression and her imploring tone turned to one of resolve. "I won't wear it."

Lily waved her off with a cheery smile. "Hey, I got the man in the end, didn't I?" Just give her an Oscar for that performance. "I was hoping you might be able to point me in the direction of a nice sundress I could use for our elopement, or maybe modify something."

"Elopement?" Olivia's face fell.

"See? You have to have a real wedding," Ginger insisted. She began fussing with racks of dresses again.

Olivia took one look at Lily's expression and gave a dramatic gasp, grabbing Lily's hand. "Look at your ring! It's amazing."

Suddenly a crowd of women gathered around, taking in the glitter on her finger and distracting Ginger. Lily owed Olivia one, that was for sure.

And the ring *was* beautiful. One of the nicest things she owned. She wasn't sure what she was supposed to do when they split up. Give it back? Keep it? Sell it? The ring definitely made everything feel more real.

"Where did you two meet?" asked a tall redhead. She held herself so erect that she made Lily think of the military. And yet she was warm and full of life.

"We grew up together."

"He pulled her out of a mud puddle, Allison," Ginger added.

"That's so sweet. My husband and I have been married for seventeen wonderful years. I wish you all the happiness." She gave Lily a reassuring smile, setting her at ease. "I'm Allison Fentriss, by the way."

"Pleased to meet you."

"I couldn't help but overhear, and all I have to say is don't let these two tell you what to do," she said quietly. "You do what feels right for you and your man. It's your marriage, your day."

"Thank you."

Wanda, Ginger's grandmother, appeared from the back room with a large box. "Allison? I have those fabric scraps for you."

"I'm making quilts for the Quilts of Valor Foundation," Allison said. "I'm going to create something special in honor of war brides—a quilt made with bits of material from wedding gowns. A lot of women got married without a fancy dress during the war."

"Speaking of which, Lily deserves a nice dress. There's no war here." Wanda gave Lily a big, hopeful smile. "And yes, I was eavesdropping as much as I could while rummaging about back there."

Allison laughed good-naturedly. "You're a good friend to her, but it sounds like she's looking to elope."

Ginger sighed, seemingly giving up her quest as Olivia assured Lily she'd find her the perfect sundress for her big day.

Lily nodded blindly, seeking the door. Standing in a bridal shop had made everything feel pretty real and it had been a busy twenty-four hours. From the ring to the prenup, but now family, too. Olivia was sticking up for her and soon they'd be sisters for a while.

And then they wouldn't be.

And Lily would be alone once more.

CHAPTER 4

*E*than tapped the window's button twice, sending it zipping downward as he called out of his SUV, "Hey, Lil!"

She was in front of Veils and Vows, looking slightly overwhelmed. Ethan knew he should get out of the car, show her some respect and not shout to her, but his leg was killing him from the weather swing. He guessed they'd have rain within an hour or two and had tossed a waterproof windbreaker into the backseat earlier.

Lily gave him a little wave, the wind opening her suit jacket, pressing her blouse against her distracting curves.

"Get in," he said, knowing he sounded gruff.

Lily raised one eyebrow, but walked around to the passenger side. She climbed in, bringing with her fresh mountain air and a scent that was feminine and somehow familiar.

"Do you have ID with you?" he asked.

"Yeah, why?"

"You'll need it for a marriage license."

"Oh, thank goodness." She leaned back in the seat. "They were trying to convince me to buy a big dress, so the sooner we're married the easier it'll be to hold my ground." She gave a shaky laugh, fluffing her light brown locks with her fingers and sending them tumbling around her face, making her look delicate and beautiful.

"My family is planning a surprise engagement party," he said.

"Oh." She looked pleased, but taken aback.

"I think we should get married before it happens."

"Okay. When is it?" She helped herself to a sip of the water he had open beside him—and left a ring of lipstick around the mouth of the bottle. It didn't bother him, but it made his mind go utterly blank.

"Next week?" she prompted.

"Uh, tonight. At seven."

She had been sneaking another swig and sprayed water everywhere. "Tonight?" She dabbed at her wet chin, then used her jacket sleeve to dry his dash. "That's really soon."

"Yeah." And right now was a perfect time to wed. There was no catering to take care of, and Leif, the chef at Benny's, had things under control leaving Ethan free to take care of things with Lily. And they had to strike fast, too. They'd been engaged for less than a day and the town was already diving into preparations like it was an emergency situation. They had to get married before things got out of hand.

Ethan had pulled away from the curb and hesitated, unsure which direction he should drive. "Are we getting married or what?" He chided himself for his gruffness.

She didn't reply immediately and he took a better look at her. She appeared tired, uncertain.

"Are you dying?" she asked.

If he'd been drinking water it would have been his turn to spray it all over the dash.

"What?"

"Or sick?" She was eyeing him carefully.

"No."

"Is there anything I should know about before marrying you?"

He felt taken aback. What had they been talking about in the bridal store? He was certain nobody else in town, aside from his doctor, knew about the chance he was developing severe arthritis. And whether he was or not, it wouldn't impact their marriage.

He paused at a stop sign, one block off Main Street. "We don't have to do this. We can figure something else out."

"No," she said fiercely. She reached over and turned down the music, sending "When Something Stands for Nothing" by Headstones almost to mute. "We both know what we're getting into and this is the best way for both of us."

He pulled away from the stop sign, his heart beating hard against his ribs as he said lightly, "Last chance to back out."

"Do you want to?"

"I'm about to drive us the next town over so we can get married."

Derbyshire wasn't far, but there'd be less chance for anyone to interrupt their elopement—which was fairly likely in Blueberry Springs, with everyone wanting to be a part of the celebration. Awesome, but slightly inconvenient.

She gave a nervous laugh. "I didn't get you a wedding band."

"I don't need one."

"Then how will anyone know you're mine?"

Know you're mine...

That sounded good.

He found himself giving her a funny look. "Well, it's not real…and rings can be expensive."

"You got me a ring."

Of course he had. It wouldn't be right for her to have a bare finger.

The only other woman who'd ever worn his ring had given it right back again after she'd found out his crash had left him paralyzed, with a very slim chance of recovery. And he expected Lily to do the same once she could take over the businesses—leave him.

"So why can't I get you one?" Lily's eyes had narrowed and she looked borderline angry.

"Men rarely wear rings and there's no reason for you to spend that kind of money on me."

"Well, my husband wears a ring, so you can stop at the jewelry store or else I'm not marrying you."

Ethan pretended to give a weary sigh as he attempted to hide his amusement. It was ridiculous for her to go to the bother and cost. Plus, he honestly didn't know how he felt about wearing a wedding band. It felt like flaunting the lie, a constant reminder of how he'd never be a real husband to someone as wonderful as Lily.

"Lil—"

"I'm serious."

He glanced over to confirm what he already knew. She was digging in.

"Fine." He turned the vehicle in the direction of the jewelry store, dark clouds starting to knit together to the north.

"Good." She crossed her arms.

"If that's how you want to spend your money."

"I also expect us to remain exclusive while married."

He braked in front of the store with a jerk and Lily's seat belt clicked, locking her tightly against the seat. His voice was shaky with indignation as he stated, "It may be a fake marriage, but I am an honorable man, Lily Harper. If I'm married, I'm married."

"Good."

"Good." He threw the vehicle into Park with a snap.

"The same goes for me. And I'm glad you chose this store. I like the rings better here than in Derbyshire."

Ethan swallowed hard, hoping his voice didn't sound pained. "You've been ring shopping?"

"You're not the only one trying to make this look real, buster." She scowled at him as she climbed out of the SUV and slammed the door.

He sat in the vehicle for a moment, finding himself smiling. It was good to have someone dish it back. It happened so rarely it made him feel a little bit alive.

Human.

Like she wasn't afraid of breaking him with her words or moods.

He liked it.

Shaking his head, he carefully climbed out, catching up with Lily, who was already taking charge inside the store. She was playing down the congratulations with a smile and wave, already choosing rings. His kind of woman. Dani had made such a huge fuss over her ring it had been embarrassing. Especially when she'd turned right around short weeks later and handed it back to him. Man, had he ever been a fool. He should have seen it coming.

"What do you like? White or yellow gold?" Lily asked.

Ethan had thought about that very thing years ago. He'd chosen yellow gold for Dani, thinking it classic. He'd placed the whole set on hold, ready for the special day when they would commit to each other for life. It had taken him several attempts to summon the courage to propose. He'd received a lukewarm yes that had turned into a no once the doctor told her there was a good chance he might never walk again and would likely live off a disability pension for the rest of his life.

"White or yellow gold?" Lily repeated.

"I don't care," he snapped. He wanted white

gold and had bought Lily's ring in white for a reason. Plus, they should match.

No, it didn't matter. They weren't wearing these forever. Just long enough for her to establish herself as the owner of Benny's and the catering company. The rings could go to a pawnshop for all he cared.

But they should still match.

"White," she decided. "It's got to be bad luck to not wear a set, don't you think?" She began skimming the cases of white bands. "Diamonds?" she asked. She glanced at him, adding, "No, too flashy," before he could reply that it wasn't to his taste.

They cruised the cases, Lily leading, Ethan pretending not to care. Wearing her ring for a year was going to feel like he was overstepping his bounds. His family was going to be mad when they broke up.

But he'd be able to give Lily what she deserved —her own restaurant—and that would make it all worthwhile.

Every once in a while her comments would draw him in and he'd find himself agreeing with her assessment.

"Do you like your engagement ring?" he asked, leaning against the case, allowing his leg take a break.

Lily held out her hand, taking in the ring as

though considering it. Her long, slender fingers looked delicate with the simple, yet generous diamond. It pleased him, the way it appeared as though he was spoiling her. Buying the ring had pushed back his date for paying back his dad and Trish, but he felt it was worth it—especially when her cheeks flushed pink and she got that cute, shy look. "It's nice."

"We could exchange it. Get you something bigger." It was only money, after all. And maybe a nicer ring would help take the social sting out of marrying a man who not only didn't love her, but would soon divorce her, while all her friends were staying together, starting families. Plus he'd seen Lily's rusted old car. This was likely the most expensive thing she owned.

She curled her hand against her chest. "No. I like it."

Their eyes met and he made a point of checking his phone for the time as a flash of something that felt like a whole lot more than a guy sticking up for his sister's BFF passed between them. It felt like a peek into the future. A future with Lily.

She returned her attention to the rings, hustling the selection process along and pointing out five different rings she'd like to see.

As the clerk lined them up on the case, Ethan realized they were all ones he'd have chosen for himself. And even though Lilypad was going to up-turn his life soon, upsetting his quiet balance, he decided that might be a good thing.

LILY STUDIED the rings lined up in front of them.

"Too expensive," Ethan said, discarding an etched band.

"I'm choosing," she said, pulling the ring back into the lineup. Out of the corner of her eye she saw the clerk watching them as though he didn't quite believe they were a couple.

"I'm being reasonable," Ethan said. She stepped closer to him, the heat from his body was pressing into hers, making it impossible to concentrate.

"And it's my choice for my husband." She could afford it—sort of—and it was one of her favorites. Plus, it wasn't as though he'd skimped on her engagement ring.

The employee was still watching with skepticism. She needed to get Ethan to loosen up. She didn't remember him being this standoffish as a teen. She needed him to warm up so they looked like they might actually be in love.

Not that he'd ever fall for her. He was using her to get what he wanted, then he'd leave her like all the others had. Only this time she was going in with her eyes open and her heart on ice.

Ethan's ex, Dani, had been the only one to claim his heart, and the woman had had everything. Grace, beauty, smarts. Someone had mentioned she'd moved to New York and was modeling for *Vogue.* She even had her own line of perfume. Lily definitely wasn't in that league. Or anywhere near it.

"I'm the one who has to wear it," Ethan said, his voice low and gravelly. He was trying to nudge the more costly ring out of the line again.

"And I'll be wearing its mate."

Their eyes met and she felt a flash of something she didn't want to resist, but wanted to explore. What was it? Longing? Lust?

"Maybe I picked out the entire set and paid for it when I chose your engagement ring." Despite Ethan's gruff tone, there was a telltale lilt of teasing there, too.

The clerk whispered something to a colleague who'd come out of the back room, both of them sneaking looks at her and Ethan. Lily found herself wishing Ethan would bend her over the display case and kiss her so hotly nobody would ever doubt they were a couple.

As if he'd ever kiss her. He'd probably look like

he was kissing his sister if he did. And that was going to be a problem, wasn't it?

"You didn't pick any out," she stated, pulling her brain back to the problem of rings as Ethan checked the time once again. Yeah, yeah, in a hurry. She got it already.

Get married before the engagement party, put the ball back into their court.

But rings were a big decision.

"You don't know that I didn't," he said lightly.

"Yes, I do." She stared him down and a smile began to play at his lips. Why did he always find their bickering so amusing? It was like he wanted her to fight a bit, wanted her to shove back.

"How do you know?" he asked, crossing his arms, leaning against the case even though there were signs saying not to. She pushed him off the glass, pointing to one.

"Because you would have marched in here with your bossy pants on and said it was what we were getting." She shifted closer, allowing her chest to brush his as she acted the part of the fiancée getting her way. "And you didn't. So I know."

He cleared his throat and tapped a plain ring with a jagged edging. "Not that one."

She pushed a similar ring that was cheaper by a few hundred out of the lineup, then gave Ethan a saucy glance. He leaned closer, her body awakening at the possibility of contact.

Instead of touching her, he reached past her, tapping the glass. "We'll see these ones next."

"Please," she reminded him.

He met her eye, his breath warm against her cheek. *"Please."*

"Much better." She turned to the rings he'd chosen and choked. He *had* to be kidding.

"The ones I prepurchased." Barely holding back a grin, he slid the chunky, gaudy wedding band onto her finger. "Mrs. Mattson?"

Mrs. Mattson. How many times had she written that in her journal, daydreaming about this moment? There wasn't enough oxygen in the world to keep her standing upright at this moment.

She yanked at the ring, ready to set it back on the counter, remove herself from this charade before it got further under her skin. She didn't care what rings they ended up with, she just needed to breathe.

The ring was stuck. She stared at Ethan in panic. He met her look with one of his own before he burst out laughing. Real laughter. Delight. Joy. Happiness.

He'd never looked sexier.

"I am not leaving with this ring!" she hissed, yanking on it.

He laughed harder, his expression open. His laughter sounded amazing. Free. Unlike the grumpy bear he'd been for the past day and a half.

"I'm serious." She continued to pull on the ring. Tears flooded her eyes as she flipped between freaking out and giggling at the craziness of the situation.

"Mrs. Soprano," he said, between shouts of laughter.

"*Not funny*! If I have to wear one, so do you!" She couldn't hold back the panicked laughter, and Ethan, weak from his own, pulled her against him, his body shaking. He felt good wrapped around her and she hugged him back, her humor dying as she became aware of how good he felt, how *right*.

Her childhood protector, her idol, her crush. He was a man, and there was an undeniable heat building between them the longer they embraced. She glanced up to see if he felt it, too, and his own mirth faded as their eyes met. A hot current passed between them, fleeting but powerful.

Ethan stepped back, but she squeezed him tighter. "I don't care if the world burns down, I'm not taking this ring home with me," she whispered, tucking her head under his chin with a sigh.

He chuckled, smoothing her hair, hugging her so sweetly. Like friends. Like lovers.

When Lily went to move away, Ethan was slow

to release her, his mood suddenly somber, and she couldn't help but wonder what he was thinking and whether the embrace had felt as right to him as it had to her.

WHAT HAD THAT BEEN? Ethan was trying to pull himself together after the shock of yearning that had bolted through him in the jewelry store. The pull he'd felt to kiss Lily, to make it all real when she'd been in his arms, had been unsettling.

She was his sister's best friend and had always had a crush on him. She wasn't someone to mess around with emotionally. It was his duty to protect her.

But she'd felt so incredible, so right.

Even now, glancing at her in the passenger seat, his ring on her finger, their wedding bands in a bag at her feet as they drove off to get married, he felt a possessiveness wash over him that he'd never felt with Dani. With anyone.

It had to be the stand-in big brother card pulling some punches. Had to be that he'd always felt protective of her. It likely hadn't helped that the store clerk had kept one interested eye on Ethan's cute and sexy fiancée the whole time they'd been shopping. He didn't blame the man; Lily was one fine woman. In every way.

At least once they were married and past tonight's party they could become ensconced in their own projects for a while. That would help. Everything right now was feeling too big. Much too big.

And maybe a little bit real.

"Stop the car," Lily said, surprising Ethan.

They were halfway to Derbyshire to get their marriage license before heading to the courthouse for a lil' ol' four forty-five "I do." Dutifully, he looked for a place to pull off as dark clouds rolled in overheard, promising an evening storm.

Was she experiencing cold feet? Maybe she hadn't liked the way he'd looked at her in the jewelry store. Because her tone certainly said she had things she needed to get off her chest. A very nice chest, too. One he wouldn't mind exploring with his mouth sometime soon.

Ethan let out a gusty sigh, trying to school his thoughts. The more he was around Lily, the dirtier they became. He was going to need...he didn't know what. Well, he did know. He needed her, but that wasn't going to happen. At least, not in that way.

Ethan pulled off the highway and into a hiking

trailhead's turnout. There was a time as a kid when he'd take that trail every other weekend with his family. Back then Mandy had been in a carrier, she was so small. Back before their parents had divorced and well before his accident had made the Blackberry River Trail virtually inaccessible to him.

Just thinking about the accident brought back that helpless feeling of being trapped in a hospital bed, unable to move, unable to care for himself. Everything had been ripped away from him by chance. Thirty seconds faster or slower on that highway and he would have missed the avalanche. One more lingering goodbye kiss from Dani, or one less, and his life would be different. He'd be in construction, married to a model. Happy.

He stared at the familiar trailhead and wondered if he'd ever feel able to take on the three-mile loop again. What if he had kids one day and they wanted to hike? Would he be able to keep up? He looked over at Lily. She was spry, athletic. She'd be able to do the trail in record time.

"You hike?" he asked.

"What?" She shifted in her seat, as if searching for clues to his question. Spotting the trail sign, she nodded. "Yeah, sure. But I was thinking..."

Thinking. Women. Never a good combo.

I was thinking we should take a break. You have your recovery to worry about and I have... Dani had never finished the sentence; her implication that she still had a life had been clear to both of them. She'd twisted off the still-new ring—leaving it on the hospital bed just beyond his reach, so he'd had to ask his kid sister to move it for him, to toss it.

Dani was one woman he never wanted to lay eyes on again.

"Sorry?" he said, realizing Lily was talking.

"Kiss," she insisted.

He stared at her blankly. What had she been saying while he'd tortured himself with the past?

"You and I," she said slowly.

He cleared his throat, buying time. Suddenly the vehicle felt too small, the late summer's sun streaking through the windshield too extreme. He put down his window, breathing in the crisp mountain breeze. Rain was coming for sure.

She wanted to kiss him.

That couldn't be correct.

"You know?" she continued. "So we look convincing."

"We don't need to kiss," he said, shaking his head too vigorously. Kissing was...crossing a line. Beyond platonic. Kissing would make it difficult to remain honorable.

"The guy in the store was onto us until you hugged me."

Ethan frowned. He hadn't thought the clerk

was onto anything other than the fact that his fi-ancée—yes, *his* fiancée—was one hot number.

"We don't have to be an affectionate couple."

"Ethan!" she cried in frustration. "Newlyweds kiss. People who rush into marriage are all over each other. You act like you're disgusted to even touch me."

Her cheeks were pink with anger.

"I'm not disgusted," he said defensively. Talk of being all over each other brought up all sorts of longing he shouldn't be feeling for the gorgeous, sexy woman beside him. He'd bet his new high res-olution monitor she was wearing deadly erotic un-dergarments beneath that short business skirt of hers.

No, he needed to stop thinking about making love to her—that was at the top of the "no go" list.

If nothing else, he could still act like a gentleman.

"Why are we even going to do this if we're not going to bother to make it look convincing?" She continued to press him. "It won't work if you don't touch me, and you flinch like you've been seized by the devil any time I reach over to play the part of adoring fiancée."

Adoring fiancée. Why did he want to savor the sound of that?

"People are going to expect us to kiss, Ethan."

"I'm sure there's a way around it." He shifted, his back bothering him from all the tensing going on.

She let out a tortured sigh. "Have you ever been to an engagement party? People kiss."

Man, she was insistent. But dutifully, Ethan thought back. His family had thrown a party for him and Dani while he was still in the hospital. It hadn't really gone over well, seeing as they'd arrived shortly after Dani had come by to dump him. Definitely no kissing at that event.

Mandy and Frankie? Kissing had been constant, like they'd wanted to rub it in to the entire world that they'd finally hooked up. Devon and Olivia? Yup. Still lots of kissing going on there, too.

Lilypad had a point. Kissing and physical affection were basic expectations of newlyweds.

But still.

"Nobody expects *me* to be affectionate."

"They're going to want at least one lip lock. Even from you."

Ethan ran a hand over his face, unsure how to proceed. He'd strived to avoid thinking about touching her, caressing her, holding her, tasting her. And now she wanted him to.

He couldn't decide if he was cursed or blessed.

Heck, his mind was already swiftly heading to the gutter, his libido on call and hurrying to be named later as an accessory in the upcoming crime scene where their friendship was ruthlessly murdered.

Lily was blinking furiously, looking so hurt he knew he had to act, figure out a way around this.

Why couldn't he just be at home with his web business like he wanted, and ignore the rest of the world and its complications?

"What would you like me to do?" he asked.

One dutiful husband-to-be, coming up.

"Act like I'm not repulsive! That...that—"

"You're not repulsive."

She turned in the seat, her expression hard. "Then kiss me."

"Lilypad, come on..." His grip tightened on the steering wheel. Kissing her felt akin to taking advantage. He was older than she was. She was someone he had to look out for. And if he kissed her...it felt like he'd be avoiding his duty somehow.

Which was all entirely stupid. He needed to get over himself. They were adults. She was sexy. And she wanted a kiss.

He was a good kisser.

Kissing her was his new duty.

She crossed her arms, chin out. "I can't risk breaking the trust of the people we love just because you don't find me desirable."

To his horror she began crying. She turned

away, swiping at her eyes angrily, trying to be tough, strong.

"You're desirable," he said quietly, shifting in his seat. It felt wrong admitting it out loud. But did she have to cry? That was so unfair.

She was still sniffing and he didn't know what to do. Mail a confession on fancy notepaper? She'd probably be appalled if she had any idea how much he craved her.

He tentatively patted her knee. It was bare due to her short skirt, and sexy as all get-out. If he wasn't careful, his hand was going to find its way higher and higher on her leg, savoring the smoothness of her skin. He withdrew it abruptly.

"See?" she spit. "See? You patted me like I'm your grandma!"

If this was what it was like to be married, maybe he didn't want it so much, after all.

"Get out of the car," she said.

"What?"

"Get. Out of. The car."

He slowly turned off the engine, taking the keys with him in case she had ideas about teaching him a lesson and leaving him on the side of the mountain. He angled his way out of the SUV, testing his leg before putting weight on it. Standing, he turned to face her, but she was already storming around the vehicle. She came up beside him, slamming his door with such force his eyebrows shot up. She backed him against the SUV, grabbed his face and pressed her lips to his before he had a chance to react.

Her lips were warm, her eyes closed. She had his head in a tight grip so he couldn't escape, and she tasted like chocolate and tears.

She didn't give up when he didn't kiss her back, just kept pressing against his closed mouth, working his rigid lips with her own.

Her body felt good against his. Those curves. Those voluptuous, sexy curves that had been haunting his dreams since her return. She was all woman. One hundred percent. The tomboy had been chased away so fully she was barely recogniz-able. She wasn't Tagalong any longer. She was the sexiest thing he'd ever…no. No comparison. She was just the sexiest thing *ever*.

She pressed nearer, so near he couldn't think. She bit his bottom lip and he opened his mouth in surprise. She took advantage, her tongue meeting his. His blood surged at the intimate contact and he kissed her back, his own desire taking over, his mind lost.

He spun her, tumbling against her as they pressed up against the vehicle's cool metal, desper-ate, their kisses bordering on indecent with their urgency as thunder rumbled in the distance.

Everything he'd held back soared through him and their kisses became frantic with need, their tongues battling as his hands lifted, cupping the undersides of her breasts. He gave a tender squeeze and she sighed into his mouth, a leg wrapping around him as though opening for him. Ethan shuddered with pent-up testosterone and fell into her heat, angling his hips. She moaned, spurring him on as his hands moved higher, his body rocking against hers. She was pert, excited, and just before he lost all sense of bearing a vehicle passed on the highway, tooting its horn and smashing the magic.

He broke away, to find Lily panting, her expression one of unhidden need, of satisfaction and desire. It was heady seeing her lips rosy, her chest heaving, the unbridled want flashing in her eyes. Want for him. She was tipping toward him, unfinished business blatant in her gaze, in his bloodstream.

He backed up another step so he didn't fall into her once again, because for the first time since their agreement, he thought Lily wasn't the only one at risk of taking things too far and getting hurt.

CHAPTER 5

*L*ily's legs were still trembling from their mind-exploding kiss and she tried to act unfazed as they walked up to the county clerk's office, a chilly breeze pushing debris along the sidewalk. But her body was stuck in the red alert zone, ready to combust with just one more world-changing kiss from Ethan.

She'd go senile in her old age, forget her own name, but still remember that kiss along the highway.

"Ready?" Ethan asked, zipping up a pale blue windbreaker before lightly tapping her elbow to get her attention. She jumped at the fizz of energy that ramped through her body like a missile ready to deploy, certain he could read her thoughts, read her excited body language. Fake fiancées didn't hanker to get it on with their fake fiancés. Not like that.

She edged away. How was she going to spend a year living shoulder to shoulder with him and not ruin things?

No love in the kitchen. That's all she had to remember. Stick to the rule.

"You okay?" he asked, taking her arm and sending a jolt of longing straight into her core.

"Yeah, of course."

"Just think…in one year you'll be the proud owner of two businesses." He gave her a half smile, seemingly unaffected by their kiss.

Right.

Platonic.

Hardly. That kiss had been anything but platonic.

But a kitchen. She could create the life she wanted, and the kiss had merely been an experiment to prove they could pull this off. He seemed unaffected and she should be, too. He was like her ex-boyfriends, just playing along so he could get what he needed, which in this case was selling his businesses for a nice wad of cash. It was just her old crush making her tingly everywhere. Nothing more.

Although he *had* reacted. Her gaze slipped

south of his belt before she caught herself and looked away.

She was going to embarrass herself. She was going to throw herself at him if she carried on with this marriage.

No. She was working toward financial freedom. She was going to help her father. All she had to do was focus on the fact that neither she nor Ethan planned on keeping their vows.

See? Now a completely different kind of sweat was happening.

"Hey?" Ethan moved in front of her. "You all right?"

"Ha, ha."

"Seriously." He pulled her chin toward him, forcing her to meet his steady gaze. All she could think of was whether he was going to kiss her or not. Whether he was the dominant type when it came to—whoa. No. *Friend.* He was just a friend. A *business* partner.

"If you want out, we're out," he said quietly. "We can find another way. It's only money."

She hesitated, then shook her head as he released her. If he could handle it, so could she.

But his gaze was still taking her in as if he was concerned about her. "It's just a document," she said. "Just..."

"Just us sticking it to a bunch of people who

won't give you the chance you deserve. There's nothing to feel bad about. If they can't handle you unmarried, then we'll give you that title."

"The lengths I'll go to for my career," she said, her throat closing up. "I hope my next husband doesn't judge me for this."

Ethan took a step back, thrusting his hands into his pockets. "Right." He swallowed, looking awkward. Finally, he took her hand in his. It was warm and humongous…what was the saying? Big hands meant big—

Don't think!

The sky opened up just then, dropping rain over them and Ethan quickly draped his windbreaker over her head, creating a shelter so she'd stay dry. He paused to sweep a thumb over her cheek, his shirt becoming plastered to his chest as he got soaked. "We're going to get you those businesses, Lily. You're going to follow your dreams and have everything you want."

She felt her bottom lip quiver.

"Just remember, no matter how real it all feels, it's fake. If we remember that, nothing will go wrong and nobody will get hurt."

ETHAN'S PALMS WERE SWEATING. The imposing courtroom with its shining oak; the judge—an old family friend—officiating. Signatures. Witnesses.

The deception suddenly felt bigger than he'd intended. He glanced over at Lily, who was biting her lip, looking at him with such trust and hope he knew he couldn't back out. She was beating back a fear that kept dodging through her, and it was currently edging to break free again. He shifted closer, taking her hands in his. Her palms were as damp as his own, but her smile made him feel less alone.

The judge began reciting his legal spiel. Eventually he paused. "Do you have rings?"

Ethan pulled the wedding bands from his wet jeans pocket. Maybe he should have kept them in their boxes instead of unceremoniously dropping them into his pocket before coming inside. He should have dressed up. Should have done her that honor. "I'm sorry I'm not wearing a suit."

Lily looked pretty in her short skirt and fitted blouse, which had managed to stay dry. "I'm sorry I didn't buy a gown."

"I'm not," he whispered. "You look beautiful."

With shaking hands they exchanged their white gold bands.

"I now pronounce you husband and wife."

Lily giggled nervously, her eyes glittering. Ethan couldn't help but smile.

He was a married man.

Someone had chosen him. Someone believed he was man enough to go the distance.

The happy feeling vanished as he realized he'd just made Lily Harper his wife. He'd promised to cherish and hold her. Protect her.

He pulled her into a tight embrace.

He had a duty to her, and what they had entered into—both the marriage and business deal—were not things to take lightly.

He would keep his vows. No matter what.

"You may kiss the bride," the judge said, a small smile teasing his lips.

Ethan swallowed hard.

The kiss.

There was no getting out of another one, was there?

Lily was gazing up at him expectantly. When he hesitated, her smile wobbled and she slipped from his embrace.

Protecting her also meant protecting her feelings, sheltering her from the gossip and doubts of others. Cherishing her, showing the world that she was a worthy queen of any man's domain.

Ethan eased closer, taking his time, taking her in. Those perpetually smiling eyes, her tempting womanly shape. He slipped one hand to her hip, sliding it around to the small of her back, folding her body close to his. She fit perfectly, like a wife should. With his right hand, he swept his thumb across the freckles highlighting her cheek, cupping her head. She'd settled her hands against his chest as though uncertain about being the subject of his focus. Her breathing became unsteady, anticipation undoubtedly building inside her as much as himself. He wasn't sure if it would be a light kiss or something out of control like earlier. Either way, he needed it to be convincing, as this was their first kiss as husband and wife.

"You're very beautiful, Lily…" Harper? Mattson? Which name would she take? Even though he knew it made sense for her to keep her own name, given the nature of their commitment, he found himself wishing she'd take his, accept it as part of the deal. She was part of the clan now—officially—and in his heart that's where she would always belong: as a Mattson.

He slowly lowered his lips to his wife's, brushing them in a teasing manner. She opened her mouth and he consumed it with his own, their kiss full of desperation.

Her hands, which had been flat against his chest, rose up, swooping around his neck, locking him closer. They paused momentarily to come up for air, then dipped into the kiss again, forgetting their surroundings.

The judge eventually cleared his throat, bringing them back to the present.

"Well," he said, "I hope you two have a nice long honeymoon planned, away from prying eyes."

Ethan gazed upon the flushed woman wearing his rings, his own glinting fresh and new, and hoped it took a long time for them to convince his business partners that Lily was the new owner.

FROM ACROSS THE ENGAGEMENT/JUST-GOT-MARRIED party, Lily could see Ethan eyeing his family with reservation. He was pulling back, putting up walls around himself, no hint of a smile in place. She kind of got it—the party was overwhelming, filled with people who were stunned and excited for them, while chastising them for rushing in without allowing them to be present.

And upset.

Members of his family were definitely upset, but desperately trying not to show it.

Lily watched from her spot with Mandy, where they were setting out appetizers. Ethan's father, Cory, had pulled him aside from where he'd been chatting with his grandfather.

As the men passed her, Ethan's dad collected her, herding the newlyweds toward his kitchen.

She gathered up a few dirty plates as she went, making herself useful. Her brother, Moe, caught her eye as she passed, giving her a subtle thumbs up of solidarity. She wondered if he and Amy still had their marriage pledge to get married when Amy hit thirty if they were both still single. If so, what a messed up family they were when it came to marriage. Her mother had only married her father because she was pregnant with Moe. Then she'd stayed around long enough to have Lily, but left soon after. Every few years she remembered Lily's birthday and sent a card, but, overall, motherhood really didn't seem to be her mom's thing.

In the kitchen, Ethan's shoulders slumped and he didn't look up as Lily placed the dishes in the sink. She went to his side, unsure what her momentary role was. She wanted to hook her arm through his, express solidarity, but felt he wouldn't appreciate her touch.

"Sorry, Dad," Ethan muttered.

"You couldn't even have us stand as witnesses? You had to run away? And today—after we'd talked?"

"I told you we were eloping. I told you we were getting married today."

"You know how important a wedding was to Trish. Are you ashamed to have us stand up for you after all we've done? Is that what this stunt was about?"

Lily felt her mouth pop open and Ethan stiffened at her side.

"Mr. Mattson—"

"Dad." Ethan interrupted her, his voice firm. "We said we didn't want a fuss, didn't want to burden you with parties and expenses."

"We're family, Ethan! *Family.*"

Cory attempted to stare down Ethan, who had looked up, his expression stony.

Her new father-in-law turned to her and she mustered a weak smile, feeling ashamed for the way they'd shut out Ethan's family.

Mandy slipped into the kitchen for more cream for the coffee and, grateful for the interruption, Lily pulled it out of the fridge, as well as a plate of cream puffs. She handed them to Mandy, wishing she could join her friend with food prep rather than be stuck in here with two volcanoes about to erupt.

"I hope you're up to the task of standing up to this man," Cory said to Lily, after his daughter returned to the living room.

"I—I am," Lily stammered.

"We know what we're doing, Dad."

"Well, you two sure don't look happy."

"Maybe because you're chewing us out for doing what we wanted."

"How do you think I felt, hearing the news from my friend in Derbyshire?" His father's voice was low, humiliated.

"I'm so sorry," Lily whispered.

Cory's shoulders fell as he took in her expression. He held out his arms, pulling her into an embrace. "Aw, *I'm* sorry, Lily. I just wanted to see you in a dress. You've always been like a daughter to us and always will be." He laughed and held her out in front of him. "And now you are! It's wonderful to have you as part of our family, and you will always be welcome here even if you and my son ran away together. We are truly happy for you." He gave a sigh and a sad smile.

Lily knew they were forgiven and that he was only expressing his well-earned disappointment.

"*We're* so sorry," she stressed.

"It's called eloping," Ethan snapped.

"Ethan," she chided.

His frown softened as he glanced at her. He tugged at his ear. "Sorry, Dad."

"We love you, Son. And we just want to be a bigger part of your life, is all. Ever since your accident—"

"I know, I know," Ethan interrupted.

"—you push us aside. Things are different for you now and it's okay to—"

"I'm happy. Okay? Let's not have a fight just because we see things differently."

The men stared at each other, shoulders stiff, fixed in what appeared to be an ongoing battle.

"I should call my dad," Lily said quietly, patting her thighs for her phone. No pockets. She was still in her suit from their morning meeting to sign their prenuptial agreement. Wow. Things had moved fast. Engaged to married in less than twenty-four hours. No wonder everyone's heads were spinning.

But her father still didn't know she'd wed or even gotten engaged.

Lily glanced around, trying to recall where she'd left her phone. Ethan pulled it off the top of the microwave, where she'd set it while arranging a plate of cheese earlier, and handed it to her. Her father was going to be delighted to hear she was working on owning a place, thrilled that her new man was Ethan. But he would also start applying pressure, thinking she had enough money to help him. And she didn't. Not yet.

As for her mother? Lily didn't even know where to find her. Her aunts, uncles and cousins might possibly take a passing interest though, as would her old classmates and friends from the city when they saw her post a line or two about her new relationship status on social media.

Ethan left the kitchen with her, acting like a bodyguard as he cleared a path through the roomful of people who felt more like family than those related to her by blood. Lily smiled in a daze, taking hands that reached out as she passed, accepting everyone's congratulations.

It was good to be back in Blueberry Springs again, back at home with the Mattsons.

Ethan set her up in Mandy's childhood bedroom—not his own—and Lily sat on the edge of the bed. She glanced at her phone, noting and discarding a text message from Tanner. He had regrets. Should have given her more credit in the kitchen. Blah, blah, blah.

What would it take to get rid of him? A message saying she'd married Ethan?

"Want me to stay?" Ethan asked, one hand on the doorknob.

Her new husband. A whole new life. A fresh start.

This was going to work.

"I'm okay," she said. Her voice lacked the perky confidence she'd expected it to have, and for a second Ethan's usual shields seemed to come down. She found herself giving him a soft smile. Ethan was always there for her. The guy looking at her now, unguarded, ready to sweep in and help if she gave the word, was the one she'd always had a crush on. He was also the man who had kissed her on the side of the road—word of which had made it back to Blueberry Springs already. And then the tender "I do" kiss. Toe-curling and real.

"Really," she said more firmly.

And just like that, his shields went up again, their little connection breaking. She smiled in relief as he left her to deal with her dad. She and her husband had a business agreement, and she knew it wasn't safe for either of them to ever let it feel like something more, for even one tantalizing second.

"I HOPE nobody gave you too much grief," Ethan said, unlocking his front door. His phone app had triggered the lights when they'd drawn close, giving the place a welcoming feel. Well, as much as the empty house could.

Maybe Lily would add a few things to liven up the place. Although, hopefully, not with those cheesy Keep Hanging in There cat posters she'd liked in high school. He'd begun giving her one for each birthday before she moved away, partly because he'd loved her delighted reaction.

"Everyone was fine." Lily looked nervous and

had both hands on her suitcase's handle, as if she was an orphan worried that one wrong word would find her turfed out of her new home.

"How did your dad take the news?"

"He asked if you're wealthy."

"Wealthy? Really?" Ethan closed and locked the door after them. He hadn't seen Mr. Harper in years and the comment surprised him.

"Sorry." She tried to brush off the subject, which told him there was something there. "He's just looking to retire and was hoping I'd found a sugar daddy in my new husband." She gave a laugh.

Husband.

Wife.

Would he ever get used to those words in relation to the two of them?

He had a wife. Was married.

His gaze slipped from Lily to his ring finger.

The gold band felt surprisingly comfortable and he liked the style she'd chosen.

"How much does he need?" he asked.

"Don't give him a dime."

He bet Lily would, though.

"We'll set you up in the guestroom," Ethan said.

Lily hauled her suitcase into the room and Ethan hovered in the doorway, feeling awkward. He should have carried her bag. Should have had flowers or a welcome sign or something.

"I made the bed for you."

He couldn't figure out what to do with his hands. They felt loose and in the way.

"There are towels in the bathroom. Do you take long showers? I don't have a real schedule...so I... can shower whenever. And I sleep on the right side of the bed."

"What?" Lily looked up, eyes wide.

"In case—in case anyone asks. You know, like in the movie where they get married for a green card? Never mind. I'm going to go do some work."

As he backed away, she said calmly, "If anyone asks, I expect you to stare them down, implying that it's inappropriate of them to think of your wife in such an intimate setting." She rested a hand on the bed, leaning forward, eyebrow raised.

"Right."

"Although maybe I shouldn't live out of a suitcase."

He looked around the room. No bureau. "What if we have overnight guests?"

"Ethan?"

"Yeah?"

"You're freaking out."

Definitely.

She moved closer, wrapping her arms around him. He froze, unsure what to do.

She'd looked happy when they'd said "I do." And yet he knew she was here for only one reason.

He knew so little about adult Lily and yet had promised her everything. Everything but the one thing that would make their marriage real.

"Hug me back," she said, snuggling closer. "I don't bite."

"Fine." He hugged her loosely, not wanting his body to take a hike down Wrong Way to Think about Your Wife Boulevard.

"Closer," she said, leaning against him. She was warm, felt right. In the back of his mind he felt a glimmer of hope. One that said, *Hey, man. Maybe this could work. Just go with it and see.*

He watched her, noting the small smile on her face, the lashes resting on her cheeks as she leaned against him, eyes closed. He wanted to brush that stray strand of hair off her cheek, wrap his arms around her soul and never let go.

What a quandary. How was he going to act like they were happy newlyweds when he was afraid to touch her, afraid to give in to that spark he felt every time their skin brushed, afraid that the next time their lips met he'd be unable to pull away until he'd satisfied them both?

He was going to have a difficult time being a gentleman, and only hoped she became like his sister had during her first year in business. Mandy had been stressed, snarly, and nobody ever saw her unless they stopped by her café.

Then again, he'd just handed Lily, an expert in the food industry, two complete, fully-staffed businesses that he ran on the side of his new web venture.

He only hoped for her sake that the string of back luck that had followed him since putting them on the market would wane. No more unexplained failing refrigeration units. No more shipments going rotten for no apparent reason. None of it.

"That feels nice," she murmured, a contented smile still on her lips.

"What does?"

"The back rub."

His hand stopped moving. Without realizing it, he'd been stroking soft circles onto her back, soothing her as though it would settle his own mind.

In some ways it had. He felt calm, less freaked out.

But it was time to let go of his wife. And yet he knew that when he did he was going to be struck by loneliness, and the fact that this was going to be a very long year.

CHAPTER 6

"Will you show me around the restaurant today?" Lily leaned against the small breakfast table in Ethan's kitchen. It was a three-bedroom house—one for each of them plus an office for Ethan—but the kitchen was minuscule. A galley affair with a dented electric stove that nobody had even bothered to level. For someone in the food business Ethan lacked most of the tools she considered basics.

However, according to the storage company, they could have her belongings here within a few days to a week, and then she'd be able to really cook up something good. In the meantime, she supposed she'd suffer through Ethan's overdone scrambled eggs.

He pushed back from the table, blinking twice.

"Right. I should probably introduce you to your staff. Transition you in."

She nodded slowly, wondering if his plan had been to just dump the businesses on her and go his merry way. Her father had been happy to hear she'd married Ethan and had asked when she'd own the restaurant outright. Despite his lack of financial stability, he was determined that she would be the first in the family to be fully independent, no longer worrying about being the expendable one on the factory floor or the girlfriend about to get kicked out of a kitchen. Even Moe worked for someone else, though everyone thought he owned the pub he managed.

Lily poked at her eggs.

"Do you normally cook yourself breakfast?" she asked. How could a man in charge of a restaurant and a catering business dry out eggs so badly?

"I usually get an egg off Leif's grill—the few benefits of owning a restaurant." He looked at his own untouched plate. "You don't have to eat these. I kind of forgot about them in the pan."

"So you don't cook?"

He wrinkled his nose in reply.

He avoided cooking, but had made her breakfast. That was sweet.

"How do you manage the catering if you aren't into cooking?"

"Lots of sandwiches," he said, eyes twinkling.

"Does your staff know I'm taking over?"

He shook his head. "Although if they have two brain cells clicking around in their heads they'll have figured it out by now."

"We'll have to act as though we're newlyweds," she reminded him.

He stood, dumping his eggs into the trash. "We should go. I have a lot to do today."

"Ethan?"

"Nobody expects affection from me." His glance took in her jeans and sweatshirt once again, as he had when she'd left her bedroom earlier, and she still couldn't decipher the look.

"I unpacked some of my things into your closet while you were showering."

He froze, his plate angled toward the dish-washer, his expression unreadable.

She added quickly, "You know...in case. I thought my stuff should be in your room. So I put my suitcase in there, but then I realized a real wife would unpack, so I took half your closet."

She grinned at him, loving her new role, as well as having a little bit of power over the man who usually called the shots.

"My things will smell like your perfume." He was blinking slowly as though trying to compute the takeover.

"You don't like it?"

"It's…" He was looking around the kitchen, his plate still in hand. He seemed lost. "It's…well. We're married," he said finally, finding a place for his plate, closing the dishwasher. He started the machine without soap. "It's smart thinking."

She paused the machine and added soap before starting it again.

"Here." She handed him a travel mug filled with coffee.

He stared at the cup for a beat before accepting it.

"Most people would say thank you," she teased. He was so off balance it was cute. It was like he'd been living as a bachelor in a locked-up bunker for years, thinking the rest of the world no longer existed. And then boom. Here it was.

He glanced at the cup again, then her. "Thanks." Ethan gave the microwave clock a quick glance. "I have to be online at eleven and there's a lot to show you."

He led her out of the house, locking the door after them.

"Can I get a key?" she asked.

Wordlessly, Ethan unlocked the door and headed back inside. She waited on the front step, waving at their lawyer as he jogged by in the late dawn fog. If memory served, that meant it was going to be hot and dry today, yesterday's rain already forgotten.

She should get active again. For too long she'd spent most of her time in kitchens, her only exercise racing from prep area to the walk-in fridge, and mindlessly chopping vegetables. She'd bet that the Blackberry River Trail where she and Ethan had stopped to kiss along the highway would be a nice place to get back into hiking.

Her mind drifted, moving on to the unspent passion that still sizzled between her and Ethan when they let their guard down. There was something there. So why did Ethan continue to pull back? Was there actually something wrong with him? Because with him amping up his computer venture and her with her foodie stuff they were going to need to burn off some stress, and what better way than in a marriage with benefits?

Not that she believed he wanted that, but there was definitely something worth exploring, if their kisses were any indicator.

Ethan returned, a spare key on a plain loop held out for her. "Most people would say thank you," he said as she accepted the key, her thoughts still on how she could get him to loosen up, give in to that something that sizzled just below the surface.

"Thanks," she dutifully replied.

"If you download my home app I can set you up with remote access from your phone, too."

She followed him to his SUV, admiring the way his shoulders swayed as he ambled along, favoring one leg ever so slightly. The tightness she'd seen yesterday seemed to be almost gone and she wondered if he was more at home with their arrangement now. Either way, he didn't seem like a man who needed to worry about having a power of attorney document on hand.

She skipped through the cool mountain morning air to the car and popped into the passenger seat. The leather seats were cold and Ethan turned on her seat warmer as well as his own, giving her a quick look to see if the gesture was all right.

"What was that phrase again? Oh, yes. Thank you," she said with a smile.

He let out a huff of amusement, catching her humored dig.

He might be gruffer than he used to be, but under it all he was still the same great guy she'd had a crush on for all those years.

ETHAN PULLED up behind his restaurant—Lily's restaurant for all intents and purposes, even though his name was still on the deed and would be until they divorced.

"I wouldn't change the name anytime soon," he said to Lily, pointing to the sign in the alley that said Benny's Big Burger Deliveries Only.

"I won't." She held her hand up as though taking a pledge, a bright grin lighting her face.

She was wearing tight jeans and a loose sweatshirt, and had her mass of hair pulled up in a loose bun. Somehow she looked even sexier than when she was wearing her tempting business attire. It didn't matter how many times he checked her out, the results were the same. Off the charts cute and sexy.

And his.

Sort of.

Plus she smelled amazing. And that was going to be an issue, seeing as he was going to have to suffer through the olfactory reminders every day because her clothes were now hanging alongside his.

Like they belonged there. Like the two of them belonged together. Like their twelve month commitment was something more.

Ethan climbed the five steps to the restaurant's back door. Five evil stairs that were easier today than they had been yesterday, his left leg loose again with the warmer weather. He turned off the alarm system, flipping on the overhead lights as he made it the few feet into the back hall, passing the new and slightly finicky walk-in fridge before entering the large kitchen just down and to the left.

After twenty minutes of giving Lily a rundown on the essential points, he sat with her in the small staff room at the back of the restaurant, sipping coffee. A fridge stood in the middle of one wall for staff lunches, a small table and chairs near it, then a few old lockers from the high school, a whole lot of boxes and old dining room furniture.

When they were back out at the new walk-in fridge he had to remember to tell Lily about its flaky power switch so she could document it if it turned off on its own again. The company he'd purchased it from and who had done the installation said it wasn't actually faulty, but that someone was turning it off. Ethan couldn't see any of his staff meddling in such a destructive way and had refused to pay the bill until he had a reliable, working fridge.

"How long until staff arrive?" Lily asked, pulling Ethan from his thoughts.

"About fifteen minutes."

"You know," she said, eyeing the space, "if we rearranged a few things the staff would have more room back here." Her phone buzzed with an incoming text and she flipped it over from its spot on the table to peek at it, gave the screen a disgusted look and marched the device over to a stack of boxes, leaving it there as though giving it a time-out.

Ethan wanted to ask if it was Tanner, but figured if she didn't mention it, it wasn't his business. Or quite possibly, she wanted to mention it, but hadn't enjoyed him acting like a possessive fool last time and bringing his fists into her conversations with Tanner.

Even though Tanner had had it coming.

"Be careful about changing things right away." *Like putting your clothes in my closet.* What was he going to do if she needed an outfit and waltzed right into his room wearing nothing but a towel?

His blood was pounding south just thinking about it.

Lily reached over and gave a wobbly chair a shake. "If I fix up the room it'll help me win them over. They deserve a nice break room."

"They might expect a raise."

She blew off his words as if they were a joke and stood, hands on her hips. Recognizing the determination in her gaze, he decided to go with it. He was feeling good today and could handle moving a few light items around to give the room more space, or whatever Lily had in mind.

"What did you want to do?" he asked, cracking his knuckles.

She turned to him with a smile so flashingly bright it took his breath away. He wanted to cross the room, gather her in his arms and kiss her senseless.

She pointed to the extra fold-up chairs piled in the middle of the room where someone had left them after Mary Alice's annual birthday celebration last April. "Put those along the wall." He complied as she slowly did a full turn of the room, finger tapping against her chin. She picked up one side of the table they'd been sitting at moments ago. "Help me with this."

He stepped over, testing its weight. It was still within the doctor's orders of not overdoing things.

"Where do you want it?"

Moving in tandem, they carried it to the other side of the room. Ethan set his end down in the commanded spot, pleased he hadn't felt any noteworthy twinges in his joints or muscles. This was actually a little bit fun.

Lily smiled at him, her enthusiasm contagious and sexy. He found himself returning her smile.

"What's next, boss?"

She gave him a smart look and bent to flip open a few boxes of supplies sitting in a cluster in the middle of the room. He liked her in jeans. The way the soft, pale denim hugged her hips. He found his coffee, taking a sip to mask the way his mouth was salivating. If he wasn't careful, he was going to find himself jonesing it big time for his wife. A wife he couldn't touch.

"These should go in a storage room," she said.

"This is it."

Her expression darkened with disappointment.

"Maybe we could stack them out of the way," he suggested.

"Good idea. I'll keep an eye out for a used shelving unit, and in the meantime…" She shoved a few boxes into a corner. "…we can create a nice open area in the middle for sitting and mingling."

He nodded, liking the overall effect already. She kept shoving boxes his way and he stacked them against the wall, careful to lift with his legs. So far, so good. He got to the last one, which was larger and heavier than the rest, causing his left shoulder to protest about the awkward angle he had to assume in order to lift. He'd pushed a wheelchair for years and had some serious arms and shoulders, but this big, unwieldy carton reminded him that his upper body bulk didn't give him license to do something foolish. He shoved the box into the corner and turned to try and dissuade Lily from moving anything bigger.

"Leif, your chef, will be here soon."

"Great. What do you think?" She was tapping her chin again. "Should I repaint the walls white or go with a pale yellow?"

"Your call."

She nodded and moved to the fridge, placing her palms flat against its white side. "Let's shove this over a few feet."

"There probably isn't enough cord."

"Pull it out a few inches and see."

"I don't think moving the fridge is a good idea." He was pretty sure, due to its size and weight, that it was firmly on the "no" list the doctors had given him.

Lily sent him a curious look and began rocking the heavy appliance, trying to get it to move. Ethan found himself nudging her out of the away, fearing she was going to pull the thing over on herself.

The fridge's feet screeched across the tile as he put physics to work, edging it away from the wall. His shoulder throbbed, reminding him that he was now overdoing it. He needed to stop.

Lily crowed in triumph and bounced over to squeeze his arms in excitement. "There's enough cord! Shove it over about four feet, Mr. Man. I'll let you know when you're out of cord."

"We need help." *He* needed help.

"Why? We've totally got this." Her eyes were sparkling despite her confusion and she gave his biceps a squeeze. She was studying his physique, trying to find the reason for his hesitation. He knew he looked strong enough, and he understood her lack of understanding at him pulling back. This was where he should tell her he wasn't supposed to do these kinds of things anymore. That pins and rods might break the tentative bone reconstruction, causing it to give way if torqued with enough force. It probably wouldn't happen moving a fridge, but he still had to be wise and play it safe.

She moved to the appliance again. "Come on, sweetie." She gave him a challenging pout that was so full of sexuality he felt his heart and breath stutter. His baby sister's BFF was *not* supposed to be hot. Not supposed to be sultry. Was not supposed to tempt him into doing stupid things or send his blood pressure sky-high with come-hither looks or ego patting. And definitely not with a sexy, full-lipped pout that made him think of frilly negligees and soft breasts ready to be revealed for his waiting hands.

Telling her about his limitations would surely end her flirtatiousness and result in that familiar, haunting twinge of pity he'd seen flash through the eyes of so many others. He couldn't bear to have his status fall with Lily, to have her subtly change the way she treated him.

He knew he had to tell her, but even more so,

he wanted for a little while longer to be the man she saw, even if it was a lie.

LILY STOOD in the break room, frozen with disappointment. They'd been moving stuff, smiling. Having fun. Even flirting a bit. Ethan was seriously buff, but he'd acted like he couldn't move the fridge, which meant something was wrong. Something he didn't trust her enough to tell her. Instead, he'd slipped from the room with a flimsy excuse about setting up the dining room for introductions.

She needed to find out what was wrong with him. Why he was shying away from pushing a fridge. Why he wanted that power of attorney.

And as for the fridge, she was moving that thing. Being small, she knew how to use her weight and the strength of her legs to make large objects succumb to the laws of physics.

She squatted at the base of the fridge again, pushing her shoulder into its side and straining to tip it enough that she could shimmy its feet over a small hump in the titles. She groaned and sagged to the floor. She couldn't do it alone. Not both tip and pull.

She pushed a hand through her bangs, standing

in time to see her husband reenter the room with a large, older man in tow. Not that Ethan was small, but this man carried himself like a marine or something. And his perceptive stare matched that assessment.

"I hear you have a fridge you want moved?" he stated. He was studying Lily as though he could tell exactly why the For Sale sign was suddenly gone from the restaurant's window and why Ethan was married.

"It's stuck on some uneven tiles or I'd slide it over myself." There was *definitely* something wrong with Ethan if he was asking a man old enough to have grandkids to do the lifting.

"This is Leif Moreau, your new chef," Ethan said, referring to the bald man wearing entirely too much cologne, which Lily found surprising for a chef.

Leif gave Ethan a look, eyebrows raised. "*Her* new chef?"

He turned to Leif. "This is my wife, Lily Harper."

Lily perked up. "This is so exciting! Pleased to meet you. I went to ITHQ. Where did you go to culinary school?" The Institut de tourisme et d'hôtellerie du Québec didn't sound like much by its name, but she'd been able to do two of the stages required for her degree in Michelin-starred restaurants, as well as one in a luxury hotel in Spain. Not bad for a kid from Blueberry Springs.

"Self-taught." The man had his arms crossed, sizing her up. "You speak French?"

"Enough to figure out studying in Québec, Canada."

"Bienvenue, madame." His accent had a slight Cajun accent as he welcomed her.

She knew her accent had more of a French-Canadian flare due to her time studying in Montreal.

"Bonjour. How long have you worked here?" she asked him conversationally.

"Since you were both kids." He tipped back on his heels as though daring her to fire him. "Career change. Still have lots of good years left in me."

"Leif used to be a police officer," Ethan said. "Anytime you have a problem customer, he'll take care of them."

She immediately thought of Tanner and looked away, worried how things would seem if her chef had to turf her ex.

"There haven't been many," Leif assured her.

No doubt. The way he was sizing her up would deter most dine-and-dashers, she was certain. Lily felt as though the man could see every page of her life before him like a movie.

She tried for a smile.

"Think you can help with this?" She leaned against the white fridge, ignoring Ethan. "I'm hoping to make the break room more pleasant."

"Nobody takes breaks in here anymore."

"Why's that?"

"Too cluttered," he said with a laugh.

She gave Ethan a smug look. "Well, let's see if we can fix that, shall we? How about you lift while I—" She didn't bother finishing her sentence, as her chef shoved the fridge into the spot she wanted in a matter of seconds, easy as cutting into Jell-O with a machete. "Well, that's perfect. Thank you."

He'd be a handy one to have around.

He smiled and crossed his arms over his barrel chest once again, his biceps looking extra beefy, to the point that all she could think of was how easily he could lift a stockpot full to the brim without spilling a drop. Again, handy to have around.

"Will I be looking at retirement since you're ITHQ trained?" Leif was watching her, not Ethan.

Wow. No beating around the bush with Leif. But what was she supposed to say? That a small-town restaurant had plenty of room for two chefs? That she wouldn't nudge him aside to make room for herself, the boss? Then again, she wasn't sure how she'd find the courage to do that when he'd been here since the dawn of time.

Ethan left the room, saying, "I'll let you work out the arrangements."

Leif raised his brows. "I don't want to come between the two of you."

"Oh, you won't come between us," she assured him. Ethan was doing a fine job of putting a wedge in there all on his own.

ETHAN PACED HIS HOME OFFICE, feeling edgy. He'd introduced Lily to the staff, then hoofed it out of there like his life depended upon it. He felt bad for ditching her, but judging from her questions she'd be fine. The restaurant needed him for only a few hours a day, after all.

But the way she'd looked at him when they'd been moving the fridge…all flirty.

There'd been a hint of curiosity, too, though. Like she was starting to realize that he might be hiding something from her. She was too smart to fool and he was going to have to admit his limitations soon.

But that flirtatious look. The hint of desire when she'd squeezed his biceps… He felt himself flexing automatically as he hobbled around his office, trying to stretch out the aches that had settled in.

He didn't want to lose the power to impress her. He wanted to be the strong, virile man she saw. He wanted to build on that, not watch it dissolve before his eyes.

Even if her admiration was based on a fake perception.

Knowing he wouldn't be able to code the complicated website structure that was next on his to-do list—thanks to Lily and that pouty look she'd given him earlier—he began phoning his restaurant suppliers, letting them know he was authorizing her to send in orders on his behalf for both businesses. Because the sooner things were in place for them to move on, the better.

CHAPTER 7

*L*ily had been working in the restaurant for a week, Ethan taking care of the catering end of things until she had her feet solidly under her. There was so much to learn about the quirks of the old place, such as the fact that the knobs on the grill didn't line up with the right burners. Just little things, as well as adjusting to being the boss and having everyone defer to her, sidestep her with uncertainty. She was exhausted, but loving every second of it.

The restaurant was already starting to feel like hers. She'd been making small changes her staff had requested, from more breaks—they loved what she'd done with the break room—to better scheduling. Even now, while she and Leif sweated over the stoves, him on breakfast duty and her creating the soup of the day, she could hear two of the waitresses laughing together down the hall as they took a quick break together.

She smiled at the sound and continued adding a pinch of this and a pinch of that, layering in the spices for her minestrone.

"Order up," Leif said. "Where's Gloria?"

"Her feet were bothering her. I'll take it out," Lily said, quickly wiping her hands and collecting the hot meals before he could say something about her pampering the waitress. She added a slice of orange and a sprig of parsley as garnish, ignoring Leif's look that suggested it was a waste, and hustled out with the meals.

Gloria had been on staff since forever and could use someone looking out for her. She was one of the most reliable employees, and Lily knew if she had her on side everything would become easier.

When she returned to the kitchen, Ethan was there, looking gorgeous in a soft, button-up shirt and faded jeans.

"Hey, baby." She stood beside him awkwardly, wanting to touch him, but knowing any physical gestures wouldn't be rewarded.

"How's it going?" He'd made it a habit of checking in each morning before heading over to use Mandy's kitchen to deal with any catering orders, and today was no exception.

"Fine. Like always."

"She's babying Gloria," Leif grunted.

"It's true," she admitted.

Lily caught Leif's smile.

She lifted herself onto her toes to give Ethan a peck on the cheek, knowing that the cook had noticed how seldom the two of them touched. Ethan's gaze softened and she decided he was a fine actor. When he wanted to be.

"See you tonight," she said. "Oh, and don't make supper—I'm in charge for the next week. I want to try some new recipes on you."

"Sure." He turned to go.

"Ethan? Can you take this to my car?"

She hoisted a box of mismatched cutlery. It jangled and threatened to give out on her as she brought it to him. She was curious to see if he'd reject the box, as he had the awkward bags of trash she'd asked him to take out yesterday. She knew he wasn't lazy and she hoped if she pushed him enough he'd reveal why he didn't want to lift or carry certain items. Was it because of lingering injuries from his accident or something else?

"It's time this stuff got taken away," she said. "It doesn't fit properly in the restaurant's bins and is driving me crazy."

"Then buy new bins. Cutlery is expensive."

"It's mismatched, like the carpeting in the dining area." Soon she'd have this place the way she wanted it to be—neat, tidy and homey. It would take time and effort, but the place would at least look like someone cared about it.

She hoisted the heavy, sagging box, hoping to push it on him, but he quickly said, "I've got to run —Fran needs her keyboard swapped out in the boutique again. Maybe next time."

Leif intercepted her, taking the box. "Watch the eggs for me."

"Ethan can carry it," she said as Leif disappeared down the back hall. Her voice trailed off as she added, "He's going that way and you're cooking."

Why did someone foil her plans whenever she tried to get him to open up?

Ethan followed Leif, stating he'd get the doors for him.

"I needed you on these grills," she said to Leif when he returned. She pointed to the stove where she was currently burning scrambled eggs as she tried to flip about twenty pancakes. Ticked off that she hadn't managed to fit into Leif's flow fast enough to save the food, she scraped the burned meals off the grill, tossing them into the full trash can.

"What's wrong with Ethan?" she asked. If her

husband wouldn't tell her, surely someone else would.

"He needed help," Leif said calmly, slipping the egg lifter from her hand and taking over once again.

"Have you seen his shoulders?" she retorted. "Why can't he carry a box?"

"I suppose you should ask him."

Lily let out a grumble, causing Leif to smile, then she sighed. She'd seen Ethan act creaky and sore from curling over his keyboard, and maybe it wasn't anything more than that. Maybe he just needed yoga and a better lifestyle.

She made a decision. "No more eggs off the grill for him," she told Leif.

He glanced at her from the side, giving a soft chuckle of amusement.

"I'm serious."

"I know, and I think it's sweet that you care."

"Of course I care. He's my husband." She slapped ham on the grill, wishing her cheeks weren't burning. "He needs a wife to whip him into shape. And I'm just the woman to do so."

***

ETHAN DECIDED it was time to finally find out what he was dealing with physically. Months ago Dr.

Leham had had him get an MRI, to see why his joint pain hadn't waned as much as the doc expected it to. Ethan had avoided going in for the results, worried what he might find. But he was a husband now and it was time to face it like a man. Especially if there was something he could do about it, because Lily was honing in, closer and closer, expecting answers.

When he arrived for his appointment, he was led into Nash's newly decorated exam room. It looked like his wife, Katie, had been there adding touches, just as she had in Devon's home. Lily had slowly been changing things here and there in Ethan's house, but not to the extent he'd thought she would. He'd been hoping she'd leave more of her imprint on the place, as her tastes weren't bad other than her choice in a husband. Then again, she'd been working fairly hard and probably didn't have the time. Or much stuff, come to think about it.

The doctor entered the room, looking at Ethan in surprise. "Well, it's about time. Here to see the results of the MRI, or did something else finally drag you in? Perhaps a foot that's turned a funky shade of green and black? If so, write up your will for your new wife, because you're toast. Congrats by the way."

"Good to see you, too, Nash."

The doctor smiled and sat on a rolling stool across from him. The man's sharp blue eyes took him in as he held the clipboard against his stomach, checking it every once in a while. "How's the pain? I've seen you hobbling around town worse than your grandfather. Are you taking turmeric?"

"It didn't make a difference."

Nash made a mark on the paper attached to his clipboard.

"You still think it's arthritis?" Ethan asked.

"It's not uncommon in people with your medical history to develop it."

Ethan must have been Attila the Hun in a past life—although maybe it was simply karma coming in strong for him laughing at Devon's jokes about their stepmom's fake boobs back when they'd been preteens. They hadn't exactly been nice about how fake the enhancements looked.

Ethan regretted their behavior—even if it wasn't responsible for his current state of ongoing bad luck.

Nash pulled up Ethan's file on a nearby computer, angling the monitor so they could both see it. He did a bit of clicking, and black-and-white images of things Ethan had no idea about filled the screen. But the resolution was fantastic.

"Nice monitor."

"Thanks. This is your MRI. These shady bits

here would suggest arthritis. Strange that the turmeric didn't help. It usually does."

"Could be something else?"

"Possibly. Food sensitivities causing inflammation. Although if it is, it's not presenting like a classic case."

"Cancer?"

Nash shook his head.

"But you never know, right?"

"It's not cancer, but as you know, nothing in life is guaranteed and something is going on there. I'd suggest playing around with your lifestyle habits, keep a journal and look for trends."

"Weather changes bother me."

"That could be related, but it's also common in limbs that contain rods and pins. Either way, that's likely to get worse as you age. I suggest you move to a more moderate climate with less variable weather patterns."

"Move?" He didn't want to live in an old folks retirement village down south, where the weather never changed. Plus he had to endure at least another year here for Lily.

"Sell the businesses. Although I'm hearing good things about your wife's cooking skills. Speaking of Lily, do you need birth control?"

"What?"

"I'm not taking new patients at the moment, but

if you and Lily need to talk birth control, come in and I'll set you up."

Ethan tried to close his mouth, but it kept gaping open.

"Erectile dysfunction?" Nash asked, obviously misreading Ethan's expression. "That can be an issue with patients who've experienced paralysis."

"It's fine! I'm…fine. Really."

"Moving regularly can help ease the effects of arthritis." He gave Ethan a wink. "So does having an open mind. The body takes hints. If our thinking is rigid that's how our joints and muscles become. I recommend taking it easy, going with the flow. Open up."

Ethan snorted before realizing Nash was serious.

"Come back in three months and we'll take another MRI to see if any changes are happening that we need to worry about. In the meantime enjoy being a newlywed."

Ethan nodded, letting the man usher him out of the office.

Birth control? Erectile dysfunction? He'd gone in to find out why he was in so much pain and hadn't come away with a single helpful answer other than to play around with his habits, go with the flow and come back later. For birth control.

LILY SPREAD her papers out in the restaurant's dining room in the quiet before the supper rush. Her office—Benny's old one—was so stuffed she could barely get to the desk, and it would be weeks before she got it decluttered enough to work effectively in there.

Lily felt someone watching her and looked up, to find Gloria gazing at her expectantly.

"Sorry?" She glanced around. There was only one table of customers and the waitresses had collected nearby to fill the sugar shakers and wrap cutlery in paper napkins.

"How did Ethan propose?" Gloria repeated, pouring sugar into a shaker. Lily's best bet was that the five-minute task would take Gloria thirty. Frustrating, but then again, during the lunch rush Gloria was the waitress to be counted on. The tight, dated polyester uniform she professed to love, though? That had to go.

Lily frowned at the list in front of her. She'd never had to deal with accounts before and had to admit some of it was mind muddling.

"My daughter had a wonderful wedding," Gloria said. "Amber and Scott had been in love for so long."

Lily nodded, vaguely recalling Amber from

back in school. She'd seen her in the news some time ago, but couldn't recall the details. "That's nice."

"So how did Ethan propose?"

Lily rubbed her forehead. Ethan. Right. She'd been cooking him both breakfast and supper this week—like a real wife might. She enjoyed their quiet meals.

The other waitresses were obviously listening in, their expressions curious.

Right! This was that moment she'd been waiting for—the one where they connected like a big ol' family. One where she wasn't just the boss and owner, but a friend.

The proposal. Right.

Lily's heart sank. It wasn't a romantic story and nothing like the moment she'd dreamed of, that was for sure.

But she knew she couldn't blow off the question. Waitresses could make or break a restaurant and she needed to bond with them, keep them happy.

She gave a small, embarrassed shrug, figuring she'd stick close to the facts. "I proposed to him."

She was met with blank stares.

"No, really," Sasha, a waitress in her early twenties, prompted as she rolled a knife and fork in a fresh white napkin. "How did he propose?"

Lily laughed. "He looked just as surprised as you do."

"But…" Tanya, the youngest—a high school student—gave her a confused look.

"I've had a crush on him since forever." Lily felt herself blush at the spoken truth.

"And he said yes? Just like that?"

"Once he got over being stunned, yeah. Kinda." She peeked up at them shyly.

"I guess he figured nobody else would take him," Tanya said to Sasha, just loud enough for Lily to hear.

"He's a keeper!" she exclaimed, jumping to his defense.

"Dani didn't think so."

"Dani's loss is my gain." The table of four was waving at her and she stood up, glad for the interruption.

"I heard she's coming to town next week."

Lily didn't dare react to the news as she walked over to the waiting customers. Dani was gorgeous and Lily didn't think Ethan had ever truly gotten over her. Just like her brother hadn't quite gotten over the woman he'd dumped in his twenties, and as a result had a silly marriage pledge with his friend Amy. Most men seemed to have a woman like that in their past. And as Ethan's wife, Lily didn't ever want to face her or feel the full effect of her lingering power.

"Hi, how's your meal?" she asked as she approached the table. She remembered to smile, not reveal the fact that she felt like she was facing a firing squad, with four sets of eyes aimed at her judgmentally. "Everything okay?"

"The lasagna tastes different," the man said.

"Today's special is supposed to be roast beef," another one said.

Their wives nodded.

"Yes, the special today is Benny's traditional lasagna—just made with fresh oregano and a bit more rosemary to give it a richer flavor."

"It's nice," one of the women said. "But are we supposed to eat this?" She pointed to the sprig of parsley.

"No, it's garnish."

"Garnish? It looks like parsley."

"It is."

"I wanted roast beef. I come in for the roast beef."

"I'm sorry, sir." The roast beef once-a-week special barely broke even, so Lily had tried offering the lasagna as a special instead. It seemed Blueberry Springs wasn't ready for that.

"If there's no roast beef, then don't expect me to come back."

Lily resisted the urge to beg, to backtrack. "Then we'll miss having you, especially if we make roast beef."

"Will you?" he asked, his bushy gray eyebrows raised.

"You'll have to come by and see," she said with a teasing smile, turning on her heel and instinctively knowing she hadn't handled that as well as she could have.

Gloria was chuckling when Lily returned to her paperwork. "You're changing too much too fast."

"All I did was take roast beef off the specials for today."

"Too much, too fast. He comes into town for that roast beef every week and has been for five years."

"Well, unless he starts paying more for it, it's not coming back."

Gloria's eyebrows shot up.

"That special barely pays for itself," Lily grumbled, taking her seat in front of the printed spreadsheets again.

The waitresses avoided making eye contact with her.

She was blowing it with them. She could feel it.

"Have you been a chef for long?" Sasha asked, and Lily threw her a grateful look.

"A few years. I've always wanted my own kitchen."

"Everyone says you married Ethan for this place because you couldn't afford to buy it," Gloria said, a sly glint in her eyes.

"Oh! I—" Lily decided to keep her mouth shut.

"Liz said she saw you two kissing out at the Blackberry River trailhead and you were all over each other," Tanya said, leaning forward.

Lily felt her face heat with embarrassment.

"I heard he can't...you know..." she prompted, her eyes shining with curiosity.

"Tanya!" Gloria snapped, slamming a full sugar shaker on the table.

Lily laughed at her reaction. "What can't he do?"

The women all resumed working, their cheeks red.

"What?" Lily asked, a feeling of dread seeping in. "Tell me."

She was close to discovering what was wrong with Ethan and her whole body felt clammy.

Tanya looked at the other women, who were suddenly frozen in place.

"After his accident—being paralyzed for a while. You know...? Everyone's saying he can't... with a woman. And that's why we never see you kissing much."

Lily gasped, dread and humiliation burning through her as she picked up the gist of Tanya's accusation.

"It's okay. I had a boyfriend who was horrible in bed," Sasha said, giving Lily a sympathetic glance.

"No...it's...we..." Lily scrambled to sweep up her papers so she could flee to the privacy of her office before she humiliated herself by blurting out something she'd regret. She caught herself. Running off to hide would be the worst way to react. She calmed herself and said politely, "It's nothing like that."

But what if it was? What if Ethan couldn't perform in the bedroom and that was why he kept pulling back whenever she got close?

No, that didn't make sense. He also avoided lifting and moving heavy things. And anyway, she'd felt evidence of his virility pressed against her when they'd kissed.

However, it was part of the overall puzzle. One she planned on piecing together sooner rather than later.

ETHAN COULDN'T CONCENTRATE. He stared at his monitor and the computer cursor blinking endlessly, his mind as blank as the page of code he was supposed to be writing.

No, not quite blank. His mind was stuck on the woman he'd married almost two weeks ago. What was he going to do? What if his arthritis or whatever it was flared up to the point where she thought she needed to stay and care for him instead of spreading her wings like they'd planned? She already had her father leaning on her. She didn't need another burden.

"I hear you're unable to keep your wife happy in bed. Need any tips?"

Ethan looked up from his screen, blinking like the cursor, and trying to figure out what his grinning brother was saying. He'd expected it to be Lily when he'd heard the front door open. She was usually home by seven and it was already eight-thirty. He'd come to look forward to sharing a quiet supper with her. It was a nice way to cap off a long, lonely day in front of his computer.

His brother, looking relaxed and athletic—no doubt just in from an after-work run—was waiting for Ethan to react. He was happily and newly married to the woman he'd fallen for in college over a decade ago, and from what Ethan had heard, having the best sex of his life. In other words, Devon was the last man Ethan wanted to hear from as he dealt with frustrating levels of unsatisfied desire as he continued through the worst dry spell of his life.

"Shut up," he said, turning back to his computer and typing a line of code before checking it in a preview application, to make it look like he was actually working.

His fingers halted over the keyboard. Wait one second. He swiveled back to his brother.

"What did you say?"

"There you are," Devon said cheerfully. "Thought you hadn't heard me." He threw himself into the armchair Ethan kept in his office for reading and lounging. The way his brother contorted his spine to sag into the plush chair, legs slung over the side, made Ethan wince.

"Who said that?"

What if it was Lily?

Or one of the town gossips? If so, it was unfair for Lily to have to deal with it. But how could he stop the wagging tongues other than to prove them all wrong by sending Lily out into the world barely able to walk from the best orgasm of her life? No, make that *orgasms*.

Why did the very thought of that make him want to grin?

Devon shrugged, picking up a stress ball Ethan used for strength building, giving it a squeeze. "Everyone says she married you for the restaurant."

He was watching Ethan as though he expected him to explode.

Instead, Ethan turned back to his computer, staring blankly at the screen once again. He'd been kidding himself that he could pretend to be man enough for someone like Lily. Everyone could see it was an uneven match borne out of something besides love.

"She deserves better," he muttered, trying to shift his mind back to the website he was building.

Although maybe bad gossip would help everyone love her all the more—a woman who not only had to put up with his grumpiness, but was subjected to poor sex on top of it.

On top…

No, no time for visions of what that might be like. Glorious. Fabulous. Completely gratifying.

He heard his brother's feet hit the floor and turned to see him sitting forward. "Whoa. What?" Devon asked in a hushed voice.

"It doesn't matter. She's not going to stay." And she sure wasn't going to see his messed-up body, laced with scars. Too many surgeries, tentatively piecing together a man that had barely survived. She was the kind of woman who probably wouldn't mind, but it was a moot point, anyway.

"What are you talking about? You've been married for less than a month. You can't break up."

Ethan froze, realizing that his mental thoughts had somehow become verbal. "Never mind. I'm just moody. This site I'm working on is kicking my balls with steel-toed boots."

"You can't be a used wad of toilet paper with her," Devon scolded. "It's a charming challenge at first—trying to make you smile—but it's gonna wear. Even on her. She likes warm hugs and you're basically an icicle."

"Devon, we're okay."

And in a lot of ways, they were. She was a fantastic cook and he left the table feeling good each morning, and not just because he wasn't eating a heavy, greasy meal off the grill. It was because...

It didn't matter. He was going to get attached and miss her when she left, which meant it was best to maintain the status quo. Be a grump, be alone. Let her be a lovable, happy person charming the world.

"She's always had a crush on you." Devon was bouncing the stress ball against the wall with a thud, thud, thud. "I would have thought that would lead to killer sex. When Olivia and I got back together, man...chafing became a problem, if you know what I mean."

Ethan curled his lip. He really didn't need to hear about how awesome their sex life was while he was living with Miss Sex Appeal and couldn't touch her.

And the rumors. How had they started?

He was fairly confident he didn't want to know.

"How is Olivia?" Ethan asked, trying to get his mind off his own wife.

"Pregnant."

"What?" He spun to face his grinning brother. "Congratulations."

Devon beamed at him, but then a twinge of worry made his grin fade slightly. Ethan had only recently learned a few of the couple's secrets from their college days and knew the reason for his brother's concern with the pregnancy.

"How's she feeling?"

"Morning sickness hasn't been fun. I keep telling her to get her sister to come down and stay a bit."

"Not a bad idea for her to take it easy. But isn't her sister a debutante or something?" He couldn't see someone like that holding the hair back for her pregnant sister while she battled morning sickness. Then again, some things you couldn't hire out.

Devon chuckled. "She falls under 'or something.' But she always cheers up Olivia. She is spunky in her own rule-following way."

They sat quietly for a moment.

"So you two are really okay?" Devon asked,

bringing the conversation back around to Ethan's marriage.

"Yeah, just...you know. A lot to process with it all happening so quick."

"Well, I think you two are great together." He stood up. "Just don't be yourself and it'll all work out."

"Myself?" Ethan felt the sting of anger.

"A grumpy donkey who pushes everyone away, believing you're too crippled to be likable. She thinks the world of you."

He watched Devon, trying to gauge how much truth was in his words.

"Try catching her looking at you, Ethan. She's got it bad." His brother laughed. "And you and those dopey eyes, like you're the nerd drooling after the prom queen. Oh, it's too funny. You guys are *married*." He let out another laugh, moving toward the doorway, then lowered his voice. "If you want to make her happy in bed, women really like it when you—"

Ethan lunged at him, shoving his brother from his office, slamming the door. Devon laughed on the other side, calling loudly, "The new town librarian ordered *The Joy of Sex*! She's a sexy beast and has everyone all fired up. Maybe she has some tips for you. Or at least a manual on how to use your body to please a woman."

Ethan didn't need tips. He needed a willing wife. A wife who actually loved him. All of him. Even the bits she didn't know about and likely never would.

IN THE GUESTROOM, Lily looked at the single bed she slept in. Her shipping container of furniture, housewares and extra clothes had finally arrived and was currently sitting on Ethan's front lawn. The question she was facing was how much she should bother to unpack, seeing as she'd be finding her own place in a year.

Sighing, she sat on the bed. She'd messed up with the ladies at work. Balancing the boss-friend-colleague thing was harder than she'd believed. She'd imagined them all as one big happy family that spent hours upon hours together, working, laughing, sharing. It wasn't like that. Not yet, anyway.

She'd stayed late at work, fretting mostly, and missing supper with Ethan.

She didn't want to talk about her sex life with staff, but she wanted to be a part of their lives, offer them a place of work that felt welcoming, enjoyable. She wanted the restaurant to be where they ran to when they had life news to share.

Maybe she could fix yesterday's faux pas. She could cook a buffet for her staff and their families on Sunday morning before opening. She'd do all the prep and all the cleanup, making it a real treat. She dusted her hands together as though removing the mental problem, and stood up to tackle the idea of unpacking herself even further into Ethan's life.

Her phone rang and she checked to see who it was. Her father. Take one problem off her plate and add a new one, that's how life felt these days.

"Hey, Dad."

"Are you the owner yet?"

"It'll be at least a year."

"Don't let him screw you over. You deserve this."

"Dad, Ethan's a good man."

"I know, but you're really reaching for this and our family has never had anything like this before. This feels too easy. Too good to be true."

"It's not." It was definitely not too easy. "And I trust Ethan."

"I don't."

"You don't trust anyone."

"For a good reason."

Lily huffed in amusement. "The restaurant will be hopping in a matter of weeks, so don't stress. I'll send you money as soon as I can."

"I don't want your money. I want you in a secure job."

"That's what I'm working on, and I'll send you money. You can't keep living hand to mouth."

Her father sighed and said, "Break the chain. Break the cycle I'm stuck in, Lillian."

She ended the call, feeling the pressure to succeed even more than before.

She went to the kitchen and poured herself a glass of wine, then headed to the front yard, passing the small bureau she and Mandy had wrestled into the entry earlier.

Ethan was on the lawn, a keyboard tucked under his arm, staring at the storage unit.

"It's going to kill the grass," he grumbled.

"Grumpy bear, it's fine. It won't be there long. And I'm sorry I missed supper tonight."

"It's fine? What are you going to do with all of this?" He peered around the open doors, contemplating her packed belongings.

Lily glanced to her right, spotting the neighbors. She waved and called a greeting, making it obvious to Ethan they had eavesdroppers.

"You're moving in?" they asked skeptically, crossing the grass.

"Of course." She held her glass of wine against her chest, feeling wary.

"I heard you two weren't... It's not our business."

Lily frowned and glanced at Ethan. His face had turned to stone and she was pretty sure she heard the keyboard's plastic casing crack from his hands tensing around it as he struggled for control.

Uh-oh.

Was he going to go all Incredible Hulk on her? If so, she couldn't wait for his shirt to come off. She'd bet he had an amazing chest.

"Maybe you should mind your own marriage," he snapped, storming toward the house.

Lily hurried after him, alarmed by how wounded he seemed this evening. She knew she'd missed supper, but this felt much bigger than that.

"What was that about?" she asked as soon as the door was closed behind them.

"You should lock your unit if you're not unpacking it. I won't be responsible if anyone takes stuff out of it." He lunged down the hallway, his forehead furrowed.

"Ethan, what was that comment about us?" She hurried after him, dread heavy in her gut. He was already sitting in front of his computer, his fingers punishing the keys. "Let's go for a hike. Blackberry River was always nice. We could get out of the house, straighten our story and spend some time together—like true newlyweds."

"I have work to do."

"I could pack a picnic. I made those biscuits you like. We could have those with butter and cheese. Maybe some cold cuts and grapes?"

His monitor went black and he pushed himself away from his desk, turning his shoulder to her as he brushed past.

Was that a yes?

She caught up with him again in the living room, where he was sorting through the day's mail.

"Is that a yes or a no?"

He didn't answer, just lowered his head even farther so she couldn't see his expression.

"Fine. That's a no," she guessed.

He was trying to shut her out.

Well, she wasn't going to let it be easy. She set down her wine on the coffee table and took one end of the bureau sitting in the middle of the entryway. Maybe if he helped her unpack it would loosen his tongue. She could find out what was bothering him, as well as what the big secret was with his health.

"Can you help me with this?" she asked. "I'm going to put it in my room."

"You're unpacking?" he asked in obvious surprise.

"Yes," she said, her voice wavering. She hoisted her end of the bureau. It was much heavier without

Mandy on the other side. Awkward, too. "Help me?"

"It's too big for your room."

"Then let's put it against that wall." She pointed to a spot in the living room. Like most of the house, it could use a few extra pieces of furniture. It was as though Ethan hadn't fully moved in, didn't really live here. "Is that okay?"

"Put things wherever." He continued shuffling through the mail. It was his third pass through the envelopes.

"Although having it in here could be an issue," she said, pretending to think things through.

He peeked up from the mail, his eyes flicking from the bureau to the spot she'd pointed to. "Why?"

"Well…" She stepped around the antique piece, then leaned against it. "I keep my lingerie in this thing. So it means there might be times when I'd have to streak across the living room to find the items I want. You usually keep the curtains closed, right?"

The envelopes in his hand began to fold as his fist closed around them.

"You know…bras, panties and those…" Nuts. She couldn't remember the name for the fancy lingerie that had garters—lingerie she didn't have and likely never would, since it didn't seem like the kind of thing you wore under jeans. She waved a hand through the air. "You know…" she lowered her voice "…all that sexy stuff."

Ethan's Adam's apple bobbed twice and his voice was rough as he tossed the mail back on the table, saying, "Our sex life sucks."

She laughed. "Paper marriages rarely include buzzing sex lives. But if you want to change that…" She eased closer, teasing him, curious how he'd react. There were sparks between them, that she knew. But why it seemed to scare him off was still a mystery.

"It's what everyone's saying." He held his ground, looking up, his expression one of hurt. He covered the flash of pain quickly, layering it below anger.

"Oh." The day's conversations flashed though her mind. "Oh, no. The waitresses. They were… We were talking and they must have…" She involuntarily gave her husband a visual crotch check, hating herself for letting their words get under her skin, causing doubts despite how her body had responded to his. The dry thrusts, his hot kisses and grazing thumbs. How heated and entangled they'd so quickly become out on the edge of the highway, their bodies intersecting in all the right ways with just one kiss.

"You don't deserve to be talked about like that," Ethan said. "I think we should break up."

"Excuse me?" She felt a flash of rage. "Oh no! No way. I'm tougher than rumors, Ethan Mattson, and so are you. You might be older than me but you do *not* get to decide my life. You don't say when we're quits just because some nosy ladies can't mind their own business. We knew this wouldn't be easy, but we made a commitment to each other."

"You deserve better than this."

"Ethan..." Lily softened her tone. "I appreciate that you're looking out for me, but all we need to do is get our story straight and spend some time together in public. And for the record, I said I proposed." She touched his hand, knowing her physical reassurances would be rejected. He didn't disappoint, and pulled his hand away, putting space between them.

"I should have," he said, his voice low. His gaze finally met hers and all she saw was pain. Layers and layers of pain and frustration and disappointment in himself.

"Talk to me, Ethan."

He remained silent and she tapped the bureau, hoping that having something to focus on might help the conversation flow. "Let's move this thing."

"I can't."

She froze. He couldn't get it up? *Oh. Oh, no.*

"But I felt…" Her gaze drifted to his crotch.

"*What?*"

Uh-oh.

"I *can*." He stepped closer.

"I know. I mean I felt…" Shoot. Best to not talk right now.

"Is that what everyone thinks? Is that why they say our sex life sucks?"

"I, um…" She closed one eye, wincing. "Kinda?"

He grabbed her wrist, pulling her out into the yard. He glanced around for an audience and, finding one in their gossiping neighbors, yanked Lily close, wrapping his arms around her. She felt frightened by his urgency until she met his eyes. The fiery demand to prove himself melted as his gaze met hers, and he tenderly brushed away a lock that had fallen across her forehead. "Is it okay if I kiss you senseless, Ms. Harper?"

For a moment she wished she'd changed her last name so he'd call her Mrs. Mattson, make her feel like she belonged—to him.

"As long as you don't try to prove to the town here on the lawn that you can get it up," she replied nervously. "That might be taking things a bit far."

He threw back his head, laughing so hard his chest bounced against hers. When he looked at her it was with such affection and openness she felt her heart drift closer toward forbidden territory. And maybe some answers.

"Kiss me, Ethan."

He didn't wait for another plea, but lowered his lips to hers, proving to all onlookers that Ethan Mattson definitely knew how to kiss, and that if they'd had a sex life, it would have been smokin' hot.

CHAPTER 8

*L*ily curled a leg around Ethan's. She wished he'd pick her up and carry her back to the house, put those big arms to good use and go Tarzan. Or caveman. Or any kind of man who had it bad for his wife like his kisses suggested.

She heard someone who sounded an awful lot like Ethan's brother holler, "Get a room!"

Taking the cue, Lily broke the kiss and pulled her husband toward the house. She didn't try to hide the way her eyelids felt heavy with desire, the way her body kept drifting back to his. Ethan stumbled, then picked up the pace, their lips colliding as they tried to get in hungry kisses while still moving toward privacy. Man, he was a good actor, and she wasn't sure a cold shower was going to get her hormone levels back to normal once they made it inside, their convincing act no longer required.

They made it up the steps before she let him crash into her accidentally on purpose, taking the opportunity to grope his back with splayed fingers, her kisses hot and furious.

They were putting on a good show, but the heat was as real as the fires of hell.

After staggering through the open front door, Lily thought Ethan would shut it behind them and let her go, then step away, cool and unaffected, like always. But instead, the door slammed shut behind him and his hands dived under her shirt, causing her to suck in a breath. Her T-shirt was on the floor seconds later, and she arched her spine, moving closer to what mattered. Ethan's kisses were those of a man possessed, and she trailed her nails down his chest, then wrapped her arms around his trim waist, pulling his tight-muscled body toward her.

They made it a few steps across the entryway before she bumped into her lingerie chest and angled herself onto it, splaying her legs so she could welcome Ethan into the V of her body. He accepted the invitation, his hands tangling in her hair as their lips continued their arousing exploration. With her legs wrapped around him, she arched, and his mouth moved in hungry strides toward her lace bra. Lily had never been turned on so fast in her entire life.

When his palms finally cupped her, his kisses slowed to worshiping speed, and she moaned. Reflexively, she reached for the hem of Ethan's shirt, eager to touch warm flesh, ready to explore. To rip the cotton from his body with her teeth, if need be. But he shifted abruptly, releasing her breasts and grabbing her wrists, so she couldn't move. He had stopped kissing her. His eyes were dark, chest heaving, he was watching her, a strange expression on his face.

"What's wrong?" She wanted that shirt off him. She wanted to touch every inch of his flesh, wanted to own it, possess it, have the right to explore, feel him, have him.

His gaze drifted to her lavender bra. He blinked a few times, then eased back a half step. Then another.

"Ethan," she whispered as she reached for him, eager to draw him close again, feel his heat, his need.

He said nothing, simply bent to retrieve her shirt, gently handing it to her, before he turned and walked away.

THE NEXT MORNING Ethan hid in his office until Lily left for the restaurant. He felt like a dork for embarrassing himself the night before and allowing the opinions of others to influence the way he treated her.

Who practically made love out on their front lawn? Who pulled off his wife's shirt as if he had the right to ravage her, when he didn't even have the courage to tell her why he couldn't move a fridge, and that under his clothes he looked like a torn-up teddy bear that someone's half-blind grandma had patched back together?

But the way Lily had looked up at him, that merry twinkle in her eyes and her sweet voice, all husky, saying, "Kiss me, Ethan..."

Yeah, that was why. It made him feel like he could fly, and believe that no matter what he could or couldn't do he'd always be her hero.

And that lacy lavender bra? It was all he could think about this morning.

Only about eleven months, one week and six days left before they crossed the year mark.

In other words, he was going to have to learn to deal with his attraction if he didn't own up and be honest with her.

He couldn't risk messing up, though. He didn't want the restaurant back and the amount of time

Lily had freed up for him already was making a difference with his web business.

So what was he going to do? Every time she looked at him it turned up his internal thermostat, as if he'd decided to have a bonfire under the desert sun while wearing all his winter gear.

He needed to tell her, needed to come clean.

She might reject him, but she also might not. The ball, however, would be in her court.

His cell rang and he pulled it closer. Gloria's number. Why was she calling him? Lily should be at the restaurant…

His heart raced as he answered the phone, fearing his string of bad luck had been extended to Lily.

"Hello?"

"Hey, Ethan."

The waitress sounded unfazed, casual.

"Gloria. What's up? I'm busy."

"Lily was wondering if you took the cash float for the register out of the safe."

"Why doesn't she ask me herself?" *Because she's afraid of you and the way you just about lost control of yourself last night, you numbskull.*

"He wants to talk to you," Gloria hollered, not bothering to cover the speaker on her phone.

Ethan rubbed the bridge of his nose.

"Hey, did you empty the safe?" Lily asked, sounding out of breath.

"No. What's missing?"

"Just the float."

"Are you sure you didn't deposit it by mistake?" There was silence. "Lil?"

"I must have put everything in the night deposit on my way home. Sorry. I'll figure it out with the bank when they open."

"You open before the bank. What are you going to do about a float?"

More silence.

"I'll see what I have kicking around here at home." He could be a good guy. Help her with the business. Keep that up front and center, so he didn't try and make sweet love to her in a broom closet.

"Thanks, Ethan."

"What are husbands for if not saving the day, on top of rocking your world on the front lawn?" he asked, then ended the call in shock.

He'd just said that.

Then again, she'd hinted that they could make their marriage a bit more...sexual. If he was going to tell her the truth and get in the ring, he may as well give her some forewarning, right?

Ethan dug through his change jar, which held a mix of coins and small bills, before deciding to haul the whole thing down to Benny's to let Lily sort through it for what she needed in her cash register.

He glanced down at his outfit of tattered jeans and an equally worn T-shirt. Walking to his closet, he braced himself as Lily's perfume wafted out, her side of the closet so much brighter and more cheerful than his, as if reflecting their personalities. He chose a crisp white button-up shirt, rolling the sleeves over his biceps, revealing the edge of one of his many scars. He added a new pair of jeans and was out the door to save the day, beg silent forgiveness.

And maybe finally tell her the truth.

In the restaurant, he noted Lily pause when she spotted his attire. She liked what she saw and the feeling was mutual. She was wearing a flirty little skirt and a knitted top that slid off one shoulder. Her tumble of curls brushed her shoulders and her legs looked amazing.

"I love summertime," he said quietly as she turned her back, no doubt a reaction to his mauling last night, followed by his sudden rejection when she'd gone to lift his shirt.

He handed her the jar of coins, striving to keep his gaze from drifting to the neckline of her top. Lavender again? Lace?

Ice shower. He needed ice. Possibly down his pants.

She hoisted the jar. "How much is in here?"

He shrugged. "Some people would say thank you."

"Thank you, Ethan," she said, with a hint of sass that went straight up his spine and into his brain. His gaze drifted to the neckline, then lower.

"You're not even going to kiss him as thanks?" Gloria asked as she walked past.

Lily's expression turned hard with hurt and rejection. "He's not into public displays of—"

She didn't get to finish her words because Ethan pulled her to him, planting a sweet kiss on her lips, his hands on her lower back. The coin jar hit him in the center of his chest as his wife struggled for balance.

"Anything for lil' Lily," he said, releasing her, satisfied that he'd taken her breath away.

Her cheeks were flushed and he gave her a wink.

He might be playing games he would never win, but he also had a duty as her husband to act like one.

"What was that for?" she asked breathlessly.

"You being you." In the restaurant he could give her a little kiss, be flirtatious without worrying about taking it too far and ripping off her shirt like some sort of savage who thought she was the sexiest, most irresistible woman he'd ever laid his lips upon.

Seriously, though. What color was her bra today? It must be strapless, as her bare shoulder was devoid of anything but a tantalizing expanse of flesh. Curiosity had him stepping closer, which meant it was time to leave. Things were heating up like he was baking in the desert again, a glimmering mirage of them with a real future taunting him in the distance.

"While you're here, can you help me?" Lily asked. She handed the jar to Gloria, instructing her to create a float.

"Sorry, what?"

"I need a hand."

He began instinctively backing toward the door, sensing she was trying to trap him into exposing the truth about his physical limitations.

He paused. It was time to man up.

Lily tucked a strand of hair behind her ear. "I want to move the cash register and resurface the front counter." She pointed to the ancient beast taking up most of the space beside a stack of menus. "Are you okay with that? It only cost me six bucks."

Ethan shrugged. It was her place now.

"So can you lift?" She cleared away the menus,

then held up a long piece of countertop plastic that looked to be cut to size.

"Uh..." He glanced at the cash register. There was no way to lift with his legs, no way to angle it so the forty to fifty pounds weren't hanging straight off his spine. "I can't, Lily."

Before he could explain why, motion outside the big bay windows caught his eye. "Is that my grandpa?"

"Just lift it," Lily demanded.

Ethan caught another glimpse of his grandfather, while trying to figure out Lily's unusual tone.

"Why isn't he... Shoot! Gramps!" He opened the door, running after his grandfather, who was walking down the street in nothing more than an undershirt and a pair of boxers.

LILY FELT as though she had been just about to get to the bottom of Ethan's secrecy surrounding his reluctance to lift things when he took off again. Then again, his grandfather did seem to be a tad underdressed for a public appearance. She joined Ethan on the sidewalk in front of the restaurant, shielding her eyes against the bright sun rising over the mountaintops.

"Gramps," Ethan said, "I don't care if you feel

like it's going to be a hot one, you can't dress like this. You need pants or shorts."

"How's it any different than what the kids are wearing today? Everything important is covered up."

"You need to wear shorts over your underwear."

"Says who?"

"Society. Besides, you don't want your one-eyed willy popping out to say hi to all the ladies."

"You give an old man too much credit. Nothing's popping and hasn't for years."

Lily hid her smile behind a hand and tried not to feel too much tenderness toward Ethan as he dealt with the situation. He was calm, kind and gentle. None of that scowling business going on. He was like the old Ethan she'd fallen for and it made her swoon just a little bit.

Yesterday she'd felt the heat. The passion.

The rejection.

Maybe she wasn't womanly or sexy enough for him. After having a supermodel for a girlfriend, who wanted the kid he'd used to pull out of mud puddles? Or maybe he was just smart enough to not mix business and pleasure, as Lily had in the past—always leading to disaster.

Plus, she'd made it clear she was in their marriage for one thing only—a restaurant. And knowing Ethan, he was probably trying to protect her, keep within the parameters she'd set out for them.

Platonic.

What had she been thinking, suggesting that?

"Need any help?" she asked, lightly touching Ethan's arm to make sure he'd heard. He looked amazing with his bronzed skin set off by that crisp, white shirt. He looked healthy and delectable, and their kiss out on the lawn to shut up the neighbors came flooding back to her mind. Steamy. Irresistible.

Yeah, a platonic business commitment was that last thing she wanted.

Both men looked at her as she repeated her offer of help.

"No," they both snapped, displaying the same defensive look.

"Wow. What are the names of the women who dented your lovely personalities?" she muttered.

The men shared a glance and Lily tipped her head to the side, feeling as though she'd inadvertently stumbled onto something.

"Okay…" She eased closer, curious.

"I don't need some woman leaving me, kicking me while I'm down," Gramps said, waving his arms. "And neither does Ethan!"

"He's a widower," Ethan mumbled to Lily.

"She left me!"

"She died. People do that, Gramps."

"Well, Dani left you."

"I'm aware of that."

"Dani?" Lily asked involuntarily. She'd heard the story, of course, but none of the details of her leaving him high and dry when she'd found out he was paralyzed. Lily was curious to hear what her husband's thoughts on his ex were. "I heard she's coming to town soon."

"I'd rather not talk about her," Ethan replied.

Did that mean he was still pining for her and had a secret hope that she'd soon reclaim him like lost luggage? Because if so, he deserved a whole lot more than that.

"She left you right when—" Gramps started to say.

"We're heading home now." Ethan began to gently guide him down the street.

Lily, knowing any offers of help would be rebuffed, stood in front of her restaurant, curious about Ethan and his ex and whether Dani might be part of the grand puzzle Lily was trying to solve. She had a feeling that if she solved it, she would also unearth the key to Ethan's heart. But the question would be whether that key would turn for someone like her.

ETHAN, sat in a corner of the living room at his dad's, watching over his newly adopted nephew, Axel. The little guy had fallen asleep in his baby swing, his newborn body all perfect and tiny, curled into the small space. Mandy and Devon were arguing several feet away about whether Gramps's recent behavior was anything new or not.

The family had gathered to discuss what to do about Gramps, and so far it looked as though everyone thought it best to throttle back his independence. The issue seemed to be how best to keep an eye on him until a spot opened up in the town's nursing home. Ethan, knowing what it was like to be on the receiving end of the family's good intentions when it came to things like this, tried to stay as far out of the discussion as possible.

He looked up as Lily let herself into the house, looking tired. He gave her a nod and she moved to join him in the corner, but was waylaid by Mandy.

Before long the volume in the house grew and Axel began fussing. Frankie was at the far end of the room, trying to fix Dad's recliner, while Mandy was still chatting with Lily.

Lily. Ethan still needed to come clean with her about his physical limitations.

"You need out of there, little guy?" He unhitched the swing's straps and lifted his nephew, who was warm, pliable and completely trusting. Ethan set him against his shoulder and rocked slowly, and the baby quickly settled in.

The room continued to buzz around them while Ethan sat in quiet contentment.

Trish sat down beside him.

"I'd like the family to take a hike together," she said.

Ethan gave her a blank look. It was a well-known fact that he and hiking did not belong in the same sentence.

"Just in the meadow, silly. Walking through the flowers is barely different than walking down a sidewalk. We'll bring a little picnic and blankets to sit on."

The meadow, located just outside of town, had a gravel parking lot and crisscross of foot-worn paths that led to higher mountain trails. It was a popular area for hikers, but he could wander the mostly level paths within the meadow without too much issue. And a picnic among the rolling grasses and wildflowers with Lily did sound kind of nice. Romantic.

He wished he'd thought of it himself. And that the rest of the family wouldn't be coming along.

"Why?" he asked Trish.

"To celebrate the newest addition to the Mattson family."

Ethan looked toward his wife. "I don't think Lily wants—"

"Axel, silly! Oh, Ethan." Smiling at him, Trish rested one hand on the back of his sleeping nephew. "You've got a one-track mind about your wife, don't you?"

He caught Lily's eye from across the room. She was watching him with an odd, soft expression and he hoped Mandy wasn't telling her silly stories about his childhood.

"You want to hold Axel?" Ethan leaned forward, prepared to go interfere with his sister's story-telling, in case she was giving Lily the wrong im-pression.

His stepmother shook her head. "Mandy says he screams unless he's in the swing, and he's not screaming so best to hold on to him."

Ethan leaned back in the chair, feeling a sudden pressure to keep the infant happy.

"We're going to hike on Sunday," Trish said, standing up. "Lily's going to need a few hours off work."

"She sets her own schedule," he replied.

"I can take the time," Lily said, joining them. "I'll bring a picnic for everyone."

Her attention seemed to be fixed on Axel and Ethan.

"He's so small," Ethan said. He could cup the

baby's entire head with his hand, feel his heartbeat through the soft spot at the top. So fragile, so in need of protection. He wished he was a stronger man so he could teach his nephew all the things a boy needed to know, such as how to live off the land for a weekend high in the mountains, how to fish and build a tree house, make a slingshot. Everything.

But that wasn't his job. Axel had Frankie, and Ethan was merely an accessory, an uncle. Although maybe there were still things he could teach the boy, ways he could be a part of his life.

"No, no," Trish was saying to Lily. "You don't need to go to the bother of trying to feed us all. This is a celebration, not more work for you."

"I'd like to." Lily looked put out at being denied the opportunity to fill eight hungry mouths.

"Fine then," Trish said softly, giving in. "We'll see you both Sunday."

"What about Gramps?" Ethan asked.

"We're going to put him in a home. He can't live alone any longer."

"Oh."

"We're hoping you can tell him."

"Me?"

"You have a good relationship with him."

"Well, I guess." That was going to be hard. He knew what it felt like to have your independence taken away. Which was maybe the real reason the family had chosen him.

"Ethan," his father said, coming to stand beside Trish, "we'd also like you to take in your grandfather until we can get him into the home. There's a bit of a wait list, but it doesn't seem safe to have him living on his own any longer."

Ethan opened his mouth to protest, but his dad continued on, not backing down even though Ethan gave him the same helpless look that had worked beautifully while he'd been paralyzed, but seemed to be losing its effect these days.

In other words, his father wasn't buying it.

"You have a guestroom and work from home. Plus you're one of the few people he listens to."

"But…" That wasn't how things were supposed to work. Cory wasn't supposed to push him around like he did Mandy and Devon. Ethan glanced at Lily, who was looking everywhere but at him. "But we…"

"We what?" Everyone in the room was watching them, waiting for his excuse.

"We would love to have Gramps," he said quietly, knowing that it would take Gramps about ten seconds to see through his and Lily's pinch of commitment.

"WHAT ARE YOU DOING?" Lily put her hands on her hips and looked up at Ethan, who was standing precariously on a stepladder, messing around with something in the ceiling tiles near the walk-in fridge in the back hallway. It was crazy early and she'd been having a Beyoncé dance party while getting things prepped for the day; she didn't need an audience messing with her "zone." But he'd marched in like he owned the place, toting one of those clear plastic boxes of his full of gadgets, and now he was setting something up in the ceiling. Her ceiling. She squinted at the device he was aiming. A camera! Seriously? "Are you *spying* on me?"

"No, solving the bad luck of this place once and for all."

"What does that mean?"

"The new fridge that turns off on its own, the missing cash float. That stuff."

She'd never found the missing two hundred and fifty dollars. Lily decided she must have made a simple accounting error and deposited it along with the day's income. But before coming to that conclusion she'd made the mistake of mentioning the missing money to her father in their weekly phone call. He'd gone into a tailspin about her being shafted by The Man. She never did manage to pinpoint who he thought The Man was, but secretly suspected he was referring to Ethan.

Either way, she now was much more careful with her accounting and kept better track of which employees had access to what.

But the fridge? She hadn't heard anything about it acting up but if Ethan was training a camera on it, she could assume something more than a faulty switch might be at play.

"Has someone been turning off the fridge?"

Ethan shrugged.

"Well, I hope a camera solves the mystery." She hated to think how much a walk-in fridge of spoiled food might cost the restaurant.

Ethan glanced down at her, his mouth holding some sort of orange thing that looked like the cap off a glue bottle. He plucked it from between his lips and twisted it onto two wires, saying, "Flip the third switch down, left side, in the panel box."

"Where's that?"

"In the office, behind the door."

She went into the room, flicked the stiff switch and returned, happy to see she hadn't electrocuted her husband.

"Well?" she asked.

Ethan carefully eased his way down the stepladder. "That should do it." It seemed like his muscles were bugging him again. His skin was slightly pale, too.

"Do you eat a lot of wheat?"

"What?"

"Your joint stiffness. It could be a wheat in-tolerance."

"Or the fact that a few hundred thousand tons of snow threw my car off the road and down the side of a mountain."

Lily winced involuntarily and he saw it, turning his shoulder to her, shutting her out. *Okay, tough guy.* So his body language was saying he didn't want empathy from anyone, but it didn't mean she had to play along.

"You were paralyzed?" she prodded.

"Yup." He picked up his plastic bin and carried it off to her cramped office.

"But now you're not."

"Yup. But there are things I can't do."

"Like what?"

He simply gave her a look over his shoulder. That broad, broad shoulder. Then he winked and thrust the bin into her arms, lifting the lid and re-moving a small camera.

What had that wink meant? He was teasing her, playing around.

"I'm going to put this one watching the safe."

She felt as though the bottom of her world dropped out, sending her into free fall. "But you and I are the only ones with access now." That was a change he'd insisted upon after the float had gone missing. There was no reason to put a camera above the safe unless he didn't trust her.

"I thought my bad luck would end when you came along," he told her.

Lily's world rebounded and her heart lifted. "Aw, thanks, Ethan." He gave her a strange look. "That's really sweet."

"My luck hadn't changed," he grumbled. "Something's still messed up around here with the fridge shutting off and the missing cash."

She nodded quickly.

"So I have to look out for you, Lilypad." He had climbed up onto her desk and started messing around with a ceiling tile.

"You don't have to do anything."

"You're my wife."

"That you don't love." *And still won't confide in.*

His eyes met hers, as if he was searching for meaning behind her words.

"Ethan, I'm all grown up. You don't have to keep pulling me out of mud puddles."

"Yes, I do." He took her in with a sweeping gaze, then said gruffly, "You're important to me."

Lily sucked in a deep breath. She was going to cry. A big ugly, happy cry.

He fitted something up in the tile, then checked his phone. He angled the camera, then rechecked his screen. "Hand me your cell."

She felt her back pockets, then rifled through a stack of papers she'd been working on earlier. She found the device and handed it to him. He tapped the screen a few times, then showed her a live video feed of her office. There they were in black-and-white. The desk, the safe, the couch and filing cabinet.

Lily felt conflicted. She loved that he was trying to look out for her, but it also meant he could spy on her at any time, as if he didn't trust her.

Ethan carefully eased himself down from the desk, swinging his legs over the side before standing beside her. "Now you'll be able to see if someone is stealing money or messing with the fridge."

She could see him watching her through the image on her phone.

"Some people would say thank you, you know," he added.

She felt the tug of a smile and put her phone in the back pocket of her jeans. She knew he meant well, that he wouldn't abuse his ability to peek in on her office.

"Thank you, Ethan."

He nodded. They were standing close, watching each other. He wasn't backing off like he usually did.

"Hey, Ethan?" she asked softly. "Can you help

me drag this couch out of here?" She hoped to re-move it, giving her more room to work. She also wanted to see if Ethan would avoid the request as usual, or whether he'd tell her the secret that kept wedging its way between them.

When he didn't move, his conflicted gaze still stuck on the piece of furniture, she took the few steps that separated them, sliding between him and the door, hoping he'd choose her this time.

"You can't, can you?"

He didn't say a word, simply kept staring at the couch. Finally, he shook his head.

"Nobody talks about your injuries. Not even you."

The room was painfully quiet.

"You can tell me, you know," she said gently, pressing a palm against his solid chest.

"Lily." He placed his hand over hers, finally meeting her gaze. "We didn't get married to fix each other or ease the loneliness. I might be able to walk, but...I can't be everything you need."

"And you think you know what that is, do you?"

"Just take what you can," he urged quietly.

"Maybe *you* need to take what you can and *enjoy* life."

He shifted uncomfortably. "Lily..."

"Trust me, Ethan." She lifted herself onto her toes, whispering in his ear, "You're more man than you realize, so you'd better let go of your fear and start acting like it. Your wife expects it."

You're more *man than you realize...* Lily's words kept going through Ethan's mind as he hiked across the meadow with his family, celebrating the addition of Axel to the Mattson clan. He was feeling pretty good, making him think that maybe she was right. For example, he'd balked at going on the hike when Trish had first suggested it, but it turned out he was fine. More than fine. He even wanted to go farther, up into the gentle hills that overlooked the town. It had been a long time since he'd gone this far on his own steam, and he was likely going to regret it. But right now he didn't care, and just wanted to enjoy the feeling of liberation.

Lily hooked her arm through his and he leaned closer, bumping shoulders with her as his stomach growled.

She sighed, obviously regretting that she'd forgotten her carefully packed picnic lunch back in the car when they'd arrived late.

"It's okay, Lil."

"You're having a good time even though you're obviously starving?" she asked.

"The best." He pointed to the others, who were up ahead. "You can run on with the crew, if you'd like."

He hadn't quite told her the extent of his lingering injuries in her office the day prior, nor the fact that Dr. Leham thought he might have a form of arthritis that could leave him immobile again, but he'd tried. And she'd essentially told him to stop living in fear and live for today.

Go with the flow.

He wasn't sure what to do with that. But he was trying.

"I'm enjoying being right where I am," she said, snuggling against his arm. Given their leisurely pace he figured they looked like a couple on a romantic stroll. He liked the image that evoked.

"Me, too."

She smiled up at him and he had to prevent his heart from involuntarily growing a size or two.

"Do you miss the restaurant?" she asked after they'd walked a ways.

"Miss it?" He couldn't think of a single reason why he would, other than it got him out of the house a bit. "Nope."

"Not at all?"

"Okay, I miss Leif's eggs." Not really. He preferred Lily's meals and the way he felt good all day after eating them. Maybe it actually was something in his diet bugging his joints, as his doctor had suggested. Or maybe it was simply the Lily Effect, where everything just seemed sunnier in his life when she was around.

"Oh, you," she muttered, apparently knowing he was kidding about Leif's cooking.

Mandy hung back from the clan to wait for them. With Axel in a carrier strapped to her chest, Ethan's sister looked happy, at peace. He hadn't even realized that she and Frankie were having fertility issues until she announced the other month that they were in line to adopt a baby.

"Motherhood looks good on you," he said as they caught up.

"Thanks. I hope this hike becomes tradition every time we add a kid to the family. It's fun." She gave him and Lily a pointed look.

"Think you'll miss working?" he asked.

"I'm not quitting," she said quickly. "Just slowing down a little."

"Right."

"How could you not miss it?" Lily asked. "Your café must feel like home."

"Home?" Mandy asked skeptically. "I don't know..."

"Yeah. You know, you're cooking and have all these wonderful people working together and you feel like…" Lily paused uncertainly and Ethan took a better look at her.

"Like you belong there?" he asked quietly.

Mandy quirked her head.

"Yeah." Lily's face lit up. "And because you own it…it's yours. It'll always be there." She frowned. "That sounds silly, doesn't it?"

Ethan thought about it. His wife had lost a lot of kitchens over the years, which couldn't have been easy if they were places where she'd felt at home and accepted. First she'd lost the Mattsons' kitchen, when her father found a new job and they moved away. Then kitchens where she'd served out her various internships for school, and finally in the city of Dakota where she'd been romantically burned.

"Benny's will always be there for you, Lily. Just like me," he said, helping her over a fallen tree that crossed the path, Mandy having already scrambled over it, baby and all.

She smiled at him and, looking over the events of the day, he realized something. Lily just might be onto something with her comments about him and his life. He might have believed he was sheltering himself from pain and from being a burden on others, but in the process of hiding himself away he was also missing out on truly living.

CHAPTER 9

"*E*than, just chill!" Lily was feeling exasperated. They were back at Ethan's house after the hike, and Gramps was scheduled to start moving in that night. "We can share your bed."

"The futon will be here next week. I can crash on the couch after Gramps goes to sleep."

"Ethan. We're married."

"Lily..."

She couldn't help but secretly wonder again if his rejection of her had anything to do with his ex. His sexy, beautiful, successful, famous fiancée, who'd left him but was supposed to return to Blueberry Springs any day now.

"We can share a bedroom," she said quickly. "I'll be working extra, anyway, seeing as Leif is getting cataract surgery tomorrow and won't be in for up to a week."

"We need to talk—"

The front door opened and Ethan's dad entered, Gramps in tow. Devon was behind them, hauling suitcases.

"I can't believe you're giving up on me," their grandfather complained loudly. "One outfit that doesn't meet your approval and I'm out on my ear and being babysat."

Ethan moved past Lily to settle him. "Gramps, it'll be okay. We've got a spare room and, honestly, working at home is lonely. I could use the company."

"Bull crap!"

Lily laughed. There was nobody quite like Gramps.

Ethan smiled. "Yeah, okay. You got me, but are you going to fight city hall?"

"I'd like to see you try," Devon said with a smile, crossing his arms over his chest.

"I want my own place."

"It was either here or my place," Devon said. "And Emma—Olivia's sister—is coming to stay for a bit and I didn't think you'd like her as a roommate."

"Is she pretty?" Gramps asked, perking up.

"Come on," Lily said, interrupting the gripe session. "I made you some mashed potatoes with extra butter." The man loved them and she'd hoped it would help ease the transition, distract him from the fact that the family was overriding his wishes.

"I'm imposing. You're newlyweds."

Lily gave a small smile. "Don't worry about us. We're all family here."

"My hearing is just fine, you know."

"It's not," Devon muttered, heading out to get more of Gramps's belongings from Mandy's truck.

"I don't want to be a burden," Gramps complained.

"You're not," Ethan said quietly.

"Says you."

"Yeah." He stood taller. "Says me."

"You called yourself a burden and now I'm one. I thought we were sticking together."

Ethan swallowed, avoiding looking at Lily. "I struggled for a while to be completely independent."

"What?" Gramps was scowling in frustration at not being able to hear him. The old man looked lost, alone, and Lily's heart went out to him. He relied on Ethan and likely felt betrayed right now, tricked into answering to the will of the family. A family who loved him and cared for him.

"Maybe I was wrong, Gramps," Ethan said

louder. "Maybe it's okay to let people help if they want to."

"Amen!" Cory hollered from the guestroom, while Gramps grumbled, "Balderdash!"

"I want to help and I'm family. That's what family does," Ethan said. "How's that a burden?"

He and his grandfather stared at each other, waiting for the other to back down.

"I love you, Gramps."

The old man relented with a scowl. "Fine. Love me. See if I care."

Lily bit back a smile as Ethan shot her a secret glance. He was trying not to smile either.

"Mashed potatoes?" she offered again.

"You bribing me?" Gramps asked.

"Yes."

"I take bribes," he said after a pause.

"That's because I make the best mashed potatoes."

"And you put up with Ethan."

"That I do. And I'll happily put up with you, too."

As they turned to head to the kitchen, Ethan held out his hand for a fist bump. *United.*

Lily grinned and whacked her knuckles against his. From the doorway, Trish shot her a grateful smile, warming her from the inside out and making her feel like she was a help, like she was part of the family.

Gramps followed Lily to the kitchen, and from there she could hear the Mattsons carrying in items, taking over Ethan's home. She really hoped nobody opened the drawers to her lingerie chest which had eventually been abandoned against a wall in the living room.

She settled Gramps at the table with a plate of mashed potatoes and gravy, along with a tall glass of milk.

Lily sat across from him, happy to be off her feet for a few minutes, happy to be feeding someone without forgetting the meal, as she had on the afternoon picnic. She still couldn't believe she'd managed to leave it in the car, or how everyone had convinced her to enjoy the hike rather than to go back for it. They'd said it was more important she didn't miss out on the family hike than for them to eat.

She hadn't quite known how to take that, but everyone had been happy. Even Ethan.

Although they had eaten in the end—in the parking lot, laughing and telling old family stories. Some of which included her, making her feel like a true Mattson despite her fake marriage.

"I know what you two are doing," Gramps said, breaking into her thoughts.

"Feeding you?" she teased. After his forgotten-pants episode she'd been taking him meals and checking up on him when Ethan couldn't. She'd discovered quickly that the only thing he'd eat off the buffet plate she'd bring from the restaurant was the mashed potatoes. Any time she slipped a carrot and half slice of roast beef beside the starchy, buttery food it was more to appease her guilt than anything else.

"Pretending to be in love and doing that marriage bit."

Lily didn't know where to look, what to say. Just on the other side of the wall were the rest of the Mattson clan who, as far as she knew, weren't yet onto their little marriage deal.

"We consider you family, little Lil. Marriage or not."

She swallowed over a sudden, insurmountable lump in her throat.

"So I'm only gonna say this once, because that boy means the world to me. Not a lot of people take my guff, and I wouldn't do anything to ruin our bond, or whatever fancy, feely thing you want to call it. You hear? I can't betray him. Especially with me now under his roof and rules.

"So here it is. You gotta take that man to bed."

He said it so seriously Lily began laughing.

"I'm not kidding around." His voice had turned

gruff and she squelched the urge to continue laughing, worried he'd shut her out. "It's to protect your interests," he grumbled, no doubt insulted by her reaction. He dug into his potatoes as if she was no longer there.

"My interests?"

She really didn't think Ethan was going to run off with another woman. Unless, of course, someone like Dani returned to town and batted her eyes three times. In the past that had seemed to be the magical signal that shut down Ethan's ability to reason and caused him to fall into step like he was a well-programmed robot, intent on doing her bidding.

"You married the louse to save on taxes, I figure. Have a prenuptial agreement, too, if I heard correctly."

Lily massaged the bottom of her foot, afraid to confirm his suspicions in any way.

"He has nothing to lose," Gramps said, then downed the glass of milk Lily had set out.

"We have a legal agreement," she said quietly.

"If you don't take him to bed," he said pointedly, "he has nothing to lose."

Lily stood, tucking her hair behind her ears.

"He can get an annulment," Gramps said louder, ensuring she'd hear him out. "Void the marriage like it never existed. Then where will you be?

Mandy said you've already been taken by a few men in the city. I trust Ethan to do the right thing, but you've got to protect yourself and consummate your marriage."

"But…"

What if he did annul their marriage? Then the prenuptial agreement would be worth nothing, since technically their marriage would have never existed. Right?

She sat down again. Gramps could be on the money, even though she didn't believe Ethan would ever double-cross her and leave her with nothing. But she also knew she was already improving the restaurant's bottom line with some strategic management. And as she had learned, greed and desperation made people do crazy things. Such as get married.

But Ethan? She trusted him, knew him. But she'd also trusted her ex-boyfriends and look how that had turned out.

LILY STOOD in the doorway of Ethan's office, where he was hunched over his keyboard with what sounded like "Hotel California" by the Eagles playing.

"I didn't know you liked classic rock," she said.

No response. His fingers kept flying over the keys, clack, clack, clack.

Last night had been the first night with Gramps under their roof. Ethan had worked in his office until well past midnight, then had sneaked into the living room to sleep on the couch. Alone in the bedroom, Lily had tossed and turned, thinking about what Gramps had said about an annulment.

She noted a plate beside Ethan, one that looked an awful lot like the one she'd placed in the fridge when he hadn't surfaced from his office that morning. She'd fed Gramps his share of sliced hard boiled eggs and fruit salad before putting the rest away for Ethan.

Even now, at the end of the day, Ethan was moving stiffly. Obviously his preferred sleeping arrangement was an unwise one.

"Ethan?"

They needed to talk about the annulment thing, come to an agreement that would protect both their interests. Or simply go to bed together. That would be fine, too.

She went back to the kitchen and grabbed the bowl of caramel popcorn she'd made when she'd come home from work, craving something sweet and crunchy. Gramps had complained that it got stuck in his dentures and had waved her away, ensconced in front of the TV watching golf, an empty cereal bowl beside him. His supper, she presumed.

She returned to the spot in the doorway to Ethan's office. Monitors were lined up in front of him, a massive ergonomical chair hiding more than half his back. There was an armchair to the right of the doorway that looked comfortable, but she didn't dare impose. To her left was a wall of book-shelves. Clear bins holding various cords, gadgets and books were neatly lined up.

He was organized; she'd give him that. Then again, this was like her kitchen—everything had a place.

She munched loudly on the popcorn. Still no response. Even with his music, he had to feel her watching him, hear her eating.

She took a kernel of popped corn and tossed it at him. It hit the back of his chair. She tried an-other, this one hitting his shoulder. Another landed to the right of his mouse. Another in his soft brown hair. She even landed one in the empty yo-gurt container to the right of his keyboard. Finally, she nailed him on the back of the neck, gaining a response. His fingers curled around to touch the spot and he leaned back, taking in his desk, which was now littered with popcorn. Slowly he turned, spotting her.

"Wow. Talk about falling down a wormhole," she said with a laugh.

"What?" He was squinting at her, his face a mask of grumpy confusion, as though he wasn't quite present on planet earth. Had to be a wormhole. Or…okay, yeah, she had no idea. Science fiction wasn't really her thing.

"I thought the animal might like something to eat?"

"What?"

"You're a bit wild, so I don't want to get too close." She tossed another piece, this one rocketing off his nose. "You were supposed to open your mouth. I brought you food."

He held out his hand for the bowl.

"No way. I'm not stepping into the beast's cage. I've seen that show *When Animals Attack*. I'll just keep tossing in food instead." She launched another piece, and when he opened his mouth to protest, it landed inside. "Nice catch."

"You're still a brat," he said, crunching on the popcorn. "Mmm. That's good."

"And you still love it—both my brattiness and me feeding you. Let's try two for two." She lined herself up like she was going for a three-pointer in a basketball game. "Ready? Three, two, one." She wasn't sure if he would play along and open his mouth, but to her satisfaction, he did. And began coughing when the piece went down his throat.

He leaned forward, hacking.

She raced to his side, ready to do the Heimlich. She squeezed between the chair and his back, wrapping her arms around his torso. She could totally close the annulment loophole with this guy, he was so broad and hunky. "Are you okay? Are you choking?"

"What are you doing?" he asked between coughs.

"Saving your life." Well, maybe not. If he could talk, he could breathe. She eased out of the cramped spot, watching him. Spotting a glass of water, Lily offered it to him.

He took a sip, giving her a look.

She eased her phone out of her back pocket. "Are you good with iPhones?"

Maybe if she could get him comfortable helping with something he knew lots about she could ease the conversation toward her annulment worries.

"I use an android, but yeah, I'm okay with them. Why?"

"I keep getting notifications that my cloud storage is full and I can't figure out how to make it go away." She'd had the problem for eons and could probably figure it out if she actually tried.

Gramps's words revolved in her head like a lit-up neon sign. *You've got to protect yourself and consummate your marriage.*

Maybe they could skip talking and hit the sheets instead. It would be so much simpler and easier in many ways.

Ethan took her phone and opened an application. "You should use a lock screen."

"I know. I've just never gotten around to it."

"Your security is horrible." He was tapping furiously, changing settings. "You need a VPN—virtual private network—if you use public WiFi, so your passwords don't get sniffed by someone untoward."

"Untoward?" She tried not to smile in amusement.

"There's no reason some of these apps need to know your location. It's an invasion of privacy. I'm also removing geolocation tags from existing photos metadata and turning off location services for photos. Disabling check-in."

"But I get rewards if I check in when I'm..." She just smiled when Ethan gave her a look. She'd turn it back on when she needed it.

"I'll also engage Find My iPhone, since it seems like you misplace your cell a lot. That way we can go online and locate it, or we can erase it from afar. I'll also add you as family to my music plan, so you can listen to something better than Katy Perry."

Lily felt the word *family* hit her like a brick to the chest.

Clearing her throat, she said, "I happen to like Katy Perry. She's better than that stuff from the past you insist on listening to."

He ignored her, still tapping her phone's screen, his eyes zipping across it as he searched, downloaded and tweaked. "I'm adding a few apps I've found helpful for catering. Let me know if you can't figure them out. And I see you've got recipe notes you haven't backed up. They'll now automatically back up to my encrypted system whenever you're on WiFi." He handed back her phone. "That should do it for now."

"Uh, thanks?" She looked at her locked phone. Wow. He was a ninja. "Did you fix the iCloud thing?"

"Yes."

"What's my passcode?"

He wrote it down and turned his back to her, preparing to go back down his wormhole, however people did that. Maybe they got sucked in? In any case, he was shutting her out now that his task was complete, and they still hadn't broached anything close to consummating their marriage.

She glanced at the numbers written neatly on an orange sticky note. "How will I remember this?"

"It's the day Moe pushed you into the mud puddle."

Lily tried to pick her heart up off the floor. Ethan Mattson remembered the date when she'd fallen in love with him. Somehow that felt entirely unfair.

———

LILY WAS GAZING at him with a mix of awe, discomfort and something else Ethan couldn't quite peg. He was fairly certain her eyes were damp, as well. That meant he'd messed up somehow.

Again.

He turned and stared at his monitor. "Anything else?"

"Uh, how's your back?"

"Fine."

"If you want the bed, I can sleep on the couch," she said quietly. "But Gramps is already kind of onto us."

"What do you mean?" She didn't answer and he turned around again. She was frowning, staring at her phone. A look of anger flicked across her face. She shoved the device in her back pocket. "Sorry. What were you saying?"

"*You* were saying something about Gramps," he corrected, watching her. Something had unsettled her, but she didn't trust him enough to tell him. That bothered him.

Then again, he still hadn't come clean about what sort of things he could and couldn't do, after all that surgery. If he wasn't letting her all the way in, why should she?

"What's wrong?" he asked.

"It's fine."

He held out his hand for her phone. "I thought of one more thing."

She took a step backward.

"Text from a hot boyfriend you're keeping on the side?" he asked lightly.

To his surprise, she handed it over. "Tanner. Can you block his number? He's still bothering me."

"Consider it done." Ethan kept his gaze on hers as he took the device, their fingers brushing, sending electric heat up his arm. He glanced at the lock screen, spotting the text notification that had bothered her. It didn't look like one that should come from an ex to a married woman. He opened the app, his jaw tight with fury.

He hit the number that had popped up with the text, calling the guy he'd punched only a few weeks ago.

"This Tanner?" he asked.

"Uh, think you have the wrong number." The

man sounded uncertain, and Ethan worked to control his rage.

Lily was watching with a look of horror and nervous delight.

"Lily's married now. To me." He made sure his voice was firm, deep, his anger evident, given the way Tanner kept imposing on Lily, who was too polite and kind to set the law on him. "If you so much as look in her direction, this little *thing* you texted a photo of will fall under one of my many knives. You understand?" He hung up before the man could sputter a reply.

Ethan took a screen shot of the harassing text and forwarded it to Scott Malone, the local police officer, as well as his friend Ginger's husband, Logan Stone, who worked in private security. Ethan's blood was boiling and the drive to murder Tanner soared.

"What else has he been doing?" he asked.

Lily was watching him, her face white. "Just that."

"Tell me if he bothers you again."

"What did you do with those screenshots?"

"I sent them to the local authorities in case he gives you any more problems." He blocked Tanner's number. The nerve of that guy. To harass a woman this way.

He glanced up at Lily. "You all right?"

She fell against him, her arms tight around his neck. "Thank you."

For one shining moment, Ethan felt like the man Lily saw. One able to protect his wife.

THE NEXT EVENING Ethan was just finishing up an email to a client when he felt small hands slip over his shoulders from behind and glide down his pecs. Lily. He caught her wrists, unsure what to do. Gramps was already asleep in his room, leaving them essentially alone.

"Hungry?" she asked, her voice hinting at things he would love to pursue if their marriage was real.

He turned his chair to face her. She was wearing a skintight dress that hinted at some fine lingerie underneath. He tried to roll his chair away from her, out of range of temptation, but promptly came up against his desk.

Her hair was softly curled, tumbling around her flushed cheeks.

She was gorgeous and the very definition of tempting.

"What are you doing?" he whispered.

"Asking if you're hungry," she replied, a glimmer of amusement in her eyes. "Want something?"

Not what was on the menu, that was for sure.

And why was she wearing heels? Was she trying to kill him with sexiness?

"There's food?" He shifted as though about to climb out of his seat and push past her. They'd had supper a few hours ago, but he was willing to overeat if it meant preventing taking things down an avenue that would merely hurt the two of them.

"Not so fast." She placed her left knee beside his hip and grasped the back of his office chair, not unlike the way she did in some of his forbidden fantasies.

He kept his hands clenched on the armrests. When he didn't push her away, she placed her right knee beside his other hip, straddling him. She lowered herself so she was sitting in his lap, her heat intoxicating, distracting.

"What—what are you doing?"

"Trapping you."

"Why?" Her body was so warm and soft, her gaze so welcoming. It would be easy to lose himself in the moment, to give in to the attraction he'd been battling so long.

Losing would feel so good.

Her fingers brushed his neck and he shivered. He wanted to stand, but knew it was unfair to reject her again. Not that her sitting on his lap was fair, and soon she'd feel exactly how he was affected.

"I want to talk to you, that's all." Her words were innocent, but her intent sure wasn't.

"Lily…"

"We're both adults." Her fingers were working magic as they trailed over his shoulders. He was relaxing, enjoying. And he shouldn't be. But he couldn't quite remember why that was.

"And a year is a long time to be celibate."

"Maybe you need to find someone on the side in the city."

Please ignore that suggestion, he silently willed.

She blinked hard, swallowed once, her nostrils flaring slightly. Then she covered her hurt with a sad smile. "Maybe the man I want is right here." She shifted so she was straddling him more fully, her core's warmth right over his. Combined with her words—total aphrodisiac. Not immune. Definitely not immune. Ego stroked? Check. Body set to sexual hyperdrive? Also check.

He'd never wanted a woman more than he wanted Lily, and that was terrifying in itself.

Today he'd felt great, with so little pain in his joints. He almost felt whole, complete. Strong. He wanted to indulge physically like he had on the hike. It had been fun, and he'd been sure that the pain he'd felt the next day had been related to sleeping on the couch more than walking in the mountains.

But he also knew from past experience that a good day was often followed by a sucker punch of a crappy day.

"Lily, tomorrow's probably going to be a bad—"

She silenced him with a finger against his lips.

Lily shifted, and he struggled not to twitch or show how affected he was by how her warmth was pressing into him, inviting him, coaxing him to allow nature and physical need to take over in a culmination of everything their species had been wired to complete. He was going to have to read-just himself given the sudden lack of space in his undergarments, but was afraid any movement might override his waning restraint.

"How about it, husband? We could have a mar-riage that fits every bill," she whispered, her lips grazing his.

His hands locked on her hips, his mouth hot on hers. She tasted like everything he ever wanted. She pressed directly over his hardness and he lost control, his hands moving to her hair, their kisses bruising. She ground her hips once and it felt good, so right. His fingers slipped up the skirt of her dress, her skin smooth and tempting.

She shuddered in pleasure and he realized what

they were doing—where it was heading. He abruptly pushed her farther back on his thighs.

He couldn't do this. He couldn't let Lily blindly get her hopes up, only to dash them when he ended up back in a wheelchair or worse. She deserved so much better, so much more than a husband who would tie her down, unable to do all the things her young and healthy body could.

He cared too much about her to become her burden, because she was the kind of woman who would stay, feel as though she couldn't just leave.

The look of hurt in Lily's eyes was so intense he froze, uncertain. He was already letting her down, hurting her feelings. He'd already screwed up.

"Lily...I don't...I don't do one-night stands." Which was the truth. If he slept with her, he wanted it to be because they both thought they had something that would last.

"We're married."

"But we're not in love, Lil. I'm trying to do the right thing here."

I'm trying not to hurt you. I'm trying not to use you just because you're here.

She blinked, her cheeks flushing. She stood, suddenly looking so vulnerable, he felt a pain in his chest for putting the hurt in her expression. The rejection.

"I'm sorry." He caught her hand as she backed

away, and she looked at him with eyes burning with shame.

"Will you ever see me as more than Tagalong Lily?"

Little did she know that was the least of his problems.

LILY HAD SENT her evening crew home early, saying it was a special treat, and promising to clean up for them. She slammed things around the restaurant kitchen, furious at herself for trying to woo Ethan and failing. She swiped at her eyes with the back of her hand and stared at the stained ceiling. Of course he had rejected her. He didn't see her as a woman and never would. It didn't matter what she wore or what she did. It didn't matter that their kisses were hot enough to melt the polar icecaps.

He didn't do one-night stands.

Why did he have to be such a gentleman?

He didn't want her. She needed to focus her mind elsewhere. If they couldn't consummate their marriage there had to be another way. Sweat equity. Common law marriage. Anything. Something to make sure her interests remained secured.

Lily put a stock pot away and groaned in frustration. Why wouldn't Ethan take advantage of what she was offering when it was so obvious they had something delicious burning between them?

She heard something bang in the back of the building and froze, uncertain. This time it wasn't just the old building shifting or the neighbor doing renovations in the store next door. She felt the back pocket of her jeans for her phone, wanting to check the back hall camera from its app. It was trained on the fridge, but showed part of the hallway, too. Maybe enough to give her forewarning if someone was inside the building with her.

Her cell wasn't in her pocket. Hours ago she'd ditched the dress and tossed on something more fitting for working out her frustration in the restaurant, and she wasn't sure if she'd even grabbed her phone in her desperation to put distance between her and Ethan.

She heard another thud in the back hall. Was it her sous-chef, Quinlan, coming to pick up something he'd forgotten in his eagerness to run to the field to catch the last of tonight's football game between a rival town?

Lily grabbed a knife as she walked around the prep island. She picked up a second knife, gripping one in each hand.

"Who's there?" she called.

She wished Ethan was here, his bulk at her side, ready to protect her. She eased around the island, keeping her back to the wall as she angled a look through the kitchen doorway and into the small hall that led to the walk-in fridge and back door.

She raised her voice. "I said who's there?"

Moments later, a scrawny black cat rounded the corner, meowing plaintively. Lily tipped her head back against the wall, her heart racing.

She placed the knives on a nearby counter and let out a breath, leaning over. The cat wound itself around her legs.

"How did you get in here?" She patted the tomcat's bony head. "You hungry?" Lily went to the fridge and took out a carton of cream. She filled a small bowl and set it on the floor.

"You shouldn't be in here." She crossed her arms, watching the cat lap up the unexpected feast. "Furry animal and all that. We'll make an exception, since the kitchen is currently closed, but don't let an inspector see you in here or they'll shut me down."

The cat finished his drink and looked up at her expectantly.

"Not too much at a time," she told it. "We don't want to give you a tummy ache, and who knows when was the last time you had food in your stomach."

She picked up the cat, which nuzzled under her

chin. At least someone didn't mind giving her some affection tonight.

"The restaurant is no place for a kitty." She began making her way to the kitchen doorway, regretting that she had to send the animal away. "Time to go back outside. But if you come again tomorrow I'll have some scraps saved for you."

She got as far as the back hallway before she noticed the door to the alley was wide open. She was certain she'd locked it behind her, an old safety habit left over from living and working in the city. Then again, how else could the cat have gotten in?

She had to be losing it. Or getting used to the security of Blueberry Springs.

"Did you open the door?" she asked the purring puss. She slowly approached the doorway, feeling as though a boogeyman was going to jump out at her. Light spilled from the outdoor light, the steps darkening as they went down into the abyss of the small lot that opened into the alley. She eased closer, holding the squirming cat close, seeing more and more of the empty parking lot with each step. Nothing lurking in the shadows. Just her old car sitting there, reliably rusted.

Feeling silly, she deposited the cat on the back step, then closed the door and latched it securely. Grasping the handle, she gave it a shake to test it.

There was no way it could have popped open on its own. She must have failed to fasten it properly.

The restaurant was quiet behind her. No humming of the various appliances keeping food chilled or frozen. No heater or air conditioning kicking in. No creaking as an early autumn wind drifted down from the surrounding mountains.

She checked the walk-in fridge's switch out of habit, finding it in the off position. She flicked it back on, feeling spooked.

Rubbing her hands up and down her arms to ward off her sudden chill, she eased her way back toward the kitchen. The whole place felt too quiet, the renewed hum of the fridge much too loud.

What if someone had come inside and was waiting for her?

Feeling wigged out, Lily turned and fled down the hallway, flinging the alley door open and racing outside. She locked the restaurant door as fast as possible, then scrambled to her car.

The cat was perched on the hood, back leg in the air as it washed itself. He paused to give her a look as if to say, "What are you freaking out about?"

Lily clung to the steering wheel, trying to calm her nerves. If the cat wasn't scared, she shouldn't be. Right?

Nevertheless, she started the engine, no longer

wanting to be in the quiet building alone. The ebony cat stood up, walked to the windshield and peered in at her with its clear green eyes. It meowed once.

Ethan had said bad luck had been following him. But what about her? She'd had her fair share, too, and was beginning to think that the quirky things happening in the restaurant were more than simple bad luck. There was someone with an ax to grind.

CHAPTER 10

Ethan had blown it. He'd known it the moment he'd pushed Lily away, before she'd gone storming off to the restaurant with hurt feelings. He'd paced and fretted for hours, worrying about her. Blueberry Springs was a good little town, but he didn't like the idea of her going out alone late at night. Especially when it was his foolishness that had sent her off.

It didn't help that she'd left her phone at home, so he couldn't check in or see whether she was indeed still at the restaurant or safe at Mandy's. Sure, he could call the restaurant, but what were the chances she'd pick up?

Around midnight he'd finally given in and checked the security footage from the restaurant cameras, seeing nothing. The fridge was on,

233

nothing interesting happening in the slice of back hallway it caught in its frame. Same with the office other than Lily arriving earlier in the evening. She could have left through the front door. Or still be there. He should have put a camera in the kitchen, as that was undoubtedly where she'd be.

He felt like a snoop trying to appease his guilt by checking to ensure she was safe. But he knew if he went to her to beg forgiveness he'd likely end up making sweet love to her on her office desk. And that would come with its own set of problems.

He resumed pacing, but by two was so exhausted from worry he stretched out on his bed to wait for her. What felt like moments later the sun was streaming through his open bedroom blinds. Morning. The sounds of his wife making breakfast in the kitchen had woken him.

He tossed on a shirt and hustled out of the bedroom, eager to verify that Lily was indeed all right.

He halted in the doorway. She was intact, cooking as though everything was fine in her world. Except there was a skinny black cat standing on his kitchen counter.

"Why is there a mangy feline on my food preparation surface?"

Lily turned her back to him. "It's not like you actually prep any food there. And he's mine."

"Yeah? What's its name?"

"Igor."

"Igor?" He couldn't help smirking.

"Yes. He's a stray in need of a home." She gave him a prim look. "Are you allergic?"

"No."

"Good. Neither is Gramps."

Ethan checked the time. His grandfather was usually up by now.

"He went out for a walk with Trish," Lily said, as though reading his mind. "She's taking him to the barber's afterward." She turned the heat off under a pan, then dumped the contents onto a plate. "Does the back door to the restaurant ever open on its own?"

Ethan's senses went on high alert. "No. Why?"

"It opened last night and Igor came marching in."

"Any signs of forced entry?" He took the cup of coffee she held out for him.

She shook her head. She had to be worried if she was speaking to him again.

"But the fridge was off again."

"Have you checked the camera footage?" He already knew there'd been nothing before he'd gone to bed.

She shook her head.

"What time did it happen?"

"Around one-thirty."

Something didn't feel right. And it wasn't just her reaction or her reaching out to him after the way he'd hurt her feelings last night. He'd be wise to have Logan Stone come check out the building and see what security enhancements could be added.

Ethan hesitated as he reached for his tablet to check the video feed from Benny's, noticing that his back barely twinged as he did so. First thing in the morning he usually had to stretch a bit before his joints and muscles moved smoothly. He rolled his shoulder, savoring the lack of pain and stiffness. That was new. Another good day instead of a crash.

But could he rely on it? Count on his body to not defeat him?

Feeling good made him worry that the next dip in health was going to be longer, more severe and more crippling. He hated using a cane. Absolutely hated it. And it would cause Lily to fuss over him, pity him, when her attention and energy would be better spent elsewhere.

"Some people say thank you," Lily teased lightly.

"For what?" he snapped, lost in his worries.

"The coffee."

He blinked at her, then realized he was indeed holding the mug she'd poured for him. "Right. Thanks."

She glanced down, suddenly aghast. "What happened to your legs?"

Pants. He'd pulled a Gramps and forgotten his pants. Boxers weren't enough to cover the angry scars left from the accident and resulting surgeries. Nineteen operations in total. Some more successful than others.

He turned back to his room, shaking his head at himself for forgetting. He yanked on a pair of jeans, taking extra time before returning to the kitchen, where Lily was waiting, a plate of eggs and sliced fruit in front of her on the counter. She was nibbling on toast and he wasn't sure whether the plated meal was his or hers, seeing as she often snitched food off the plate she prepared for him. He'd even seen her sit across from his grandpa and steal the odd scoop of his mound of mashed potatoes. The first time he'd seen it he'd expected Gramps to stick a fork through the back of her hand, but instead his expression had simply softened, and at his next available chance he'd scooted the plate ever so casually a little closer to her.

"Well?" she demanded. Man, she had that wife thing down pat.

"Well what?" Ethan grumbled, standing across from her. The cat—Igor—had come over and was weaving his way around Ethan's ankles, purring and acting like one more thing Ethan would miss when Lily left him next year.

"Are those from the accident?"

"What's it to you?" He pulled the plate toward him, planning to eat while standing. "Is this for me?"

She nodded, then stole a slice of orange, as well as a wedge of peeled kiwi, setting them on the counter in front of her. "I'm your wife and I should know where every scar is located."

"Yeah? You want to see them all?" he challenged, ignoring the food.

"Yes."

"Fine." He whipped up his shirt, revealing one of the angriest scars—from the wound that had put him in a medically-induced coma for two weeks. The one next to it had been created as the surgeons went in to repair the internal injuries from his car's bent metal, which had not only ripped him open but skewered him as well. "How's that for the appetite?"

"Oh, Ethan." Her expression softened from annoyance at his reluctance to share to one of sympathy, understanding. He waited for the pity. He waited some more.

She came around the counter, moving closer and he forced himself to stand his ground. Her hands slid under the cotton hem as he dropped his shirt, her palms flat against his skin, his scars, his old wounds. "It must have hurt so much."

He felt his walls begin to crumble.

She rested her head against his chest and he didn't know what to do. Comfort her? Appreciate the fact that she hadn't cringed in disgust?

"I had no idea you'd been hurt so badly."

"Yeah, well, I don't do well with pity." He tried to gently nudge her off him. "So you want to learn how to run the catering business today?"

She kept her arms wrapped around him. "Are you scarred everywhere? Is this why you limp and don't lift big stuff?"

It felt as though her image of him was shifting, but he wasn't sure if she thought he was strong for enduring so much, or if she thought he was broken and fascinating.

He found himself lifting his shirt again, showing her the surgery scars, pointing them out, giving them a name and their results. "Reattached ligament. Gave me back 50 percent movement in my arm." He continued on, pointing to places his pants covered. She took inventory, nodding, her eyes sympathetic the entire time.

When he finished, feeling somehow lighter for sharing, she wrapped her arms around his neck, snugging her body against his.

"You're amazing."

"Excuse me?" He slipped his hands around her small waist, liking the way she felt against him.

"To have endured all of that. I think I would have given up."

"You don't know what it's like to be unable to move. To not be able to make love to a woman." He hadn't meant to say that last bit. He closed his eyes, shutting off that part of him. When he opened them again Lily, his wife, was watching him with a look of caring and compassion. She gently placed a kiss on his jaw. He didn't flinch, simply allowed her to administer her chosen form of remedy for his brokenness.

She kissed him on the mouth, slow and sweet.

"And can you make love to a woman now?" she asked gently.

"Yes." He was getting caught up in her kisses, the power of holding her, in having the strength to do so, in the fact that they both desired each other. She now knew his biggest faults and still seemed to think the world of him. He couldn't imagine a better aphrodisiac.

"Want to show me?" she whispered.

He didn't need prompting to accept the invitation.

LILY COULDN'T STOP GRINNING. She could barely walk straight and yet felt like she was floating on a cloud of happiness. She'd been wrong. Ethan wanted her. Crazy levels of want.

In other words, it was all good in her world. Life was exquisitely beautiful.

She wanted to sing, wanted to dance.

She was making lunch and humming to herself in the kitchen while Gramps read his paper at the table. Buttermilk pancakes from scratch and a homemade whipped cream and brown sugar sauce to pour over them. She'd had to zip into the restaurant for a bit after Ethan had illuminated her on all the reasons he was an awesome husband. A husband she planned to bed again and again if at all possible.

The way he'd moved so tenderly made her dream of a real marriage based on love.

A real husband. A large family.

Igor rubbed up against her and she automatically reached down to stroke his back. As she did so, the question of the turned-off restaurant fridge jumped back into her mind. Last night had someone walked in, turned off the walk-in fridge, then left again? She'd distracted Ethan from checking the footage earlier, and she wondered if he'd had a chance to watch it when she'd gone in to work.

She found herself smiling again as he entered the room. Lily didn't know whether to look at him and expect a kiss, or pretend his presence didn't affect her. He'd said he didn't do one-night stands, even with his wife. So where did that leave them, now that they'd crossed that line of physical intimacy?

She switched the pancake flipper from hand to hand, waiting for a cue.

"I think I'll go read in my room," Gramps muttered from his spot at the table. He scooped up the cat. "Call me when there's lunch." He hoofed it into his bedroom, cat under his arm, closing the door behind him.

Lily bit back a grin and sneaked a glance at Ethan. She was going to miss Gramps when they found him a room in the nursing home and he moved out.

"Hey." Ethan planted a kiss on her temple as he moved around her. He looked limber, spry almost.

"Hey yourself," she said softly, flipping a pancake and sending it over the side of the griddle she'd unpacked from her storage container which was still parked on the lawn. Her hands were shaking. He'd kissed her! Unnecessary, and done because he'd *wanted* to.

She plucked the pancake off the counter and seeing she'd ruined it, tossed it in the trash.

"You making lunch?"

"I'm breaking the stir-fry spell with a few carbs."

"The sauce looks good."

"It is good."

"Can I try it?" He lifted the spoon to his lips, burning his tongue and wincing.

"It's hot," she warned.

"Thanks for that." He gave her a wry look.

She turned to face him more fully, suddenly at a loss over how to talk to him. The morning had changed things for her, but what had it meant to Ethan? Did he finally accept her as a woman, as a wife, and not just a tagalong?

"It's good, though. Really good." Ethan dipped the spoon back into the pot to take another sample.

"Hey! We're all sharing that." She wrinkled her nose at him double-dipping the spoon after licking it.

"We've shared worse," he said in a low voice, leaning closer, his tone suggestive.

"Will we again?" she whispered.

His lips hovered above hers. "I'd like to."

"Right now?"

"You're burning the pancakes."

"Who cares?"

He reached around her, plucking the pancakes

from the griddle with his bare fingers and tossing them onto the nearby plate. "Nice griddle."

"Is that a euphemism?"

He chuckled and ducked his head to dart a kiss against her neck. She sighed, finding the feel of his lips against her flesh so gratifying.

She waved at her throat, angling it toward him. "Again, please."

He complied, and before long the entire lunch was forgotten.

ETHAN WAS THE MAN.

He'd satisfied his wife not once, but twice in one day.

He spun in his office chair. Even his joints were feeling pretty good.

Sex was the best cure for whatever had been on that MRI.

Or maybe it was just the Lily Effect kicking in once again. He'd been feeling increasingly decent ever since she'd come his way, joined his life.

Lily was incredible. It was the only way to describe her. He wanted more. So much more. She was patient, funny and encouraging. And oh-so-responsive in bed.

They'd skipped lunch and gone straight back to

getting acquainted on a more intimate level. They'd resurfaced in time for him to take a conference call with Burke Carver's tech guy, and Lily's pancakes—the ones that had actually made it to the griddle—had been stuck in the fridge after Gramps had scored a few.

Lily had gone straight in to work and was likely feeling hungry by now, even though she worked in a restaurant. Ethan didn't see her as the type to stop and feed herself when others were hungry and jobs needed to be done.

He checked in on Gramps, who was doing his stretches in the living room, made sure the cat had found the litter box and food he'd picked up for him an hour ago, then packed Lily's uneaten lunch into one of her picnic baskets. There were little signs of her throughout the house now, giving it a cheerful, lived-in feeling.

As he searched for paper plates—he didn't have any, it turned out—he scrolled through the restaurant's fridge camera footage on his cell phone. Beyond what he'd already viewed last night, there was nothing of note, other than some interference that had created gaps in the last twenty hours or so of motion-activated recording. Useless—that's what his footage was.

He called Logan, who said interference was fairly common, particularly when there was construction occurring nearby. With the store that shared a wall with the restaurant undergoing renovations they either needed to temporarily suffer through the interference or upgrade to a multifrequency unit. He opted for the latter, asking Logan to also ensure that the new fridge camera caught more hallway as well as the switch. Logan said he'd track down a new camera and get it installed by nightfall, freeing Ethan to go woo his hungry wife.

Whistling to himself, he decided to walk, since the weather was beautiful. He honestly hadn't felt this good in years.

"Either!"

Ethan turned to see Devon, the usual hated nickname not managing to dampen his good mood. Devon could sing the whole "either or, Ethan snores" chant he'd made up when they were kids and not get a rise out of him. Not today.

"What's up?" Ethan asked.

"Is that…?" Devon leaned closer, his tie waving in the light breeze as he peered at Ethan. "Is that a *smile?*"

"Go take a hike."

"Got some skin-on-skin time with the wife, did you?" Devon fell into step beside him, jauntily swinging his briefcase. Olivia had given him a makeover during his mayoral campaign and it suited him, although it still sometimes surprised

Ethan when he remembered his romantically allusive brother had married.

"How's Olivia?"

"Morning sickness is hard, but the food Lily cooked up for her helped."

That sounded like Lily—always looking out for others.

"And Olivia aced her fashion design project for her online class." Devon was studying him and Ethan felt his defenses go up. "You seem different. It's like…someone oiled the Tin Man."

"Shut up." He couldn't hide his grin.

"And is that a picnic basket? Very romantic." Devon laughed at Ethan's fake scowl as he walked backward down a side street, parting ways with a wave.

Ethan continued on, letting himself into Benny's through the main door. The place was busy with the midafternoon coffee crowd, people waving hello as he walked through the restaurant to the back, feeling silly for carrying a picnic basket. It was too romantic for a guy like him. Too obvious he was smitten with a woman who planned to move on in a year.

He ditched the basket and found Logan Stone standing outside the kitchen, looking up at the camera Ethan had installed in the hallway. So much for subtlety.

Ethan waved him into the office—Lily's now. It smelled like his closet, and the old couch that had lined the wall was gone, freeing up an impressive amount of space. Lily had a good eye for what a room needed and he was going to miss the cozy touches she'd added here and there to his home when they parted company. Maybe there was a way he could convince her to stay.

Ethan sat on the edge of the desk, while Logan filled the doorway. The man immediately spied the camera above the desk, aimed at the safe.

"I guess I should have hidden those better," Ethan said, as the PI stepped inside, shutting the door behind him.

"It's not bad to show people you're watching. I could add a few more cameras if you're concerned."

"Maybe one in the kitchen. Just a subtle one." He felt uncomfortable with the idea of spying, but he'd been worried about Lily last night working in here alone, unable to see her. He was turning into a worrywart. All the oddities that had occurred lately could be explained away. The fridge turning off a glitch in the appliance's computer, the missing float a mixed up accounting error, the back door just the cat taking advantage of a not-quite-latched door.

There was no reason to be paranoid.

Logan scrawled a few words on a notepad.

"The back door is secure, as is the front, although you could upgrade the rear one with a stronger lock. However, if someone really wants in they'll just destroy the jamb—it's a common workaround for thieves when entering older buildings." Logan crouched in front of the safe and tried its handle. Locked. "This is a decent safe. Honestly, for Blueberry Springs your security is not bad. Do you have motion notifications set up on the cameras for after hours?"

Ethan nodded.

"How much more security do you think you'd like?"

"Enough that I don't have to worry about Lily."

Logan let out a huff of amusement. "Honestly, Ethan? There's never enough security to make a man not worry about his wife." He stood with a half smile, his gray eyes sparkling.

"You're probably right."

"Want a tracer on her car?"

"A tracer?" That felt…invasive. As if he didn't trust her. He shook his head. "It feels like this place has had a lot of bad luck and weird things going on. I just want to keep her safe. I want that ex of hers to stand down, too."

"Any further contact?"

"Not that I'm aware."

"Good. I've issued a watch with the local police." Logan frowned in displeasure.

"What?"

"It's hard for one officer to keep a town safe."

"Welcome to Blueberry Springs," Ethan said with a chuckle.

Logan gave a small smile that almost belied his serious expression. "I'll make sure Tanner is taken care of if he decides to grace our town with his presence."

Ethan nodded, not wanting to know what all was implied with that statement.

"I'll add a camera above the back door to watch the alley, and a few more IP cameras around the place."

The camera above them was an IP camera—connected to the internet, allowing him to check in remotely, as well as view uploaded footage from anywhere.

"Maybe we'll skip the kitchen for now," Ethan said. "I don't want Lily's staff thinking we're spying on them."

"I can hide one."

"I'd better run it by Lily first."

"Sure. Just let me know. And if Zach Forrester —a buddy of mine—comes by to look in on things, don't worry, he's sound."

"Thanks."

Logan left and Ethan stayed put, thinking.

A few minutes later, Lily appeared in the doorway. "I heard you were here." She took a few steps inside her office. "Acting like you own the place?" Her tone was teasing.

He swung himself off the desk. "I asked Logan to install more security."

"How much is it going to cost?" She crossed her arms, chin lifting. She was serious now, the teasing gone.

"I'll pay for it."

"I don't want to be spied on. If you don't trust me, tell me."

"This is for your own security. The back door? The missing money? Your ex? All valid reasons to up the security around here."

She gave him a dark look. "You're overreacting."

"You're underreacting."

They faced off for a moment and all Ethan wanted to do was step forward and claim her mouth with his own. He decided to go for it, moving slowly, cupping her head, letting her anger soften before kissing her.

"I brought lunch," he said, tipping his forehead against hers. "It's the stuff you made, but I thought you might be hungry."

"Are you trying to change the subject?"

"No, I *am* changing the subject. There is no try, only do."

She rolled her eyes at his *Star Wars* Yoda impression.

"You coming?" he asked from the door.

"You already know I'd follow you anywhere," she said with a smile, and Ethan felt it slip all the way into his soul.

LILY KNEW she was looking for hints that this might be real, and felt the picnic here in the town square had to be a pretty good one. He had finally let her in, not shutting her out. And he was adding security to her restaurant, which, even though it felt a bit over the top, was a protective move, securing her under his wing.

Ethan sat on the blanket he'd laid out in the square, his body a powerhouse that made her mouth water.

"You're handsome, you know that?"

He paused, his arm deep in the picnic basket. "And you're downright sexy."

She giggled, feeling suddenly shy in her jeans and sweatshirt. She smoothed her messy braid. "Thanks."

"Let's see what you made us." He began unpacking the basket, his knee pressing against hers as they sat side by side.

Lily inhaled the moment. The warmth from the autumn sun, the mountains around them looking so large and unreal, but most of all the man beside her. The man she was utterly, hopelessly in love with. She leaned against his shoulder and he gave her knee an affectionate squeeze. Little gestures always felt so much larger coming from him.

He smiled. "You look happy."

"I am."

The cream sauce she'd made was thick from being in the fridge, and they used it like a spread on the pancakes before devouring them.

"Mmm. I was starving," she said, finishing off her first one and licking the stickiness from her fingers.

Ethan was watching her and she froze with awareness as a hot current pulsed between them. He gently brushed a crumb from the corner of her mouth, then slowly leaned in, kissing her deeply. She lost track of the world around her as she wrapped her arms around his shoulders, scooting closer. He pulled her into his lap, his arms strong and sure. She moaned into his mouth as they kissed in the middle of town, not caring who saw them, who saw her loving her husband. This was what she'd been waiting for. This moment, right here, right now.

"Did I tell you I got a new contract for the catering company?" she said as they came up for air. A gray jay was hopping closer, angling toward the forgotten food. Ethan flung a piece of pancake across the grass, feeding it.

"I've been hearing good things about the changes you've made."

"Really?" She'd taken a lot of ribbing over her garnishes, the roast beef special and the like.

"Alvin said he liked the new lasagna."

"Who's Alvin? And I only added more seasoning."

"He's the town's biggest curmudgeon."

"Nice."

"You have a way of winning people over, Lily."

"And have I won you over?"

"Since day one."

"Yeah?"

"Yeah."

"And have I won you over as your wife?"

"I'll be lonely when you leave me."

"What if I stick around?" She felt her heart racing, expecting rejection for dancing over the line of their commitment, suggesting he give her more than what either of them had signed on for.

He shrugged, a small smile playing at his lips.

She was still in his lap, his eyes so blue in the sunshine, his focus solely on her. It was heady and overwhelming. He kissed her again.

She wanted to sing, she wanted to dance.

"Are you busy tonight?" she whispered.

"Not in the least."

"Good. I'm going to make you fettuccine Alfredo and then…"

"And then…?"

"I promise we'll do something just as fun as this morning."

CHAPTER 11

*E*than massaged his tight thigh muscle, wishing he'd felt up to hiking with Lily today. The physical crash he'd been anticipating had arrived in full force, just hours after the picnic in the park and the wonderfully rich pasta dinner Lily had made for him.

He struggled not to feel sorry for himself, to focus on the fact that Lily and Mandy had gone together, taking time off, renewing their friendship.

But yesterday…yesterday had been incredible. He'd felt amazing. Strong and alive. Fully human. He'd made love to his wife twice, then again in the evening, and it had simply, hands down, been the best sex he'd ever experienced. She'd suggested sticking around after their commitment and he'd been too choked up to reply.

He wanted that. Wanted to take it for granted as the ending of their story. But today his joints ached and his stomach was in knots from the constant clenching and worrying about pain. His brain felt foggy and he couldn't concentrate on work or anything around him.

He needed to tell her about the MRI results and the possible implications. He had to face the truth, the reality. All of it. Not just tell her he was having a bad day when he bowed out of a hike, as he had today.

At least she hadn't stayed back to baby him, but had simply told him to take care of himself, and left.

It had surprised him, actually. He was used to his family trying to dote on him, and it lit the idea that maybe, even if things went south for him, Lily was the kind of woman who wouldn't perceive him as a burden. She would still maintain a life for herself even if he became physically limited.

He opened a can of Mountain Dew—his go-to when he needed a kick—and forced himself to work for a few more hours, until a phone call from his former real estate agent interrupted him.

"Ethan? I know you pulled the restaurant off the market, but I have an offer I promised I'd pass along."

"What do you mean?" Ethan stretched in his office chair.

"This guy called up—he'd asked about the restaurant back in early August, I think. Maybe the end of July? Anyway, he was disappointed to hear it was off the market. I told him to make an offer because, hey, you never know, right?"

"Well…"

"He's offering thirty over list price."

"What? Why?" Who would pay that much? It would take eons to make that back in a small town, and he knew they hadn't undervalued the business. "Is he rich? Who is it?"

His agent laughed. "He'd rather remain anonymous at this point, for privacy reasons."

Had to be a wealthy conglomerate.

"He said he saw something in your gem and didn't want to lose it."

"Lily's the person to talk to, since she's taking it over."

"He's actually hoping she'll stay on as chef."

"I don't think she's interested in working for someone else."

"He didn't give me any numbers, but hinted that he'd pay her the equivalent to what they make in city four-star restaurants."

"That seems…generous." Lily could flip the restaurant and make a profit, start her own dream restaurant—one where she could use her own recipes and have a kitchen designed exactly the way she wanted, without finicky fridges or other problems.

"He was really excited about the restaurant, but couldn't buy it earlier due to a family issue. He was upset he'd missed it."

Ethan massaged his knee. Maybe he could convince Lily to move somewhere warmer, like Nash had suggested. He could do his web stuff anywhere with an internet connection, and she could find a city full of foodies. She could play and experiment.

He knew she said she liked Blueberry Springs and didn't want to change Benny's, but the place was holding her back—cooking lasagna and roasts off someone else's recipes every day wasn't her reaching her potential. It was barely following her dreams and he could tell she occasionally became frustrated.

Or if she decided to stay, she could work for the new owner and not have to endure the financial risk or long hours. She could live more. Smile. Be free while still supporting her dad.

Ethan ended the call, promising to take the offer to Lily.

He tried to go back to work, but eventually gave up in favor of a walk, hoping it would help ease the ache in his joints. Go with the flow, right?

Ethan reached the end of his sidewalk before he spotted the last woman on earth he ever wanted to see.

Dani Demare. His ex-fiancée.

She was the definition of hot due to a curvy lankiness. Her hair was perfect and shiny, her features straight and symmetrical. But to him, she was too skinny, too moody, too selfish.

He nodded and continued on his way, wishing he didn't feel so darn crippled.

"Ethan!"

He knew he'd bristled and that she'd likely noticed. He stopped but didn't turn around. She caught up with him on her high heels.

"Hi, Ethan!"

"Hi," he grumbled.

"I've been living and working in Milan. I'm in town for a few days."

"How nice." He'd heard she was an international model now. Which suited her more than staying home and playing nursemaid.

"I heard you were walking again." She was eyeing him, had no doubt noted the way his shoulders had filled out.

"Have been for years."

"And you're married!" She plucked his hand to study his ring, as if she had the right to touch him, and he had to force himself not to pull it out of her grasp. There had been a time where he'd loved every drop of attention she sent his way.

"I have to be somewhere. Nice to see you."

"I heard you married Lily Harper."

He began walking, feeling as though talking about his wife with Dani was a form of betrayal. Illogical, but it was what it was.

She caught up to him. "It's nice you're giving her your restaurant. Her family never had much and I heard she likes to cook."

She was walking gracefully beside him, her impossible glittery heels clicking on the concrete underfoot.

"You have a web business now?"

He grunted in acknowledgment, wishing he could go fast enough he could ditch her and her high heels.

"Do you like it?"

"Yup."

"My cousin Burke Carver said you're working for him."

"You're related?"

"He's my cousin—you know that, silly." She latched on to his arm, bumping her chest against him with a giggle. She used to do that all the time and it had been one of his favorite things. Not so much anymore. It made him want to peel her off him.

She gave a pout. "Will you make me a website?"

"I'm busy."

"My modeling company gave me a budget and said I could hire anyone I wanted. And I want you." She was looking at him in a way that suggested she wanted him for something other than his web skills.

He extracted his arm and stated, "My docket is full."

"It's mostly just photos."

He continued walking in silence.

"You can't fit in your old fiancée?"

He didn't reply. If he shut her out, she'd go away. Yes, it was rude, but it was effective.

"I understand if your wife is the jealous type. You and I always did have a good thing." She pouted again when he gave her a dark look, but quickly changed her tact when she saw it wasn't having an effect. "I can offer you ten grand."

"For a website?"

"It'll need a shopping cart."

That was a whole new level of headache. One he could easily accomplish, but still. He didn't want to work with Dani, didn't need headaches even if it meant paying his father back sooner than he'd planned.

"I have fan gear. About twenty-five products."

Fans. Fan gear. Of course. "Something like that will cost more like seventeen grand."

"Okay."

"Okay?" He stopped moving. She had to be kidding. Hadn't she done any shopping around? She could get a site for considerably less than that. His price was a "go away and leave me alone" price.

"There are a few of us looking for sites and I told them you were really good."

"You don't know that."

"Burke hired you."

Yeah, okay. Burke wasn't the type to hire just any old hack.

"I'll pay whatever you ask." She was easing closer, like the experienced temptress she was. "So will Tanesha and Fiona." She batted her eyelashes and gave him a sweet smile. "You were always so clever."

"Right. That's why you left."

"Oh, Ethan. It wasn't that." She smoothed a hand down his arm, her fingers curling around his biceps, her expression one of morose. "It was just the timing."

She looked at him, her expression sincere. "Ethan?" Her tone was soft, one asking for forgiveness. "Please?"

"I'll think about it."

"How about all three of us for forty thousand.

I'm the only one with a cart and we'll pay you ten up front."

"That's ridiculous." Forty grand for three simple sites? He shook his head. "What's the catch?"

"We need the tax deduction." She smiled, that perfect model smile he'd see on the cover of magazines every once in a while in Mary Alice's convenience store. "Lots of models need sites. I'll give you tons of referrals."

Easy sites. Ridiculous profit.

Man, that was tempting. Especially since it could be a quick boost to his financial goals and could help him and Lily move if she chose to sell the restaurant.

But working with Dani? He wasn't so sure that was something he wanted.

"I work under strict contracts," he said. "I'm very particular and you'll get only three edit passes —after that any changes are subject to additional charges. And you can't call me up at any time with emergency alterations. I only build the site. Someone else will have to maintain it for you."

Dani launched herself into his arms, her perfume strong and cloying. "Thank you!"

Nuts. He'd kind of just accepted the deal by listing his conditions, hadn't he? Well, he supposed at least he'd get a chunk of change he could send to his parents to repay his debts.

He just hoped it was worth the torture of having Dani in his world for the duration of the contract, because he had a pretty good feeling that even though these sites were going to give him what he wanted in terms of cash, he was the one who was ultimately going to pay. Especially when Dani finally released him and he saw Lily standing on the street across from him, her arms slack at her sides.

* * *

LILY TRIED to hold her head high as she crossed the street to where Ethan and Dani were standing. She'd expected Ethan to be doing his cold, scowling grump act, but instead Dani had been all over him, hugging him, her hand against the back of his neck like she had the right to touch him. It was intimate, that touch, that hold.

And the worst part was that Dani had almost as much claim on him as Lily did. Maybe even more so where Ethan's heart was concerned. Because as wonderful as yesterday had been, Lily wasn't delusional. She knew she didn't possess Ethan in the way Dani once had and possibly still did. When she'd suggested to him during their picnic that she "stick around" after their year's commitment he hadn't actually replied beyond a smile and a nonchalant shrug. She'd taken his response as an affirmative, but what if he'd just been being polite?

And what if she was just being annoyingly insecure?

She needed to get a grip.

She sucked in a slow breath to calm herself and joined the exes on the sidewalk.

"Hey," Lily said lightly. Dani was decked out in a designer outfit that clung to every curve, her toned arms looking strong and tanned, not pale like Lily's, from spending time in the kitchen.

"Oh, Lily!" Dani turned, cooing over her and her hiking outfit of leggings and oversize sweater. "You look so healthy and robust."

Lily gave an unimpressed blink.

"I'd heard you two married." Her gaze traveled over Lily again, this time giving her the distinct impression she'd somehow come up short.

"Right. So I'm going to go in and cook us supper, Ethan." To spite Dani, she pulled Ethan into a kiss. It was fierce and possessive and totally returned.

Wow.

Dani might make her feel like less of a woman, but Ethan made up for it with his kiss. She broke apart with a sigh as she slowly released him.

"See you inside," she whispered. To her surprise, Ethan linked his hand with hers.

"I'll come with you."

"I thought you had a meeting," Dani said sweetly to Ethan.

"It's with my wife."

"I always heard the way to a man is through his stomach," she said, with a laugh that made Lily cringe as she scurried away with Ethan.

Inside the house, he let out a sigh. "She offered me a job."

"A job?" Jealousy stirred inside Lily.

She felt like she'd finally just started to win him over, and now his ex was snooping around. And if push came to shove...

No. She was married. To him. He was loyal. He'd chosen Lily and there was no room for insecurities because they would only ensure disaster.

"Website. Shopping cart," Ethan was saying. "Big money."

Of course. She was flaunting whatever she had to sneak her way back into his life. She knew it, Dani knew it and Ethan probably did, too.

"Did you take it?"

He sighed. "Yeah."

She didn't know what to say so she moved to the kitchen. Dani would get her hooks into her husband, and it wouldn't take long, if one conversation had turned her into his customer.

Lily mindlessly began pulling out ingredients for her favorite comfort food, bread pudding.

"She's very pretty still," she said, hating herself for revealing one of her insecurities. So much for being tougher than them. She whisked the egg, sugar and milk mixture with more vigor that was technically required.

"Yeah, I guess."

"Ethan…" She tore the day-old bread to shreds.

"She's not my type."

"You were engaged." She stuffed the bread into a pan, drowning it in the sauce.

"Is me taking her seventeen grand for a five-grand website going to be a problem? Because that's the only reason I said yes."

"Why is she paying you so much?"

He threw up his arms, his movements stiff, his scowl back in place. "Who cares? It's money."

He was closing Lily out, his choice made.

"You know what?" She pushed away from the counter and shoved the pudding into the oven. "Fend for yourself tonight. I'm going to go do some work on the catering business. Pull that out of the oven in forty-five minutes and bon appetite."

She headed outside, angry with herself for not being stronger.

The door opened behind her and she turned around, hands on her hips. She didn't want to fight, but she also didn't want Dani in their lives. Not yet. Not ever.

"I'll say no if it makes you feel better."

Her eyes dampened. "Ethan…"

"You're more important." He eased down the steps, favoring his left leg. "Look, I suck at this. Just tell me what you want and I'll do it."

"You shouldn't have to give up a lucrative contract. I know you want to pay back your dad."

"Just say the word and I won't work with her."

"I'm sorry. You should take it. I just didn't expect to find her hanging all over you and I got jealous."

He pulled Lily against him, resting his head on top of hers.

"That's okay, I don't like Tanner."

"Nobody likes Tanner," she said, causing them both to laugh.

For a moment she felt like she could have it all. Love, family. Everything. As long as Dani stayed at bay. And maybe even if she didn't.

THINGS HAD BEEN awkward that morning, and not just because Lily had avoided him at bedtime, "accidentally" falling asleep in front of the TV with Gramps. Ethan could pinpoint the time of change.

It had been when Lily had seen Dani hugging him. And seconds before that, when he'd accepted her job offer.

His picnic with Lily had felt special, fun. A lot like love starting to bloom in the garden of their friendship.

He was becoming a sap. *Garden of their friendship?* The statement was both poetic and true. But now he was even hesitant to run the restaurant's offer of purchase past her.

She had told him not to give up the lucrative contract with Dani, knowing it would open doors for him. And it would. But he didn't want it coming between the two of them.

The front door opened and Ethan turned in his chair to call to Lily. "Going for a hike?" He planned to go with her today even if it killed him. They needed to talk, needed to spend time together.

And he needed to figure out how to prove that she was the woman he wanted, not the one on his monitor with the airbrushed cleavage and expanse of exposed thigh.

She appeared in the doorway, her gaze going straight to the screen behind him. Igor, who had been washing himself on the armchair in Ethan's office, stretched before meowing a hello to Lily.

"I thought I'd join you tonight, if you don't mind," Ethan said. He'd taken a dose of prescribed pain meds he usually avoided unless absolutely necessary, and was as set as he'd ever be.

She shrugged after a moment's pause. "Fine."

He turned to the screen. "How much of that do you think is airbrushed?" He casually clicked out of the program, knowing he was treading on thin ice. He should have thought to close down the program before she'd come into the room.

"You'd know," Lily muttered, disappearing from sight.

Ethan sighed in defeat. The cat gave him an unimpressed look before lifting a back leg so he could wash his backside.

"I feel like you're calling me names," Ethan muttered to Igor before joining Lily outside a few minutes later. "Where are we hiking to?"

"Just through the meadow."

"Sounds good." Not too strenuous.

They began walking in silence, waving as they passed various citizens.

"What was your favorite part about training as a chef?" he asked as they crossed a wooden footbridge, taking them into the meadow which was thick with white flowers.

"The challenge. It was hard but fun and learned new stuff every day." She quickly added, "You're limping worse today."

"Yeah."

Not before long, Ethan spotted Devon, Olivia and another woman standing among the white flowers. Valerian. That's what it was—the secret ingredient that Olivia had needed for some new makeup product line. In the end her family's company had made a deal with the town that had helped Devon cinch the vote as mayor, as well as saved the local area from a hydroelectric project that would have flooded the entire meadow.

"Hey, Ethan!" Devon waved them over and Ethan moved that way.

"There's the happy couple," Devon said when they reached them. Ethan cut Lily a look. She hardly seemed happy. "This is Emma Carrington, Olivia's sister."

"Pleased to meet you," Ethan said.

Emma was graceful like Olivia and had long, wavy hair. She shook their hands.

"Emma's taking over the All You line for the family firm," Olivia explained.

"Olivia thinks that going to school, having a baby, designing wedding dresses for Ginger's clients *and* taking care of a whole new product line is too much," her sister said with a laugh. "So here I am! I have to start learning all she does so I can take over the harvesting of valerian for our new all-natural products."

"That's cool," Ethan said, feeling the need to fill the quiet.

"We launch the products next year."

Ethan noted a tremor of uncertainty in Emma's smile, but it was Lily's flat, "Congratulations," that really caught his attention.

She looked a bit tired, more drawn, and he stepped a little closer, worried she was working too hard. Maybe they could take a weekend away somewhere. Do something other than work.

"Do you two have any kids?" Emma asked.

"Us?" Lily asked, her surprise obvious.

"We just got married last month," Ethan explained.

"Are you married?" Lily asked Emma.

"I think she has a crush on someone, but she won't say who," Olivia mused. Emma, Ethan noted, didn't meet her sister's eyes.

"Well, we were just going for a walk," Ethan said, extracting them from the conversation. "We'll let you continue with your quest to rape the land."

Devon grinned at the joke meant to ruffle his feathers, and gave him a brotherly shove.

Laughing, Ethan steered Lily away and continued walking.

"Do you want kids?" Lily asked, once they were out of earshot of the others.

"Yes."

"Me, too. But not—you know…"

With him. She wasn't envisioning kids with him. Was that what she was going to say?

He snagged her hand as they approached a bench near the rolling hills that led higher into the mountains, the trail eventually ending at an aquamarine lake. He pulled her down beside him on the seat, worried he was losing her.

"You doing okay?"

"Fine," she answered immediately. "And you?"

He'd absently begun massaging his knee. "Yeah, the usual."

"You were good for a week," she said, pointing to his leg.

It had been a darn fine week, too. One he'd like to repeat on several levels. Many of them involving his wife.

"You should try cutting out wheat and other inflammatory foods. It might help your joints."

"Okay." He had a suspicion that it might be either wheat or dairy, if anything. But those were often staples in Lily's recipes when she wasn't making stir-frys, which, in his mind, involved a fair amount of prep. She had been working hard, learning both businesses, and he didn't feel it was fair to inhibit her cooking with possible dietary restrictions as he tried to figure out which foods gave him issue through the process of painstaking elimination. Especially with wheat and dairy, which were found in practically everything.

"Want me to try stir-frys again?" she offered.

"I don't want to put you out." He stood, ready to prove himself on the daunting trail that led ahead. But Lily turned back toward town.

"Where are you going?"

Her gaze landed on his knee and the look hit him like a punch. She was returning home because she didn't think he could make the hike. She was being held back by him.

And that was about the worst thing he could think of.

⁂

LILY WANTED LAST WEEK BACK. The one where she and Ethan had made love and kissed like crazy and didn't dodge each other.

She slapped five more ham sandwiches onto a tray for the town hall meeting and grumbled to herself, wallowing in her own anger.

It didn't help that Dani had made herself at home in Ethan's office that morning. They were going over her site together, and every time Lily glanced in there was a big, beautiful shot of Dani on Ethan's screen. Perfect. Womanly.

Sexy.

And even worse was that the real deal was sitting right there beside her husband, laughing and acting coy. She'd had Lily's cat in her lap while she'd stretched out all languid and tempting on the futon, which had finally arrived. Every time Lily peeked in to see if they were hungry, Ethan would click out of whatever program he was working in as if he had something to hide, making Dani's image vanish from his monitors.

Lily hated it.

Plus she was pretty confident it was something in his diet making his joints sore, and when she'd suggested she could cook for him, he'd said he didn't want to put her out.

He was her husband. She loved to cook. How could something like that possibly put her out—especially if it helped him and allowed him to move more freely?

So she hadn't cooked. And he'd been happy about it, making his own dairy-and-wheat-free breakfast.

Lily slapped the last of the sandwiches onto a plastic tray in the back of Mandy's café, and walked them over to the town hall. She wished she could expand her restaurant's kitchen so she had enough space to do her catering prep there instead of mooch space off of Mandy. Next, she headed to her restaurant, where she discovered the fryer wasn't working.

"How much is a new one?" she asked Quinlan, her sous-chef.

Leif had enjoyed his week off for his eye surgery and had decided to tack on a week's vacation, as well. She was beginning to think the man was never coming back and that she'd have to continue juggling everything on her own indefinitely. It was hard to believe she'd once wished she'd had the kitchen and its responsibilities all to herself.

Quinlan pondered her question about the fryer for a long minute before shrugging. "Five hundred? A few grand?"

She didn't have a few grand. Or a few hundred. She'd just sent what she had to her father in hopes that he'd be able to start taking his blood pressure meds again.

"Less than what you owe for the fridge that doesn't work properly," Gloria stated.

"What?" Lily turned to the waitress.

"The walk-in fridge? The guy came by and said he's gonna sue you if you don't pay for it."

Lily gave her a confused look. She didn't see that as an outstanding liability on any of the documents she'd been given.

"Ethan refuses to pay the bill since it turns off all the time," Gloria said.

"So it is faulty?"

Gloria gave her a dry look.

She was more confused than ever.

"I'll talk to him." Later. The fryer problem had to be solved now. "Maybe we can fix this thing." She knelt on the floor and popped open its side panel. Wires hung loose. "Look at this."

Quinlan got down beside her. He smelled of garlic and radishes. "Someone damaged the wiring harness."

Lily stood and turned to face the mostly empty kitchen. "Who? Who did this?" She turned to Quinlan. "Did you do this? Is this because I'm new? Because I'm the boss? Because you don't want me to fit in and belong?"

He gave her an uncomfortable look and she realized just how irrational she sounded. She needed to get a grip.

"We lost fifteen orders this morning because of the fryer," Gloria stated. "We should get a new one. Want me to call Ethan?"

"No. *I'm* the boss. *I* can handle this."

She sucked in a breath. It wasn't a big deal. It was fixable.

But who was doing this to her? And why?

She sniffed and watched as her cook fiddled around with the wiring from his spot on the floor. "Try the on switch," he suggested.

She flicked the switch with vigor.

"Ow!" He swore a blue streak as he leaped away from the fryer. "Turn it off!"

She hit the switch again as a popping sound cracked the air, followed by the scent of smoke filling her nostrils.

That couldn't be good.

Quinlan was sucking the tip of his thumb and he pulled it from his mouth to look at it.

"Are you okay?" Her foul mood dissipated as she realized he was hurt. "Let me see." He already had a blister on the end of his thumb from an electrical shock. "Quinlan..."

"It'll be fine." He went to the ice maker and wrapped a cube in a damp cloth, applying it to his thumb. "Not the first time I've been burned."

Lily looked at the staff who had gathered in the kitchen. She couldn't imagine any of them doing this. None of the cameras that had been installed by Ethan or Logan would help pinpoint who had damaged the fryer seeing as none of them were in the kitchen and so many people had come and gone through the building between last night and this morning. Waitstaff, cooks, dishwashers, cleaning staff.

"When did stuff like this begin to happen?" Lily asked.

"A few weeks before you came along," Gloria stated.

That meant it had less to do with her and more to do with Ethan. How was she supposed to fix that?

Quinlan was staring at his thumb and Lily edged him to the side and began prepping the vegetables for the day's soup. "Go. Take care of your injury."

"You need help in here."

"And you need to deal with that burn."

"You're a stubborn woman."

"I know."

"Leif always says Ethan's lucky to have you."

"Well, someone tell him that."

Quinlan grinned. "Want me to call my uncle?"

"Why?"

"He's an electrician."

"Yeah, okay. Sure."

Quinlan left her in the kitchen, down a chef and a sous-chef. Just what she'd wanted when she'd started.

She rolled her shoulders, building herself back up again. She wouldn't let this get to her. She was stronger than this. It was her turn at bat and all she needed was to put an efficient system into place so she could take a break between the lunch and supper rush to rest—definitely not to hurry home and check on her husband.

Love had to prevail, and the less interference from her right now, the better.

But she was definitely going to go check on her husband.

Hours later, Lily dragged herself home for a break before the supper rush. She'd been putting out proverbial fires all day and it felt nice to breathe air that wasn't laced with grease. She would have been tempted to quit today if it weren't for the knowledge that the place would soon be hers.

She let herself into the house, letting in Igor who'd been sitting on the step, and found Ethan dozing on the couch. His long lashes brushed his cheek and his hair was damp. Gramps sitting in the backyard with his paper. She was fairly certain it was the same paper he'd been reading for a week, but he was happy, wearing pants and staying out of trouble.

On the coffee table in front of Ethan was a coffee mug, key chain and signed glossy headshot of the one and only Dani Demare.

Disgusting.

Lily shook Ethan awake. "Who keeps messing with the restaurant?"

"What?" He stretched. "Mmm. I had the best massage."

"Massage?" It was three in the afternoon. He was napping and had had a massage, while she'd been dealing with restaurant issues of his creation. Any sympathy she felt for him went out the window.

"I feel great."

"Someone ripped the wiring out of the fryer today."

"What?" He propped himself up, the hair at the back of his head sticking out.

"I said—"

"I heard you." He rubbed his face.

"Who did you tick off, Ethan?"

"I haven't ticked off anyone."

"Absolutely no one, thanks to that sunny disposition of yours?"

His growing scowl deepened.

"Because unless you tell them to leave the place alone, the deal's off."

"What?" He swung his legs over the side of the couch. That had his attention.

Hers too. She wasn't sure why she'd said it, only that she felt like she was going to get screwed. She could feel it coming in like a storm over the mountains, ready to lay her flat. Standing up for herself would help him treat her seriously and realize that he couldn't take her for granted, couldn't screw her over, intentionally or not.

"Don't make me repeat myself, Ethan. You heard me just fine. And as for that fridge bill that they're threatening to sue over? You're paying it, because otherwise I'll be on the hook with frozen assets and four grand that wasn't written into our contract."

Ethan stood up, his expression unreadable. "Lily, there's no way I'm paying for it."

———

"I'M NOT PAYING it because they didn't fix the problem," Ethan stated, struggling for calm against his anger. "It still turns off, doesn't it?"

"You have to pay it," Lily stated. "They said they found nothing wrong, so the warranty won't cover the visits. It's only a few hundred dollars."

"For each visit. I've had them out five times."

"Your stubbornness could impact my ability to run the business."

Ethan sighed, realizing she was right. He'd wanted a reason to believe the fridge issue wasn't in fact his staff turning on him.

"Fine. I'm sorry. I'll pay it first thing Monday." Somehow.

"Thank you."

It was time to make amends and make his wife happy again. He'd fix whatever it was with the fridge and tell her the truth about the outlook of his MRI.

He'd also tell her he'd terminated the contracts with Dani and her friends, had refunded their deposits even though the sites were almost complete, and had moved on. No more Dani in his life to bother her.

"Would you like to watch a movie with me?" he asked.

"I have to work, Ethan. A restaurant, remember?"

"You can take an evening off."

"I can't keep taking time off with Leif still out, plus Quinlan hurt his thumb."

"Staff are insured."

"Ethan, you're missing the point. It's me at the stove or nobody today." She looked like she was drowning under the weight of the place.

It was probably the best time he'd ever have to tell her about the offer. But first he had to get her through the evening shift.

"I'll come help." Ethan stood, expecting to be shut down.

To his surprise she said, "Fine. See if you can keep up." She lifted her chin and turned to leave.

"Oh, I'll keep up." Or die trying.

Half an hour later they were elbow to elbow, having a contest over who could debone a chicken the fastest. She won and he was officially dying. Well, not quite, but he certainly hadn't let her win. His wife was a ninja with a butcher knife.

"You seem more spry today," she said, elbowing him aside to place her chicken pieces in a large pot.

"You trying to make me feel better about losing?" He moved on to the pile of potatoes she needed peeled.

She laughed, dishes clinking in the background.

"I think it's dairy causing inflammation, by the way," Ethan announced as he finished peeling the potatoes. He'd been tweaking his diet and was seeing some positive results.

He trapped her against the counter with an arm on either side of her, not caring if the dishwasher saw them. Lily looked startled and tried to escape his hold. "Are you going to forgive me for whatever's going on in your head?" he asked softly.

"You have seminude photos of your ex on your computer." Lily blushed, looking away, embarrassed.

"You're the only seminude I ever want to see on my screen," he said softly, knowing nobody else would be able to hear them over the sound of the dishwasher working in his corner of the kitchen.

285

Lily rolled her eyes, pushing against him, but he held his ground. "You're beautiful."

"Ethan..." Her tone wasn't patient. "I said take the contract, not ogle your ex."

He had never expected jealousy or insecurity from Lily. Not just because of their arrangement, but because she was...Lily. Strong. Capable. Sexy as all get-out. She was number one.

"I canceled the contract with Dani this morning."

"What?" Lilly gaped in disbelief, her expression conflicted.

"It was making you uncomfortable." He shrugged as if it wasn't a big deal, even though it put him further behind in his goals to repay his dad. He'd had to use his credit card to repay the models, seeing as he'd already given their original deposit to his father. But so what? If those contracts made Lily unhappy, then they made him unhappy, too.

"I didn't expect you to let her invade our home," Lily grumbled, scrubbing her hands in the nearby sink. She dried her hands and turned. Ethan slung his hands around her waist, drawing her close.

"I like the sound of that."

"I don't." She tried to shove him away. "And I don't like you giving up jobs just because I..."

"Matter to me?"

She frowned, almost as though forcing herself to find that new hardened Lily who had slipped away almost as soon as they were married.

"'Our home.' That's the thing I like to hear."

"Ethan..."

He kissed her neck and felt her soften ever so slightly. He believed that she wanted this—them—but there was something holding her back. Something that overrode that flash of the future that kept flickering before them. One where they had it all. Love, health, devotion, companies they enjoyed, even kids.

"We're a good pair." He watched her struggle to sort through her emotions. Was he laying it on too thick? He didn't want to scare her away and she had been pulling back a bit lately.

He lightened his tone, releasing her from his embrace and tossing a handful of potato peels into the nearby compost bin. "So let's enjoy our year together before you go find your Mr. Right."

Or see that Ethan might indeed be that man.

Her eyes flashed with anger.

Had he dialed it back too far? Maybe it was time to bare it all and show her just how much she'd come to mean to him.

"Lily, I got an offer."

"What kind of offer?" Her hands stilled as she

reached for her stock pot as though she was sensing something big on the horizon.

"For the restaurant."

"It's not for sale," she whispered. "We have a contract."

"We'll take the money and you can build your own restaurant with your own menu and make it exactly like you want."

"I'm buying Benny's, Ethan." Her voice was growing louder and the dishwasher looked up from his spot in the corner.

"And because you *are* the owner I think you should take a look at it."

"Ethan, don't you get it? I don't want to sell!"

"You could earn a profit and turn around and do what you really want."

"This *is* what I really want!"

"This place is stifling you and your potential. This isn't what you dream of. Sell this old building. Find something bigger and better. Or work fewer hours as the nonowner, but still be in control as the manager and chef. Let go of the financial risk and headaches."

Choose me. Choose having more time to spend together.

"You don't think I can do this? Is that it?"

Ethan crossed his arms, trying to hide his frustration. "You're not even considering this. They offered to keep you on as the head chef with a big raise."

"And be at someone else's mercy again. Haven't you been listening? I don't want to work for anyone. I want to work for me." She jabbed her chest with a thumb.

"But this could be good." She could go anywhere, be anyone. She could create the menus she'd dreamed of as a teen. "You don't have to stay here. You could support your dad."

Her grew eyes wet. "I can't believe you're trying to sell this place out from under me. I should have known better. I shouldn't have trusted you."

"Lily, come on. You know I'm not trying to do that."

"If you don't want me in your life, just say so."

Ethan leaned back on his heels in surprise, and from the corner of his eye saw the dishwasher scoot out of the kitchen.

"What are you talking about?" he said gently. "I'm doing this because I *do* want you in my life."

"Then why do you keep pushing me away?"

"Lily." He struggled for patience, to react calmly, to help settle things instead of make them worse. "I'm not the man you see. I want to be but I—"

"Quit making excuses. If you don't want me, tell me. Don't hide behind this 'I'm not a man' crap. You've always been a man, Ethan Mattson, so stop fearing being one. You punched out Tanner, you hike up mountains, you make love like you could go for days and you do good things for others. What's more manly than that? So quit hiding behind your fear and embrace who you are, what you have."

"I don't want to be a burden, okay?" he cried. "An MRI says I'm likely to end up in a wheelchair again. You don't know what that's like, Lily, but it's no fun for anyone."

She was pale as she stared at him with disappointment etched in hurt. "So instead you deny me the love of my life? Every day you push me away, insulting me by insinuating that I'm shallow enough to care about a limp, a few aches, the possibility of disability? How dare you decide who or what I want in my life."

She spun on her heel, storming out of the kitchen. Gloria entered with a stack of dirty dishes, raised one brow and deposited her load before leaving him alone again.

Ethan leaned against the counter and let out a jagged sigh. How had he managed to mess up so badly, when all he'd wanted to do was to give Lily security and a home—the things she needed to settle down and be happy and free at long last.

LOCKED IN HER OFFICE, Lily tried to keep her tears from falling. She stared up at the ceiling, blinking. Then, realizing that Ethan could be spying on her through the camera above, she stormed off to the ladies' room so she could be angry, frustrated and confused in peace.

Then you'll go find your Mr. Right. Why would he say stuff like "our home," only to follow it up with a reminder that he had no plans to hold on to her after their agreement ended?

And why would he give up a contract with Dani for her when he kept pushing her away? Was he really worried about becoming a burden or was that just an excuse? Because, in her mind, if you loved someone nothing else mattered. People you loved couldn't be a burden. Ethan had even said as much to Gramps.

The real question was why he was taking offers on her restaurant. She shouldn't have trusted him. She shouldn't have mixed love and kitchens.

She splashed cold water on her face and studied herself in the cracked mirror. She looked tired, old. Defeated.

What if the restaurant failed? She'd still have to buy it, wouldn't she?

All she wanted to do was skip out on responsibility and eat cookie dough with Mandy, or laugh with Gramps in the kitchen while she mixed up another batch of mashed potatoes.

But this was her dream. Not all days could be perfect.

That fight with Ethan, though…it had shaken her to her core. Had she overreacted?

Straightening her shoulders, she headed back to work. Sitting in the bathroom moaning about her life wasn't going to fix things.

She left the ladies' room and ran smack into Tanner. He was lanky as ever, a mop of hair falling over his forehead, the dimples bracketing his smile giving him a charming innocence. One she knew he didn't possess.

"What are you doing here?" she demanded.

"Hey, babe."

"I'm nobody's babe and certainly not yours."

"Let's chat," Tanner suggested.

"Let's not." She wrenched her arm from his grip, realizing they were creating a small scene that had the coffee drinking gossipers in the dining area stirring. She led her ex into the staff room.

"Why are you here? My husband made it clear I'm not interested."

"You didn't return my calls." Knowledge dawned in Tanner's expression. "You blocked my number."

"My husband did."

He gave a huff of a laugh. "I can't believe you married him. Although I always knew you'd come running back to Blueberry Springs and to Ethan. That's why I made him an offer he couldn't refuse."

"What does that mean?"

He smiled and opened his arms, as though showcasing the building she was supposed to own come next summer.

No. No way.

How could Ethan even *dream* of bringing that offer to her? Not only that, he'd given her an emotional sales pitch in his attempt to persuade her.

She couldn't trust him. She couldn't trust anyone. She needed out of their marriage agreement even if it meant suffering a financial fallout.

"I'm never working for you ever again," she said to Tanner.

"I'm trying to make amends. I love you, Lily. I want to spend the royalties from my cookbook on you and show you I still care. We belong together. We had good times."

"I'm not interested."

"Maybe I could help out? I overheard a waitress say the fridge turns off on its own."

"And you know how to fix that?"

He was smiling smugly. "I do."

She didn't know whether to believe him.

"It's hard being the boss." His tone was kind,

soft, understanding. He was trying to draw her in, give her someone to lean on for a while. But she knew she couldn't trust him. She couldn't trust anyone.

"Let me help." He began walking toward the door, no doubt ready to take over, take charge, put her in the corner again.

"No."

He turned, eyebrows quirked.

"I said no. This is mine."

"Lily," he said smoothly, "I'm not going to take advantage of you. You completely misunderstood that I was trying to protect you. We loved each other and my feelings for you haven't gone away."

"I'm not interested."

"I said, let me help."

"Please leave."

"You can't be serious." Tanner was staring at her in disbelief. "My name can help you."

"I said no."

"You'll regret this."

It wasn't quite a threat, but it made her uncomfortable just the same. "You're right. I probably will regret it, but that seems to be a theme in my life whenever it comes to restaurants."

If she was going to fail, she was at least going to do it on her own terms.

CHAPTER 12

"*D*id I remember to tell Lily to sleep with you?" Gramps asked, his brow furrowed in confusion. He'd had a full day of doctor's tests and Ethan had picked him up a few hours ago, bringing him home.

"Gramps, you're tired. I think it's time to call it a night." Ethan stacked their dirty dessert dishes on the counter and began ushering his grandfather toward the guestroom, wondering when Lily would come home. Since their fight she'd been avoiding him, sometimes not even coming home at night.

"I did tell her." Gramps nodded and absently tapped the air.

"You're a good wingman," Ethan said automatically.

He needed to talk to her. He'd definitely had it

wrong, and of course she wanted the restaurant. She loved the trials and tribulations of the place just like he did with his tech work.

He should have known better, should have listened instead of spewing out his own dream of the future. One where his likelihood of disability was out in the open.

He checked his smartwatch as a notification came in for the restaurant's alley motion-activated camera. Maybe Lily was on her way home and they'd finally be able to sit down and talk things through, now that they'd had time to cool off.

Gramps was frowning, licking a remnant of chocolate icing off his bottom lip. "Yes. Yes, I told her if she didn't consummate your marriage that you could annul the whole thing and she'd be out on her ear without a restaurant."

Ethan nearly ran into the doorjamb leading out of the kitchen. "Say that again?"

"Have you seen my toothpaste? I can't find it anywhere."

"It's in the bathroom beside the sink. What did you say to Lily?"

"That sounds about right."

"Lily told you about the contract?" Why would she do that? It was risky, too risky.

"What contract? The prenuptial agreement? Oh,

I figured it all out. Marriage to save taxes and what-not."

Ethan studied his grandfather with renewed interest. He might be starting to slip a gear here and there but Gramps was still a smart man. Ethan guided him to the bathroom. "Brush your teeth first? I think you forgot last night."

"I'm not a baby. I can choose whether or not to brush."

"That's true," he replied mildly. But inside, his world was dropping out. He and Lily had made love and it had been wonderful. Then she'd pulled back. He'd had a million excuses in mind as to why, but maybe she'd taken him to bed as a way to protect her interests and nothing more. But how could she fear that he, her old childhood friend and protector, would take advantage of a loophole he wasn't even certain existed?

And then the offer on the restaurant... She'd acted like he'd been trying to swipe the whole thing out from under her.

What was going on inside her head? And how could he show her he wasn't the man she was assuming he was?

Then again, maybe it was exactly like she'd said and she only wanted the restaurant.

Not him.

Lily walked into the bedroom to find Ethan already sprawled out on the bed, gazing at her. She was exhausted and didn't want to sleep on the futon in his office. She wanted a real bed, one without her husband in it.

Without the man she'd trusted to always have her back.

She put her hands on her hips and waited. Usually he asked if she wanted the bed and would make the move. Tonight he did not.

She heaved a sigh and snatched up her pajamas.

"We need to talk," he said quietly.

"About what?" she snapped. "The fact that the offer you almost accepted on my restaurant was from my ex-boyfriend? How about we start with that."

"What?" Ethan looked momentarily confused.

"Give me some respect. You know who the offer was from and still took it to me." Ethan was shaking his head. "You may have acted as though you cared, but you always planned to double-cross me."

"Whoa." He stood up, hands out, his face a mask of anger. "You slept with me to ensure I couldn't get an annulment, so let's be fair about where we point fingers."

"I'm not going to let you screw me over."

"Screw you over? I was stupid enough to think you actually wanted me. We had a commitment to each other and I have never once let you down."

Doubt was nibbling at the cornerstones of Lily's argument. She wanted to trust him. She really did. But she also knew she couldn't continue on with these kinds of thoughts always piping up in the back of her mind. She needed to be the full owner, even if it meant financial hardship as she renegotiated new deals with vendors.

"You said whenever I wanted out of the marriage, I could get out. I think it's time."

He was staring at her, stunned. "But you—"

"I'll deal with the suppliers and hope their new discounts are deep enough I can keep things afloat on my own."

He sat on the bed, no longer looking her way.

"Ethan…" She felt tears well up. She'd made the wrong decision. "You knew this day would come. I have to protect my interests."

"If two months is enough, then fine. I'll talk to John about drawing up divorce papers." He stood, his voice calm, his face revealing that he was anything but calm on the inside.

ETHAN COULDN'T CONCENTRATE. He stared at his computer screen, the blinking cursor taunting him.

Lily wanted a divorce.

A few hours ago he'd moved Gramps into the old folks' home, a spot opening up last night.

Lily hadn't come home last night. He was starting to believe tonight would be the same story. Even Igor hadn't come home yet.

His old, quiet life—the one he'd once cherished—had returned to him, only he no longer wanted it. He didn't want a silent, empty house. He wanted family. He wanted someone in the other room cooking or reading the same paper over and over again.

He'd failed to make Lily feel as though she was safe and belonged in his life. And now she was going to own the restaurant prematurely and possibly struggle financially because he'd messed up.

His phone rang and he picked it up. "What do you want?" he snapped, annoyed that someone was interrupting his pity party. He didn't have them often, but when he did, he liked to have them alone.

There was silence on the other end of the line. He hung up and moments later his computer screen flashed to a video chat app, ringing filling the room once again. It was Dani.

Great. She must have finally received his canceled contract and refund.

He clicked the accept button and his ex-fiancée's smiling face filled the monitor.

"Hello." He aimed for polite, but knew he fell a bit short.

Just because his wife had seen the truth—that he was a crusty, difficult man sure to become a burden—it didn't mean he needed to tick off a woman who'd already seen that truth so many years earlier. A woman who could possibly send work his way in the future, seeing as he no longer had a wife running interference.

Dani laughed uncertainly. "Ethan? How are you?"

"Sorry to have terminated our contract on such short notice. I assume you got the deposit back and saw my referral to a friend who can finish the project?"

He'd been so close to completion it broke his heart having to give it up. But it had been the right thing to do even though it hadn't helped save his marriage. He'd been focusing on the wrong thing, evidently.

"Was it something I did?" Dani seemed earnest, as well as disappointed.

"No, no. Unavoidable time commitments. But Darrel can complete the sites." His cursor hovered over the red button that would end the call.

"You should have kept the deposit. You did most of the work."

"It was nice working with you. A fun challenge. Maybe in the future we can work together again."

"Is this about Lily?" Dani gave a small shake of her head, sending her hair waving. "Never mind, I know the answer. She's smart." She was sitting forward, watching him through their screens.

He wasn't sure what she meant, but suspected she knew why he'd canceled the contract.

"I was making a play for you, Ethan." Dani gave a small laugh, acting flirtatious. She batted her lashes and gave him a shy smile. "But you didn't even notice, because you're so in love with her. I'm guessing she knew."

Ethan scratched the back of his neck, feeling uncomfortable. Had Dani truly been making a play? He'd assumed she was just being her usual flirty self and had offered a ridiculous sum of cash for the site because...well, he'd assumed she'd wanted to appease her guilt, buy his forgiveness.

Her making a play for him didn't make sense, though. She'd left him quite soundly.

Dani laughed again. This time for real. "You should see your face."

"I'm sorry, Dani. That ship has sailed," he said awkwardly. She was already back in Milan for a photo shoot or conference, or else something vital to her superficial world where everything was perfect. She wanted a career, not love. At least not love with a man who couldn't physically keep up to her lifestyle.

Just like Lily.

"You can't blame a girl for trying. It was selfish of me to leave you when you needed me the most."

He watched her through the screen. She seemed genuine and he sat back, thinking. He'd never expected her to apologize, and he wasn't sure what he was supposed to say in reply.

She gave that same uncertain laugh again. "I've always felt bad for the way I left you. You're a good man and I should have stayed by your side."

"Easy to say now that I'm walking again and you have your career," he said lightly.

"Yes, but no less true."

Silence stretched between them.

"She's leaving me." Ethan wasn't sure why he confided in Dani. He supposed it was because she'd bared her soul a little bit, so it was his turn.

"But," he added quickly, "it doesn't mean I'm on the market." He arranged the paper clips scattered on the desk beside him. Behind a stack of papers he found a piece of caramel popcorn that Lily had tossed at him all those weeks ago. He toyed with it before dropping it in the trash.

"Ethan, I am so sorry. I can tell how much you care for her."

"You're sorry?" He added his own uncomfortable laugh to the conversation. "Weren't you just saying you wanted a second shot?"

"I know when I've lost, but you're still a catch, Ethan Mattson."

"A man who hobbles around like his grandfather whenever the weather changes? Hardly a catch."

"Is that why Lily is leaving you?" She sounded surprised.

"It doesn't matter why."

"If that's her reason she's just as stupid as I was," Dani said vehemently. Ethan looked up. "I wanted the job and thought caring for you would hold me back, but what I really needed was you and your love and support. I hope she wakes up and doesn't take that for granted."

"No, I made that choice for her." And it was true. He had. He'd been doing what Lily had said during their fight, and had been pushing her away. Just subtly, here and there, not quite believing that she might truly love him, want him and his uncertain future.

Ethan sat silently, thinking. He'd spent many hours angry at Dani, feeling abandoned, miserable at the hand fate had given him. If it hadn't been for that accident he probably would have married her. He knew now that it wouldn't have lasted, because they didn't have what he and Lily did. He wasn't even sure what they *did* have, only that it felt so much more consuming and real. And like a fool, he was letting it slip through his fingers.

"Ethan?" Dani said.

"Sorry, Dani. I have to go talk to my wife."

LILY FELT as though her heart had broken. She'd asked for a divorce.

She sniffed back her tears, determined not to wallow or second-guess herself. She was preventing disaster, preventing being taken advantage of. She wanted this quirky, much-loved kitchen she was standing in, and she wouldn't be screwed over this time. She was well on her way and there was no turning back, no getting sidetracked into someone else's fantasy. She didn't want to move away, didn't want to build a fancy new place where she could build her own menu and be totally free.

She wanted the security of Benny's.

Right?

If she did, why did it feel so wrong, so painful, choosing it?

She needed to smarten up and get down to work.

Focus on what she'd come back to town for. Financial independence. Her own business. She'd known she and Ethan would go their separate ways and that was what they were doing. Just like they'd planned.

Only a lot earlier.

Lily slipped her phone into the kitchen's speaker dock and turned up her playlist of songs that helped get her in the mood for creating. It was time to expand her dessert menu with one new offering, and she'd get her new, flaky piecrust recipe right even if she had to stay here all night.

She'd discovered with the roast beef fiasco that adding an item to the regular menu or specials wasn't nearly as risky as deleting one. If she offered new items that became favorites, she could slowly phase out the old, less popular ones.

She laid out her recipe notes and then walked down the hall to the walk-in fridge to collect a flat of eggs. She left the hall light on and returned to the kitchen, picking up a jug of vinegar as she passed the wet goods shelf. She just about had the eggs safely on the counter when next door the owner began his evening renovations, hammering against the wall, causing the lights to flicker. She flinched, sending eggs tumbling onto her notes. Several cracked open and she quickly wiped the moisture off her papers, the ink smearing.

At least she had digital backups. The only issue was that she was going to have to ask Ethan how to access them.

She blinked back her fatigue and tears. After taking down the camera Ethan had placed in her office, she'd spent the night at her desk trying to sleep and wishing she'd left the couch in there. She'd been hoping to sort out what to do with her life and how best to proceed, but by dawn was still at a loss.

The song playing on her phone ended and one from Ethan's family plan started up. She walked over and silenced the device.

No thinking about Ethan. Not tonight. It had been a long day of her snapping at her sous-chef and the waitresses, and it was time to unwind and celebrate what she *did* have.

She swiped at a tear. She should be happy. Elated. She was going to be on her own to make the restaurant exactly the way she wanted.

Rolling the dough, she focused on feeling contentment. Comfort. This was her home. The kitchen.

The dough tore and she growled in frustration. She crumpled it into a ball and reworked it, knowing the crust wouldn't be as flaky now, that the feeling of contentment she was searching for wasn't going to come and that she'd ruin whatever she tried to create.

Gramps had moved out today.

She sniffed back the tears that threatened to fall.

She was going to miss him. Miss living with Ethan.

She swiped at her cheeks with the back of her flour-dusted hand.

There was a lot to miss, moving out of that small house. Sharing meals, jokes, time.

Her tears fell in earnest as she realized how much she was about to lose by choosing the restaurant. She was going to lose Ethan and his family. Possibly even customers. Because who liked a woman who had stayed with a kind, upstanding hometown man such as Ethan for only two months before leaving with two of his businesses?

She gave herself a shake. It wouldn't be that bad. She needed to stay strong. She'd been on her own without the Mattsons before. She could do it again.

But what if everyone steered clear of her restaurant out of loyalty to Ethan?

There was another loud bang in the back hall, this time sounding almost as though it was in her restaurant instead of on the other side of the wall. She shook her head, wondering if the neighbor had finally broken through. She stepped out of the kitchen to check.

"Hello? Georgie, did you come through the wall?" The hall was dark and she flicked the light switch. Nothing. Had the bang loosened her wiring? She flicked the switch two more times before giving up. Maybe Ethan had been right about this place falling apart. It was a money pit.

Enough light filtered into the shadowy hall from the kitchen that she could make her way to the back door, where the other switch was located. Maybe it was just this one that had broken.

She squinted as she reached the walk-in fridge, surprised to find it open. Odd. She was certain she'd closed it. Was it another glitch in the appliance? Maybe Ethan was right and it was faulty, because there was nobody else in the locked building who could have opened it.

She reached for the door, feeling a current of air, then caught a shadow moving out of the corner of her eye.

Lily turned to defend herself, but was shoved inside the fridge. She stumbled backward across the raised threshold, landing hard on the cold floor. The door swung shut, the latch snapping into place with a resounding clang. Something scraped across the door, as if she was being barricaded inside.

"Hey!" She leaped up, slamming her body against the door. It didn't budge. She pulled hard on the handle, working it, fearing it was going to snap off in her hand when it wouldn't open.

Panic set in. She was trapped, locked in. She pounded on the door. "Let me out!"

"You think you're too good for me?"

She froze, recognizing the voice. "Tanner?"

"Think you deserve to move up in the world without me? Think you're better than me? Think you deserve more than being a lackey?"

"Tanner, let me out!" She thumped the metal door and screamed until her voice broke, hoping that the workers next door would hear her through the thick walls that separated them.

The world around her was silent, except for the clicks and hums of the fridge she was in. She waited for a minute. Had he left? She sat heavily on a crate of oranges and tried to figure out how to convince Tanner to release her if he came back. If not, at least there was enough oxygen circulating through the cooler that she could stay locked in overnight. It would be chilly, but not life threatening.

"Let's see how you feel with a little heat under you."

"Tanner? Let me out!" She leaped up to bang on the door again, the tone of his voice sending shivers down her spine, creating a panic that made her heart thud madly in her chest.

"Tanner!" She banged against the metal, the darkness feeling too close, too frightening. "Ethan!"

"He can't help you, Lily. Goodbye."

She smelled smoke. Lots of it. The fridge's air intake. It was coming from there—a hole she could escape through. She began ripping at the metal grate, hoping she could find a way to worm her way out. The grate was secured, screwed firmly into place. She was trapped.

"Help!" She screamed until her throat was raw. She threw herself against the door again, hoping something would move on the other side, magically release her. The smoke abated for a moment and her panic shifted down a notch. He was just trying to freak her out. She only had to stay calm and he'd let her out again.

"Tanner? Let me out so we can talk."

Nothing.

She coughed. Smoke was still coming in. Lily pushed a crate against the intake and shoved lettuce leaves into the gaps, hoping to create a seal.

The fridge kept pulling in more air, sucking, sucking, bringing with it more and more smoke.

Tanner was silent, possibly gone.

The fire could be real, not just a scare tactic.

Suddenly everything popped into focus. She was going to die in the fridge tonight.

She hadn't gotten her life right. She needed more time. She wasn't ready to die.

She'd been so determined to be independent, to own something, so certain she couldn't have love in the kitchen that she'd pushed everything good in her life to the edges. Ethan, his family, everything.

He was more important than the impossible task of trying to be friends with her employees. That wasn't how it worked. She needed to be the boss. Definitively. She needed to make menu changes and stand behind them, win people over to the restaurant she wanted to have—the one Ethan had encouraged her to create before he'd known a crazy man had made the offer to purchase Benny's.

He *did* know her. It was she who hadn't been listening.

Love, family and belonging wasn't something she needed to find in the kitchen; she needed to find it with Ethan.

If she got out of here alive, she promised herself she'd find the strength to step beyond the shadow of her fears, her false need to defend herself. She was going to claim love, claim Ethan.

ETHAN NEEDED to talk to Lily. He'd been stupid. She was the woman he wanted, needed. He should have done everything in his power to protect her, to be the man he'd want her to be with. One who wasn't curbed by his fears, who didn't hold back, keep secrets or push her away.

He turned down Main, enjoying the briskness in the night air that told him fall was coming soon. He spotted Mandy's big truck parked along the curb outside her café, his sister and grandpa climbing into it.

"Mandy? Gramps?" he called as he approached. "What are you two doing out so late?" It was almost midnight.

"Gramps had a mashed potato emergency," Mandy said, pushing her bangs off her forehead.

"At this hour?"

"I didn't get my evening mashed potatoes," Gramps complained.

"So you made some for him?" Ethan asked his sister. She gave a nod. "Where's your little guy?"

"Sleeping," Mandy said grumpily. "At home with Frankie. Like I should be."

"Tell Lily I still expect mashed potatoes even if I don't live with her any longer."

"You've been in the home for five seconds. You could have just called her, you know."

"I don't like it there. I miss Lily."

"So do I."

Mandy bristled with an awareness.

"Better she leaves you now rather than later," Gramps exclaimed. "Dani left you and my wife left me. Women aren't worth it! And judging from your expression it sounds like Lily just took your heart and—"

"Did Lily leave you?" Mandy interrupted, turning to Ethan.

"I don't know," he said honestly. "Gramps? If you'd known in your twenties that Grams would pass on before you, would you have not married her?" Ethan didn't wait for an answer. "Of course you would have, because love is worth the risk. I love Lily, Gramps. So enough with the "leaving" talk and being better off without her stuff you're leading up to."

"I thought we were commiserating," Gramps said, acting betrayed.

"We were. But I'm done. No more looking back. Not for me."

Gramps was watching Ethan with his foggy blue eyes. Finally he harrumphed with a hint of a smile. "Fine. Your life."

Ethan hugged his grandfather, then helped Mandy get him into her truck. "And be nice to those nurses, okay? They just want what's best for you."

He closed the truck door before Gramps could grumble at him, and took the alley that went behind Benny's with a new sense of resolve to make things work with his wife. He could smell the faint whiff of smoke, not uncommon due to forest fires that came through the mountains, although this one seemed a bit late for the season. Ethan signed into an app as he walked, to see where Lily's phone was located. No point going all the way down the alley if Lily wasn't there.

She was.

He heard a meow and glanced down to see Igor run up like a shadow in the dim light, then take off toward the restaurant. Ethan frowned and picked up his pace as much as he could.

As he came closer to the restaurant, the cat grew more frantic, as did the smell of the fire. Only now the scent was strong enough that he could tell it wasn't a forest ablaze.

He hurried around the corner of the building adjoining the restaurant, his heart stopping when he saw smoke oozing out through the crack under the back door of Benny's. Lily's car was parked in the narrow gravel lot.

Ethan scrambled to call 9-1-1 while limping up the steps to the burning building.

"Lily!"

He quickly gave dispatch the pertinent information and then pocketed his phone as he pushed his way through the closed back door, smoke billowing out with alarming persistence. There were no customers this late at night. Lily was likely the only one inside.

He ignored the questions whipping through his mind and only thought about rescuing her.

"Lily!" he hollered, groping his way down the dark hallway. The door was open behind him, but the darkness was encompassing. He could see lit up areas ahead of him, where the flames were concentrated. The heat surrounding him grew by the second. He lifted an arm to shield his face, bending to keep as low as possible without crawling. He moved past the walk-in fridge as he struggled to navigate of the dark hallway, through air thick with smoke. The heat in the kitchen was already extreme. He was too late. Something crashed in there and the heat intensified, his skin feeling as though it was peeling off him, his lungs no longer able to draw enough air to keep him upright.

He staggered back down the hall, coughing, leaning against the wall to try and keep low without collapsing onto his knees. He paused against the walk-in fridge. The metal door was warm like the air around him, and he could see flames licking the ceiling behind him, lighting up the hall.

He had to get out. Now.

He pressed a hand against the fridge's metal door, bracing himself against a wave of light-head-edness. His hand curled around the handle he'd pulled open a thousand times. It didn't feel right. There was a metal pole stuck through it, creating a barricade. He paused instead of making his way to safety and fresh air, his mind puzzling over this ir-regularity. Knowing it was irrational, he stayed put, yanking at the rod that had the door barred and finally hauling it open.

Lily fell against him, her lungs wheezing.

"Lily!"

Ethan bent instinctively, catching her with a shoulder against her stomach, hoisting her over his back. The muscles on his left side protested but didn't let him down. He could do this. He *would* do this.

He staggered down the hall, knowing it would be better if he could stay low, out of the thick blanket of toxic smoke that was choking them both.

His steps unsteady, he broke out onto the back landing, his legs threatening to crumble as his lungs drew in rich oxygen. He stumbled down the steps in a barely controlled move, tripping over Igor en route. Just as he was about to hit the ground, his brother caught him, barely holding the three of them upright.

"What took you so long?" he asked Devon hoarsely.

A fire truck was pulling up, and bystanders were gathering.

"Anyone else inside?" Devon asked, as he helped Ethan lower Lily, who was conscious and coughing, to the ground.

She was alive.

He'd never felt so relieved in his entire life. Not even when his paralysis ended.

"Is there anyone else inside?" Devon repeated.

Lily shook her head as Igor leaped on her chest and began head-butting her and purring loudly.

A firefighter rushed up to them and placed an oxygen mask over Lily's face, easing her coughing. Her eyes were wide as she stared at the bright, burning building, and Ethan felt her fear right to his core. He pulled her against him, unable to speak.

"What happened?" Devon asked.

Ethan swallowed hard and coughed, his lungs aching. "She was locked in the fridge." His raspy voice trembled with rage. "Someone did this to her. I need to find out who it was and kill him."

Devon sat back on his heels, wiping his mouth with a hand.

Lily was trying to speak, pointing at the flames. Her chest was working hard to draw air. Ethan leaned over his wife. "Lil. Lilypad. It's okay. You're safe now. Just…slow it down. Small breaths. You're in good hands. You're with me. You're safe."

———

"TANNER TRAPPED ME. He started the fire," Lily croaked, pulling the oxygen mask from her face, not even recognizing her hoarse voice. She watched in horror as flames stretched toward the sky. She would still have been in there if Ethan hadn't saved her. Her throat felt scratchy, her world black with panic. Her lungs were screaming at the effort of drawing a breath.

Ethan had been sitting beside her on the back bumper of an ambulance, both of them wrapped in blankets and breathing through oxygen masks to ease the effects of smoke inhalation. Now he was up and moving.

Lily bent over as a dizzy spell racked her. With Ethan no longer at her side her ability to remain strong began to dissolve.

Her kitchen. It was gone. Everything gone. She'd lost it all. There'd been no contingency in their agreement for a fire.

She was shaking. Tanner had pushed her into

the fridge. He'd locked her in and set the place ablaze.

Igor was still rubbing against her ankles, happy she was alive.

She glanced over as a flurry of activity caught her eye. Ethan was storming at a tall man, slamming him up against a brick wall in the alley, an arm against his throat. Tanner.

"You!" Ethan shouted. He was clearly livid, a stream of threats spewing forth as he held the helpless man against the wall.

"It was an accident! I only wanted to scare her!"

"You locked her in the fridge! In a burning building!"

"I went to get help, but I got scared. It spread so fast."

"I don't give a—" Ethan's words gave way to curses. "She's my wife!"

"She was mine first, and I warned you. I kept popping your shoddy locks to sneak in and turn off your precious fridge, stole your money—everything I could think of to interfere and give you the message to sell to me, to let me have her. But you didn't take the hint. You didn't accept any of my purchase offers, lowball or high. I knew she'd come back to you, but she's mine! Mine!"

Lily stared in wonder as Ethan pulled back his fist to deck Tanner. But Devon was there, catching his brother's arm just after he made contact with Tanner's mouth. In a flash, Ginger's husband, Logan, snagged the now bleeding Tanner, throwing him to the ground, pinning his hands behind his back while Scott Malone, the local officer, cuffed him.

Devon continued to hold Ethan back as Lily watched from her spot at the ambulance.

She didn't know what to think, how to react.

"Hey, hon, let's check you out." It was Amy Carrick, one of the bartenders from the local pub, who also worked as a volunteer firefighter and EMT.

"Ethan..." Lily's voice trailed off, unsure what she had to say about her husband defending her, about Tanner and his mixed-up head, which had cost her her dreams and almost her life.

She watched Devon push his brother back as he continued to try and press forward, land another punch. Ethan was no longer the wounded, broken man she'd known two months ago. He was everything.

Her everything.

Amy fussed over Lily and her blood-oxygen monitor while firefighters doused the flames in her burning building.

Ethan was walking toward Lily, his arms held out as though he was too puffed up with adrenaline to lower them back to his sides. He caught her eye and the transformation was immediate. His arms dropped; his angry scowl melted and a look of love replaced it.

Then worry and alarm overtook him as he strode toward her, his limp barely noticeable, he was moving so fast.

He brushed off Amy, who tried to place an oxygen mask on him again. He yanked Lily into his arms and she inhaled slowly, some of the restricted feeling in her chest easing off.

"I love you," she whispered.

He clung to her, his face buried in the crook of her neck.

"I love you, too, Tagalong."

The old nickname warmed her, made her feel bigger and more loved than she ever had in her life. She'd tag along anywhere he was going.

Ethan Mattson was the true prize, the thing she'd been looking for in kitchens around the world. And it had been right here in Blueberry Springs all along.

Love.

Belonging.

Ethan.

ETHAN SAT beside Lily on the ambulance's metal step and watched her dream restaurant go up in flames. She'd wanted that ratty old place even though it wasn't what he'd thought she needed. He had a lot to learn, a lot to not assume about her. Himself as well, if he was honest.

"You okay?" He flexed his fingers, still wanting to wrap them around Tanner's throat. He hoped Scott would put the man behind bars forever and then some. Maybe let some larger inmates beat him up a few times for good measure.

Ethan still couldn't believe how close he'd come to losing Lily. If he'd stayed talking to Mandy and Gramps for even one minute longer...

He didn't want to think about it.

He pulled Lily against him once again, unable to let go, unable to get over the awful relief that was still terrorizing him with the fear of near loss.

She was watching the flames lick the dark night sky.

"It's insured," he said, his voice husky, slightly choked. His throat hurt from the smoke, but he knew it couldn't be as bad as Lily's.

"I don't care about the restaurant," she said, pulling the mask away from her face. She swallowed hard, tears falling from her eyes.

"We can talk later. You've been through a lot."

"We're going to take you to the hospital in a

minute," Amy Carrick, the EMT stated, packing up her supplies.

He held her close and rocked her slowly. To their right he could see members of the Mattson clan hustling toward them, their faces pale, their eyes wide. He gave them a reassuring nod and then waved them away, keeping them on the other side of the police barricade. The night had a chill to it, the fire contained within the restaurant, and he pulled Lily's blanket up under her chin so she'd feel warm, safe and protected.

Like he hoped she always did when he was at her side.

Behind them, the police car rolled away with Tanner.

"I thought the restaurant was your dream," Ethan said, his mind stumbling over her earlier words, about not caring about Benny's. He smoothed the hair from her forehead and gave her a kiss.

"I thought the kitchen meant family and love." She paused to cough and he resisted the urge to tell her to stop trying to talk. "But it means responsibility and making decisions that won't always make people happy. You can't be friends when you're the boss, and I thought owning it would mean being a deeper part of it all."

"And it doesn't?"

"Not as much as being part of your family."

"You'll always be a part of the Mattson clan, Lil. No matter what you and I decide to do."

She slipped her hand into his. "I want to be part of *your* family."

He shifted so he could see her better. "What are you saying?"

"That I love you. As a husband. I want to be married to you for real. More than I want..." she gestured to the restaurant from under the blanket "...that."

"Well, I can see why. Even I'm a cut above the smoking remains of a stagnant old restaurant." He gave her a wry smile, trying to counter her seriousness, the pain etched in her face.

"Ethan..."

"I know, Lily. And I want you to know that I love you, too. I don't want you to ever leave me. I want you to live in my house, sleep in my bed and make my remaining days the best I've ever had."

Her eyes welled with tears.

"Because any day you're in my life, Lily, those are the best ones for me. Always."

EPILOGUE

*E*than looked out over the Blackberry River falls and down at the town below. He'd made the climb, remembering all the quirks of the old trail he used to take with his family. The tree that forked halfway up its trunk due to a lightning strike; the large, dish-shaped boulder he and Devon used to fight over sitting on.

It had taken him well over an hour to make his way up the trail, but it was worth it. Not just because he got to enjoy his new inflammation-free joints, which felt so much better thanks to his no-dairy diet, strictly enforced by his wife, but also because he and Lily were having a commitment ceremony. It was a beautiful, sunny, crisp October morning and they were surrounded by people they loved, people who expected Ethan to lean on them whenever he needed to. Because they were family and that was what family did.

"How are you doing?" Lily asked, sliding a hand behind his back to hug him to her.

"Pretty good, thanks." He kissed her forehead, thinking how lucky they were and how close they'd come to missing it all.

He hadn't gone back to creating Dani's site, but had been working with modeling agencies and their websites, growing his business, while Lily steadily expanded her catering clientele. They'd received an insurance payout for the restaurant even though it was arson—Tanner was serving time for that, as well as an attempted murder charge—and Lily had decided to rebuild. Not right away, but possibly in six months, once she had a better idea of what she wanted—and whether she even wanted her own restaurant.

"You look pretty," he said, leaning closer to give her a kiss.

She'd made the hike in a flowing white sundress that looked very bride-like. He'd heard that Olivia had altered something for her, but hadn't seen it until this morning, when they'd met at the trailhead. He hoped the ceremony and the party planned back in town would feel enough like a true wedding for her. She'd insisted this was all she wanted, but like any man smitten and head over heels at long last, he wanted to give her everything, from the moon and stars to the oceans and mountains.

"There she is." Ethan called over his sister-in-law, Olivia. "You made my wife look ravishing."

"She's naturally beautiful," Olivia said with a smile, giving Lily a hug.

"How are you feeling?" Lily asked.

"Much better. My sister was out visiting and cheering me up. She'll be back soon to work on the cosmetic line I started."

"I heard she's taking over for you," Ethan said.

"She is. She'll launch the whole new line."

"That's pretty cool that she can go from modeling to in-depth product work like that."

"Well, she's the youngest in the family," Olivia said with a laugh. "Anything is possible!"

"Hey!" Mandy said as she came over. "I resemble that comment." She winked at Ethan and gave him a light punch in his biceps. "I'm glad you two are doing this."

"Thanks, Fluff," Ethan said, feeling a tad choked up.

"Oh, don't give me that," Mandy grumbled.

He smiled. The nickname worked every time.

"When was the last time I had a brownie?" he teased. "I think they're fair payment to prevent me from using the old nickname."

"When was the last time you babysat your nephew so I could bake?" his sister retorted. Axel was currently asleep in a sling attached to her, adorable and innocent.

"Touché."

Mandy grinned.

"Family…" Olivia said to Lily with a shrug.

"I love it," she replied, hugging Ethan's arm.

People were gathering in the small clearing, just about ready for the ceremony. They began to head that way, but Olivia paused, looking uncertain. "Oh, and, uh…the old family friend who proposed to me?"

"Luke Cohen?" Lily prompted, having apparently heard the story—one Ethan knew nothing about, but would have to ask her to tell him later, by the sounds of it.

"I need a way to get him to Blueberry Springs."

Lily's eyebrows shot up. Oh, yeah. Definite story there.

"Why?" Ethan asked.

Lily said quietly, "Emma has a crush on him?"

Olivia nodded mischievously and Ethan figured that romantic set up looked like a giant bomb about to explode. Olivia's ex-suitor with her sister. Oh, boy.

"Do I hear matchmaking happening?" called Ginger, hustling over. "Who are we setting up?"

"Luke and Emma," the woman chimed together.

"Excellent. Let me know what I can do to be of assistance." Ginger rubbed her hands together. She caught Ethan giving her a look and said, "What? It's what I do. And might I just say you look lovely, Lily. Ethan, tell her how gorgeous she is."

"You're gorgeous," Ethan said, loving how his wife gave him a bashful smile.

"Shall we?" Devon called, prompting the group to gather together.

Ethan held up a finger, requesting a moment as he made sure the camera he'd set up to film the ceremony onto a screen he'd left in Gramps's room at the center was still online. The satellite was ready to stream and he nodded at Devon, who invited everyone to gather around.

"Ready?" Ethan asked Lily.

"Always." She wrapped her arms around him, going in for a cheek kiss. But instead of flinching as he had months ago, Ethan angled his jaw, kissing her lips with a passion that promised so much more. Released from their pasts, they were ready for a new beginning. One of love, trust, and most of all, each other.

WHAT'S NEXT?

A NEW BLUEBERRY SPRINGS ADVENTURE AWAITS...

Love? It's not in the plan.

Dive in to Luke and Emma's story, The Wedding Plan, today and continue the Veils and Vows adventure!

VEILS AND VOWS

Find love in unexpected places with these sweet marriage of convenience romances.

The Promise (Book 0: Devon & Olivia)

The Surprise Wedding (Book 1: Devon & Olivia)

A Pinch of Commitment (Book 2: Ethan & Lily)

The Wedding Plan (Book 3: Luke & Emma)

Accidentally Married (Book 4: Burke & Jill)

The Marriage Pledge (Book 5: Moe & Amy)

Mail Order Soulmate (Book 6: Zach & Catherine)

ALSO BY JEAN ORAM

Read, Dream, Laugh & Love
Sweet, Laugh-out-Loud Romances

FREE EBOOK

Have you fallen in love with Blueberry Springs? Catch up with your friends and their adventures...

Book 1: Whiskey and Gumdrops (Mandy & Frankie)

Book 2: Rum and Raindrops (Jen & Rob)

Book 3: Eggnog and Candy Canes (Katie & Nash)

Book 4: Sweet Treats (3 short stories—Mandy, Amber, & Nicola)

Book 5: Vodka and Chocolate Drops (Amber & Scott)

Book 6: Tequila and Candy Drops (Nicola & Todd)

Companion Novel: Champagne and Lemon Drops (Beth & Oz)

THE SUMMER SISTERS

Taming billionaires has never been so *sweet*.

Falling for billionaires has never been so sweet.

* Available in paperback & ebook & audio! *

One cottage. Four sisters. And four billionaires who will sweep them off their feet.

Falling for the Movie Star

Falling for the Boss

Falling for the Single Dad

Falling for the Bodyguard

Falling for the Firefighter

ABOUT THE AUTHOR

 Jean Oram is a *New York Times* and *USA Today* best-selling romance author. Inspiration for her small town series came from her own upbringing on the Canadian prairies. Although, so far, none of her characters have grown up in an old schoolhouse or worked on a bee farm. Jean still lives on the prairie with her husband, two kids, and big shaggy dog where she can be found out playing in the snow or hiking.

Become an Official Fan:
www.facebook.com/groups/jeanoramfans
Newsletter: www.jeanoram.com/FREEBOOK
Twitter: www.twitter.com/jeanoram
Instagram: www.instagram.com/author_jeanoram
Facebook: www.facebook.com/JeanOramAuthor
Website & blog: www.jeanoram.com

Made in the USA
Middletown, DE
15 December 2022

18638183R00208